HOOFBEATS

a monster romance

Val Saintcrowe

Punk Rawk Books

HOOFBEATS
© 2023 by Val Saintcrowe
www.vjchambers.com

Punk Rawk Books

All characters appearing in this work are fictitious. Any resemblance to real persons, living or dead, is purely coincidental.

All rights reserved. No part of this book may be used or reproduced in any manner whatsoever without written permission except in the case of brief quotations embodied in critical articles and reviews.

ISBN: 9798376928288
PRINTED IN THE UNITED STATES OF AMERICA

10 9 8 7 6 5 4 3 2 1

HOOFBEATS

a monster romance

Val Saintcrowe

CHAPTER ONE

FOR MONTHS, ALL anyone who was anyone could talk about was the new house being built on Tralgam Square, which took up practically an entire city block. It was indeed quite the tidbit of gossip, for I heard about it, and no one talked to me, at least not anymore.

I saw the house, of course. I could not help but be curious about it. My maid Janet and I would press our faces against the glass of the windows of my family's carriage every time we went past it, noting the progress as the weeks ticked on and on, watching as it went from framing to walls to the roof going on.

During all that time, all that anyone knew about the house was that it had been commissioned by a certain gentleman named Granville, and that he had spared positively no expense in having it built.

Little was known about Mr. Granville.

Only that he had made his fortune in the import of teas and spices, that he owned a great number of ships that went to the far east for such things, and that he was not, so far as anyone knew, married.

During dinner, the house and Mr. Granville became a subject of conversation that my brother and I could converse about, which was a welcome change, because my brother and I found little to say to each other normally.

The truth was, no matter how it was that my brother

thought to excuse himself, I blamed him for my plight. I saw no one else who was quite responsible for it, after all.

He, being the sort that he was, blamed me.

Years ago, when he first spoke to me about my being ruined, he bandied about all sorts of insults for me, using words that I had hitherto only barely heard, for they were not to be spoken in front of ladies, not daughters of earls as I was. Of course, these days, I was hardly considered a lady anymore anyway. It didn't matter what he called me, even if it was most offensive and horrid.

Then again, he didn't say these words or insults so much anymore, it was true.

No, anymore, we did not speak overmuch. So, Mr. Granville, his truly colossal house, all of that, it was welcome. It brought some livelihood to our dinners again, as we speculated on who he might be and what he might be like.

"He has, it's said, a membership at Brakestills," said my brother idly. Brakestills was my brother's gentlemen's club, where he spent a great deal of his time.

"Oh, truly?" I said. "Well, it seems they'll let anyone in these days."

My brother chuckled. "My thoughts exactly. I am quite scandalized by it. However, I suppose he has paid for it through the nose. I think he has made an endowment, in fact. Enough to fix the Brakestills roof."

"Well, then," I said. We had repaired our roof recently, and it was for that reason I had not been able to afford new clothing and was instead wearing patched dresses—not that it mattered. No one ever saw me except Janet and my brother and the other servants. "I suppose they must do what they must. Roofs are necessary."

"Yes, but no one will ever speak to him," said my brother.

"Certainly not," I said.

Of course, we had no intention of ever associating with a man like Mr. Granville. Mr. Granville was not titled and he was not our sort of people. He was an upstart. He had new money he'd gotten from *trade*. He was a curiosity, but he would never be our equal. So, there was no real talk of ever welcoming him into our society or being welcomed into his.

Then one night, my brother said, "I suppose that if his money is good enough for Brakestills, it may also be good enough for us."

"For us?" I said. "I don't know what you mean. How would we have any of his money?"

"I am thinking of proposing a business arrangement, of course," said my brother. "I could discuss all of it with him at the club. I wouldn't need to go to his home or anything."

"Well, you wouldn't need to," I said. "But one does wonder what it's like in there."

"One does," agreed my brother. "Perhaps, if it was necessary, I might venture inside. I doubt it would be necessary, though. A man like Granville, some upstart idiot, would be easily tricked into parting with a great sum of money, I think. Don't you?"

My brother and I had long been titled and practically penniless. My brother had sold what properties he could to fund our lifestyle, but this house in town and one estate in the country were entailed and could not be jettisoned. We did get some income from rents on that country estate, and it was enough to feed us and keep our servants and that sort of thing. It was likely enough to keep us quite comfortable, in fact, but my brother had a gambling habit, and that was where too much of the money went.

"Well, what sort of business arrangement?" I asked, pushing peas around on my plate. I was not certain that a man like Granville was an idiot. I thought it must take a certain cleverness and drive to rise from nothing to this, to splendor and grandeur, even someplace as distasteful as Tralgam Square.

"That hardly matters," said my brother. "I am an earl. He will do whatever it is I suggest. I am positive of it."

"Yes, you're likely right," I said. I assumed he was. People with money like Mr. Granville did not come and build ostentatious houses on Tralgam Square for no reason, after all. They wanted to be accepted. They wanted to be like we were.

They never would be.

We did not live anywhere near Tralgam Square.

We lived in the staid and traditional and, frankly, shabby part of town where people of our sort lived. The other part of town, Tralgam Square, was only recently fashionable. It was settled by young dukes and new-money upstarts. Why, there was a house there that may or may not have been owned by a courtesan—a *woman* held the deed, it was said, a woman of ill-repute. It was all right for a certain sort of person—a daring sort, I supposed. There was nothing about our sort, however, that was daring.

Eventually, the house was finished, and the furniture was moved in.

Janet and I sometimes lingered, telling the carriage driver to make up some excuse for why we tarried there on the street, watching the fine chaises and tables and the paintings be carried in over the threshold.

Of course, it was gauche to watch, and we—our sort—were above such things, so I could never stay too long.

Did I think about Mr. Granville himself, about his person? Did I imagine him in romantic ways, the way I knew some other girls in town were doing?

I'd like to say no.

After all, I was on the shelf, ruined, quite old (four and twenty) and I was in no position to marry anyone, new money notwithstanding. But we all knew it happened, that sort of thing. Granville wanted association with a title, my brother wanted his money…

I didn't think a man like Mr. Granville would marry a woman like me anyway. He would have his pick of other girls.

But… did I catch myself sometimes in ridiculous and stupid reveries?

Well, perhaps. Sometimes.

Janet and I did not see Mr. Granville alight from the carriage when he arrived, top hat on his head, tailored suit over his broad chest, dark hair pulled back from his face. But he was seen. He was seen in his finery and it was known that he had four hooves and that he had a tail that swished when he walked and that he stood much taller than most men.

Mr. Granville was a centaur.

It was quite a blow.

Not only because no one had quite realized centaurs even existed. Oh, there were always rumors. There was some town to the north that claimed they were always battling off dragons, for instance, and Janet had told me that her own sister worked for werewolves. Werewolves! And they were *our* sort of people. So, people spoke of these sorts of things, but truly?

A centaur.

In Tralgam Square?

Well.

Everyone was in an uproar. It was whispered in the streets and doorways and at balls and teas. The horror of it, the unbelievability of it. A centaur! What was the world coming to?

Well, I did not go to teas or balls, it's true. I never got invited anymore. Neither did my brother. When one is the guardian of a ruined woman, it is as much your fault as it is hers, as everyone knows. And as I have said, I blamed him entirely.

My brother and I spoke about it at length at dinner, of course. We lingered long over our astonishment that such creatures even existed, and we spoke about how he even functioned. Why, how did he sleep? *Where* did he sleep? Could he sit on all those chaises we'd watched brought into his house? Why did he need such a house? A centaur surely did not expect to entertain.

"And now your schemes of tricking him into a business proposition are out of the question, of course," I said.

"What?" said my brother. "Don't be foolish. Now that I know he's a centaur, I know that he's even more desperate and even more likely to be an idiot. I shall get even more money from him. I shall enjoy this, I think."

"Oh," I said. "I see. So, you're going to speak to him, then?"

"Yes, at the club, of course," said my brother. "He'll be ever so grateful, I'm sure."

"Have you seen him there?"

"Well, not yet. But he wouldn't have gone to such trouble for a membership and then never arrive, would he?"

I obviously didn't know what it was that Mr. Granville the centaur might do. I found myself rather curious to see him. I thought a lot of people might be curious, in fact. So, when the invitation came for the ball, I wasn't surprised.

Well, I was slightly surprised that I'd been invited, that both of us had, because we didn't get social invitations anymore. Perhaps Mr. Granville didn't know that I was ruined and had thus destroyed the family name entirely.

But I wasn't surprised that he was having a ball, or that he'd invited everyone with a title in all of town.

"Well," said my brother. "No one will go."

"Of course not," I said. "No one would dare be seen there. In Tralgam Square. At the house of an upstart. Of a *centaur*."

"No one," agreed my brother.

I DIDN'T EVEN have a ball gown anymore, not one that fit, not one that was fashionable, not one that I had never worn before. But between Janet and myself and one of the other servants who was handy with a needle, I managed to cobble something together, something respectable, anyway.

I had two dresses in shades of powder blue. I was able to use fabric from the skirt of one to make sleeves—puffy sleeves—and a bustle, and to lower the waistline. When it was done, it looked as if the two shades were meant to go together. I thought it was quite fetching.

Then came the problem of how I was going to get there. I couldn't go alone. A woman could not attend a ball alone. Well, perhaps a widow could or a married woman whose husband was away or otherwise engaged in some respectable activity. But a young woman like myself could not attend a ball alone. I was really not supposed to go anywhere alone.

Janet, being my maid, was not an acceptable chaperone.

However, I was ruined, so such things were far less important than they might have been. I did go here and there as I wished. However, in the evening, for a ball, well, I didn't know what I was going to do.

Two days before the ball, my brother mentioned at dinner that he was thinking about "looking in" on the ball.

"Oh, were you?" I said. "I happen to have been coincidentally altering an old ball gown. Just in case we might get some invitations this year."

He looked me over, raising both of his eyebrows. "You just happened to do this?"

"Let me come along," I said. "I've never seen a centaur, not a real live one. Not up close." It cost my pride to do that. I didn't like my brother very much, and I didn't like begging him, but he was the person with all the power in the household, so sometimes I had to.

He shrugged. "I suppose it doesn't matter in the end. It's not as if anyone else will be there."

"No, surely not," I said.

Of course, I knew better.

Everyone was there.

Everyone came, and they all arrived around the same time as we had, nearly two hours after the time we'd been requested to arrive. They all came to "look in," just to stay for one glass of bubbly sweet wine and then to disappear. They all came to get one look at the centaur.

And we knew this because as we all jostled out of our carriages and inside, this was what everyone was saying to each other.

"Just a look, of course. I wouldn't *stay*," they said.

They caught me in their gazes, and they shuddered. How horrid to be in the same house as one such as me. How positively wretched.

My brother grimaced at their looks. How he hated being

weighed down by me, by my reputation.

Inside the house, it was all white. There was a white marble staircase dominating the foyer, the steps wide and shallow enough that a centaur could ascend them. There were white marble pillars reaching all the way up towards the upper stories of the house. The floor was white and tiled. There was a chandelier lit entirely by white candles — a huge thing that must take the servants a ridiculous amount of time to see to. Even we had gas lamps in our home now, though my brother's gambling habit had been quite impaired by the expense of having them installed.

We went through the white foyer into the ballroom, which was not white. It was rose and gold and the entire ceiling was a painted fresco of the sky, fading from night to dawn, the edges of mountains tinged pink around the edges.

The room was too much.

It was what might one expect from new money. No elegance, simply extravagance.

However, it was also breath-taking, like something from the ancient world, something from a cathedral, some work of art.

In the center of the ballroom stood Mr. Granville.

From the waist up, he was an impeccably dressed gentleman, and from the waist down, he was a chestnut stallion. He towered over the guests, and when he walked, the clop of his hooves sounded throughout the room.

There was no music yet.

He bowed at the waist, gesturing with one hand at the crowd as they filtered. "Welcome," he said in a deep voice.

He was handsome.

I thought it was an odd thought to have about a man who wasn't really a man, but he had finely wrought features, a straight nose, kind and amused brown eyes, and his hair was long and lustrous. It gleamed in the light of the ballroom and he smiled out at the gathered assembly of our sorts of people with magnanimity and triumph.

The music began, and everyone danced.

Mr. Granville did not dance, however. Indeed, he seemed

alone. Though he walked amongst his guests, they seemed to shy away from him. They did not speak to him, but when he was far away, they openly gaped.

I found myself feeling an odd sense of kinship with the centaur. It was the way they treated me.

I don't know if I put myself directly in his path or not, but when I saw he was coming for me, I did not move out of the way.

He saw me, and his expression changed. Something went darker in his eyes, something that made him look less like the amiable gentlemen and somehow dangerous.

Still, I did not look away.

He halted, probably six feet away from me, a look of alarm crossing his countenance. He glanced over his shoulder, as if he was contemplating some sort of escape.

But when he looked back at me that expression on his face was even darker, and he was determined, and he came for me straight away.

He was huge.

I had to crane my neck up to see him when he was directly next to me.

He inclined his head and he said, "I know it is not appropriate to speak to a lady one has not been introduced to. Forgive me, but I seem to have no ability to stop myself."

Well, truly, he should have received calls from all the gentlemen in town, welcoming him, before he sent out his invitations for this ball. He was a new-money upstart, and he could ignore the rules as he wished.

"I am Miss Llewellyn," I said to him. Up close, he seemed more handsome. He seemed dashing and terrifying and exciting, and I had an odd thought of somehow hauling myself up on his back, riding him astride like a man would ride, and clinging to his human torso from behind, pressing my breasts into his back—

I didn't know where such a thought would have *come* from.

"I know who you are," he said. "Perhaps it's fortunate that I have reacted to you, at that."

Reacted?

He reached down and took my face in one of his hands. His palm was huge and thick and warm but just like any man's hand, truly. He should not have touched me in such a way, because it was improper and far too intimate. He dragged his thumb over my cheekbone.

I felt it go all the way through my body, settling somewhere shocking, and it made me think thoughts about Mr. Granville that I would not have thought otherwise, thoughts that made me realize he was, well, naked all over that stallion part of him and that he must keep a horse-sized male organ between his hind legs, in front of that tail of his, and—oh, dear.

I should have jerked back.

He bared his teeth at me and his dark eyes flashed, and he looked like some sort of beast, and I was frightened and excited and all lit up inside in a way that I had never felt before.

Truly, I was a ruined woman, but I'd hardly enjoyed being ruined, which really did seem a pity to me, in the end. Why must I experience all the consequences of such an action and never have experienced whatever was supposed to be so enjoyable about it?

However, I had since heard, from Janet—not that she really knew, because she wasn't married either—that women didn't enjoy it anyway, and that I should never have liked it no matter what Oscar had done.

"Pardon me," said Mr. Granville in a gravelly voice that seemed to burrow into me, that made my nipples stand at attention under my corset. "My apologies, my lady." He dropped his hand. He shook his head, and he uttered a horse noise, like a whinny, stamping down his front hooves noisily.

I did jerk back then, frightened of being trampled.

He took off, away from me, quite quickly.

I gaped into his wake, wondering at all of it.

My brother was there, right on the heels—hooves—of Mr. Granville's leaving me. He was furious. "What was that?

How could you allow him such liberties? You truly are nothing but a slattern, aren't you?"

"Well," I said, and my voice was shaking, "one can't *be* a slattern with a *centaur*, can one?"

"HE WANTS TO marry you." My brother shook out his napkin, glaring at me across the table as if I had somehow started all of this.

"But..." I clutched my own napkin, horrified. "But..."

"I'm considering it," he said.

"Laurence!" I dropped my napkin. Right on the floor. I was too shocked to retrieve it.

We were having dinner. It was four nights hence from the ball. We had not stayed. Indeed, no one had. The entire place was cleared out in one hour, everyone having looked in. And afterward, there was a sort of level of embarrassment amongst all the people, for everyone had indicated to everyone else they would not be caught dead in the centaur's house, and yet everyone had appeared.

"He was at the club today," said Laurence. "He approached me. I had meant to approach him, mind you, so I decided I didn't mind. Before I could even mention a business arrangement, he spoke to me of you. He asked if you were receiving gentleman callers."

"He is a centaur," I said, in a choked voice.

"Yes, everyone knows this, Phoebe," he said to me. "I didn't know what to say. You do sit out in the morning sitting room every day, don't you?" Morning callers were actually received after luncheon. I think at one time they may have come in the actual morning, but that was back when people actually rose and were moving that early. If a person had an active night life, which many people did in town, one would not be awake before noon anyway, or at least not in any shape to receive callers.

"He is a horse," I said. "The bottom part of him, that is. I can't *marry*..." I swallowed hard and retrieved my napkin.

Primly, I folded it on my lap. "I don't think it would work."

Laurence grimaced and turned bright red. "The devil take me, that's not an appropriate subject for the dinner table."

"Well, I think it's—" I let out a shaking breath and stared into my plate. "You must find out from him what he expects, don't you think?"

"I'm not going to ask him about—"

"Well, if he's talking about marriage, that's what marriage *is*." My voice had gotten rather high-pitched.

My brother pointed at me with his knife. "If your reputation wasn't in tatters, you wouldn't even know about such things." He went back to cutting his meat. "Of course, no one else is ever going to marry you, so I hardly think you're in any position to quibble."

"Quibble," I repeated. "Did you look at it?"

Laurence set down his knife. "Certainly not."

"Well, it's just *there*, I suppose. He doesn't wear trousers."

"Phoebe, if I say you'll marry him, then you will."

"Well, tell him to call on me, then. I shall get a look at it myself."

"I don't believe we're really talking about... about... at the dinner table." He let out his own high-pitched noise.

"Is that what you said? That he could call?"

"I did, in fact," said Laurence. "It solves a number of problems for both of us, don't you see? You are never going to get another proposal of marriage, and he can take care of you, and if I get shut of you somehow, perhaps I can repair the family name and find someone who will marry me. So, if I tell you to accept him—"

"I do have the right to refuse, actually," I said. "That is the one thing a lady has. The right of refusal."

"Oh, please." He rolled his eyes. "I am your guardian, and if I say—"

"Yes," I said, nodding. "Yes, if you could be *shut* of me, it would please you."

He sighed.

I gazed into my plate again. "Is he coming tomorrow?"

"This could be your only chance to marry, do you

understand that?"

"I do indeed," I said. Yes, this could be it for me. Otherwise, I would grow old here, with my wastrel brother who gambled everything away, and I would dwindle, living a life lived on the fringes, repudiated for all time for having been deflowered by a servant. I was already ruined. A centaur's wife, then.

I would not dismiss the option out of hand.

CHAPTER TWO

THE BUTLER WAS in a tizzy the next day. Truly, everyone in the household was. We hadn't had a caller in some years. It was a momentous occasion, even if the caller was a centaur, and even if certain servants were horrified that he would defecate anywhere, as a horse would. There was a contingent that said they weren't mucking the place out like a stable until my brother put a stop to it all, saying that no one would continue to insult our guest, not even if he wasn't present.

"Mr. Granville will be treated the same as any other gentleman caller," my brother said to the servants.

Indeed, no gentleman caller's visit was ever given such care.

The menu for tea was fussed over and changed and the cook made ever so many different sorts of biscuits. There were towers of sweets taking up every spare bit of space in the room, far more than anyone could ever eat.

Of course, no one knew what sort of appetite a centaur had, nor what he really ate. What if he was expecting hay or oats or some sort of horse food? Did he have two stomachs? Could he eat meat? Horses did not. It was all quite confusing.

Luckily, one did not eat meat at tea as a general rule, though butter and cream featured rather heavily. Hopefully, he would manage. He could not have made it so far in society without eating what humans ate, after all?

The servants were nervous but excited. A change of routine was always thus, I supposed. I couldn't say that I felt any differently.

I paced in the sitting room amongst the towers of sweets and my hands shook.

But I didn't have long to wait, for he arrived quite as soon as my brother had said I might receive a visitor. I saw him alight from his carriage, which was rather large, and I thought it was odd for a centaur to ride in a carriage when he could likely pull one, but he poked out his head first and then out came his front legs, and he didn't seem that much different than a human man, except for the fact he had all that horse body behind him, of course.

He came directly to the door, and I thought he might have seen me looking out the window, and that embarrassed me, so I tucked myself in away and planted myself in a chair. I picked up a book as if I had been reading all along.

I was thus engaged when Mr. Granville was announced.

"Mr. Enoch Granville," said the footman, showing him in.

I got up and put down my book and stood there, hands clasped in front of my patched morning dress, and he ducked in through the door and stood there, looking at me with his flashing dark eyes.

"Mr. Granville," I said.

"You don't have a chaperone," he said.

"Oh," I said, "I suppose I don't."

"Your brother isn't here?"

"I don't think he's yet roused himself from bed today," I said, which actually surprised me. He knew as well as anyone that Mr. Granville was coming. *Enoch*, I thought. I rather liked the name. But my brother often drank very heavily when he was out gambling, and he perhaps was feeling too poorly to get out of bed today.

"I see," said Mr. Granville. "Well, that's..." He let out a heavy sigh and his nostrils twitched. "I should not have expected otherwise."

I bowed my head. "You... you said you knew who I was.

At the ball. I can only assume that's because my reputation preceded me. So, you know that a chaperone is considered sort of... pointless at this juncture." Oh, dear, that wasn't the sort of thing one said to a guest, was it? I flushed. "Apologies, sir, I don't know—"

"No, it's my fault," he said. "I am the one who did not greet you properly. I apologize for my disrespect, Miss Llewellyn." He crossed the room then and bowed to me. "A pleasure to see you again. How are you this afternoon?"

"I am quite well, thank you." I gestured, cringing. "Do you... we weren't sure... if you sit?"

His nostrils flared again. His eyes seemed to darken, and his countenance took on that wild element to it that I had noted at the ball.

My pulse quickened.

He cleared his throat, getting himself back under control. "Ah, indeed." He looked at the seat next to the table, and then the empty space next to it. He settled down there, somehow graceful, tucking his hind legs down and then his forelegs. Now, he was like a man seated on a horse who had lain down. He smiled at me. "Will you offer me tea now?" There was a roughness to his voice.

It made my body tighten again, my breasts going taut under my corset. What was it about his voice? I couldn't say I minded it, except for the fact it was a bit alarming. He was... well... what he was, after all. I didn't know where it ended, if it indeed could end. And I didn't know how to talk about that either. "Obviously, if you would like tea, sir," I said. "How do you take it? Sugar? Cream? Honey?" I turned to the tea pot and began to pour.

"Just the tea is fine for me," he said.

"Oh, do you take cream?"

"Not usually."

"Can you... that is... does your kind have milk?"

He chuckled softly. "Ah, of course. Yes, well, I was born human. I acquired this body through magical means. It was a curse, you see. Begged from a witch by a, um, well, at any rate, from a certain perspective, it may be said I deserved it. I am a human altered by magic, and thus, the horse parts of me are not, erm, well, you won't find me grazing or anything like that, if that is your question."

"I'm sorry," I said, offering him his cup of tea. "It's horribly rude of me—"

"Yes, just as it was for me to point out your lack of chaperone or the way that your brother treats you." He accepted the tea. "I am usually not so uncouth, madam, but I must say you put me out of sorts rather badly."

I spilled the tea I was pouring for myself.

"Oh," he said. "Apologies." His voice went deeper, more scoured at the edges. "I didn't mean to alarm you. I suppose that wasn't quite a proper thing to say either. It's, erm, the curse, though, I'm afraid."

"The curse that made you a centaur?" I held a spoon of honey over my tea cup, watching as the dollop of honey slowly descended.

"Indeed, that's also not quite an appropriate topic of conversation." He was rueful, clutching at his tea cup saucer. He was too far away from the table to set it down.

"Oh, no? I am curious, I must admit." Leaving my own cup of tea, I got up and crossed the room to another table, one with a towering display of biscuits.

"Where are you going, Miss Llewellyn?" he said. "May I assist you?"

"No, no, you are seated already, and you have your tea." I tugged gently on the table, and it came closer to him.

"You can't be moving furniture, madam!"

"I am quite capable," I said. "It is a small table, not the least bit heavy. I managed to nudge it even closer to him. Then I moved the tower to the edge. "There." I gestured. "For your tea."

He inclined his head and set it down. "I apologize—"

"We should have realized a chair would be no good for you, sir," I said. "When you call again, we shall have it set up more comfortably."

He looked up at me, though even standing, I was not much higher than him when he was seated in this way.

"Again? I must say I find that encouraging." He gave me a smile. It was like his triumphant smile in the ballroom.

It dazzled me. My breath caught in my throat. "Would you...?" I gestured to the sweets. "I am already up."

"I couldn't ask you to serve me, Miss Llewellyn." His eyes were hooded now, his voice husky.

"I..." It was hard to think of words, and I wasn't sure why. His voice? His expression? The way my whole body was still taut all over? "That is what a hostess *does*, sir."

"Please sit down," he urged me. "It's easier if you're not so close."

What did that mean? My heart sped up again and I sat down. I stirred my tea. I gazed at him.

He watched me with a singular gaze, his tea forgotten. He seemed to drink in the sight of me instead.

My breath came out shaky, too loud. I reached up to absently finger the collar of my dress.

We were quiet, just looking at each other.

He was very handsome.

I tried to gather my thoughts, get back to one of the threads of conversation that we'd left dangling.

But then the door to the sitting room banged open and my brother came in. He was dressed, but he looked ashen. He was stinking of drink, a sour smell that seemed to permeate all of the air.

"Oh, he's already here," said Laurence. He came over and sat down in the chair that Mr. Granville could not seat himself in. He turned to me expectantly.

I knew what he wanted and began to fix my brother's tea the way he liked it. Three lumps of sugar, a dollop of cream. I stirred it, watching him.

Laurence was looking at Mr. Granville. "Now, see here, Granville, there are some things that must be discussed. Some *thing* like you marrying a woman... well, how does it even work?"

"Laurence!" I admonished. He must still be drunk.

Granville only laughed, though. He picked his tea back up. "You're not schooled in such things, Lord Crisbane?"

That was my brother's title. He was the Earl of Crisbane.

Laurence's ears turned red. "You can't deny this is irregular, though, Granville. Are you going to wish... perversities from my sister?"

Granville looked at me.

My heart stopped beating.

"Perversities," repeated Granville softly. Then, he cleared his throat and looked into his tea. "Nothing your sister doesn't wish, obviously. If you are concerned about her safety or harm coming to her, you should not be."

"Oh," said Laurence, nodding. He turned to me, squaring his shoulders. "Very well, then. I think that settles it, doesn't it? She'd be quite happy to marry you, wouldn't you, Phoebe?"

"I haven't asked for her hand," said Granville in a low and even voice.

"But that is the reason you are here," said Laurence, turning to look at Granville. "Is it not?"

Granville looked up at me again. His expression went wild again, and my stomach turned over. "Oh, there can be no question that I want her, I suppose. No question of that at all. I am rather mad for her, truth be told. But I don't wish to..." He let out a huff of air. "You are frightened of me, madam."

"No," I breathed. "No, I..."

"You have just assured her that there is no need," said my brother.

"Yes," said Mr. Granville, eyeing me. "Yes, I suppose I have. And that is what I wish to convey. There is no danger at all, Miss Llewellyn. So, if you please, allow me to court you."

He was lying.

There *was* danger.

I could hear it in his voice, the way his tone lilted around the words.

I swallowed hard.

He tilted back his head, seeming to drink in my reaction, as if my fear pleased him.

My heart went badly out of rhythm in my chest.

"Why?" said my brother, breaking in, and it was almost as if he were breaking a spell. "Why her? What has she done to drive you mad?"

I set down my tea. Now that my brother mentioned it, it didn't make any sense, did it? It wasn't as if I'd done anything. I hadn't moved away when Mr. Granville had come for me at the ball, I supposed. But he'd acted as though there was something about me then. And he'd said that thing about "reacting" to me, whatever that meant.

My brother set down his own tea with a clatter. "Oh, dash it all. What am I saying? I don't really care why, frankly. If you want her, take her. It's all the same to me, and—"

"Why?" I broke in, gazing earnestly at Mr. Granville.

Mr. Granville met my gaze again, and it felt as if the air went electric, like a storm was gathering and it would pelt us both with driving rain. "You are singular, Miss Llewelyn."

I drew in a gasp.

He inclined his head. "To centaurs, that is. No one knows why exactly, but there are some women who affect us in a certain way, for whatever reason."

I swallowed. "What... what way?"

"It's nothing to be frightened of," he said, but that wild look was back in his eyes and his expression was hungry, and it *was* frightening, only, well, in a sort of delicious way. For even when something is frightening, there is a thrill in being desired, isn't there? And, for me, having been ignored and cast aside and denigrated for years now, to have someone look at me like *that*, I... "It's nothing to be frightened of at all. I shall be as careful with you as I am able, I swear it to you. It would not please me for you to be damaged."

"But you want me for..." *Fucking.* Oh, dear, I couldn't believe I'd just *thought* that word. How frightfully improper of me. "Marriage."

"Yes," he said. "I don't know if I've ever wanted in this way, in fact."

"A-all right," I gasped. Why I was simply acquiescing to this, I didn't know. I had not seen... *it*. His prick, which was a horse prick, which was... I had seen horse pricks before and they were—well, anyway, this was *mad*. I shook myself. "All right, you may court me," I amended. "Since that is all you have actually offered, as you have pointed out. You have not asked for my hand."

"I have not," agreed Granville.

"I don't see why there's any need for courting," said Laurence, who had picked his tea back up. "You'll never have another offer of marriage, and we both know that, Phoebe. You seem rather... I don't know... disgustingly besotted with him, to be truthful, so I don't think—"

"I most certainly couldn't be besotted," I said. "I don't know Mr. Granville well enough for such a thing. And that is the purpose of courtship."

"Just so," said Mr. Granville in a gravelly voice. A strand of his dark hair had come free from the leather strap that bound it at his neck. He tucked it behind one ear, eyeing me.

I wondered why his hair was so long. Men didn't typically let their hair grow so long. Was it... like a mane?

I liked it.

"I'm only saying," said Laurence, "that if you'd like to draw up the papers, I'm amenable, Mr. Granville."

"We'll go at the pace my lady desires," said the centaur, looking at me as he spoke to my brother.

"Well," said my brother, "I think my sister should be convinced to pick things up from a trot to a canter." He snickered to himself at his stupid joke.

I felt my stomach twist, and it was equal parts excitement and dread. This prospective husband of mine was half *beast*. What was I getting myself into?

CHAPTER THREE

I NEVER WENT to promenade in the park anymore. A promenade was done to be seen, of course, and no one wanted to look at me.

But the following day, in the afternoon, when people did such things, I arrived, since it had been proposed to me by Mr. Granville. I arrived on horseback, accompanied by my brother, who had complained the entire way of how he didn't see why Granville couldn't simply come to our home, because then, my brother wouldn't have to bother with being a chaperone.

I told him that he could simply not accompany me to the park, and I didn't need his presence, anyway.

But he was sure that everyone would take this as the reason for my having been ruined in the first place—his complacency with chaperoning me.

It was his fault, as I've said, but it was not because he wasn't watching. Or, well, I suppose one might make an argument that was a component in it all, but there were other reasons why my deflowering was all because of his bad behavior.

Anyway, I didn't like to dwell on all that. It was a painful memory which I pushed to the back of my mind whenever I could manage it.

Mr. Granville trotted up to us, dressed from waist to head quite properly, complete with a top hat sitting upon his head. His hair had been tied back again, but I supposed the breeze had pulled it free, because there were more strands out, framing his face, and he was heart-stoppingly handsome.

He pulled up to my horse, grinning at me. We were eye to eye, at the same level, and it felt rather intimate and easy.

"Good afternoon, Miss Llewelyn," he said in his deep voice.

"Good afternoon," I breathed, for the sight of his seemed to have stolen my own voice. "You're looking well."

"You're a vision," he said, his grin going rakish. "Do you fancy going off the promenade? There's a lovely small trail this way, quite good for some fresh air." He gestured.

"That sounds wonderful," I said, beaming at him.

"Off the promenade?" groaned my brother. "Just ask her to marry you, the devil take you both."

"Lead the way?" I said, deciding to ignore Laurence, which was quite enjoyable, I must admit.

Mr. Granville tipped his hat and took off.

I turned my horse and sent it off after him. She was a dependable mare who was often my mount, and she was the sort of horse who followed whatever horse was in front of her. She went off after Mr. Granville easily enough, and we were soon off and running through the park, far from the promenade.

My brother kept the pace with us as we went down the small path single file, as we leaped over a small stream, as we headed into a wooded area of the park.

But then I looked back to see that Laurence had dismounted, and I pulled up on the reins to turn around.

Laurence waved me on, cupping his hands around his mouth. "I'll catch you up!" he yelled after me. "Go on without me."

I debated for one second, but I really didn't like Laurence's company, and I didn't want to wait for him, so I spurred my horse on.

And that was how Mr. Granville and I ended up deep in the midst of the woods, standing together in a clearing, ringed by fir trees, where the afternoon sun beamed down on us like golden streams from the heavens.

He tilted back his head and his hat fell off, and he let out a deep, bellowing laugh as he reached after it.

I started to dismount to get it for him, but he stopped me.

"Please, Miss Llewelyn. I would not have you serve me." Except that was a lie too. He wanted my service in some dark and perverse way, and I knew it and so did he.

I stayed on my horse, and the hat rolled away. I gazed at him. The light made his hair glow as it settled around his face. He was like some magical being bathed in liquid light. My breath caught in my throat as I looked at him. He... oh...

He stepped closer. "I have a house in the country," he said.

"Most people do," I said.

He laughed. "Yes, I suppose you would think so."

I felt heat rush to my face. "Well, I suppose *most* people don't, but I meant—"

"If we marry, we could ride there," he said. "But here, in the park, I can't imagine what they'd think if they saw you on my back."

My eyes widened, thinking of the image I'd had in my head before, of doing exactly that.

"I can't abide a saddle, though," he said, coming even closer, his voice reverberating through me. "You'd have to ride bareback."

I had thought my eyes could not widen further, but I was wrong.

"Oh, *that* is what scandalizes you, Miss Llewelyn? My back between your thighs?" He laughed again. His laughter seemed to shake the fir tree branches.

My jaw worked. "I am... obviously... *all* of it scandalizes me, sir."

"Terrifies you," he breathed.

"You... you are lying when you say there's no danger," I breathed.

He raised his eyebrows, a challenge. "No, I'm not."

I gasped. "You... *that* is a lie."

He touched my face again, like he had at the ball. His fingers barely grazed my jaw line. Then they went lower to brush against the skin of my neck. "All right, the truth is, centaurs sometimes go out of their heads. Sometimes near women like you. But here we are, and I'm all right, aren't I?"

"*Are* you all right?"

His grin went nearly wolfish.

I shuddered.

"You're a terribly troubling distraction to all of my plans, Miss Llewellyn. Perhaps you can also be an asset to them. Well, this is what I tell myself, anyway, but I think... perhaps I'm already out of my head for you. I want you to say yes."

"Because you..." I swallowed. "Because you want to..." *Fuck me.* "Bed me."

He laughed again, softer. "I don't think it'll work on a bed, actually."

"I don't think it'll work at all!"

"I know it will."

"You've done it before, then."

"Well... I've never trained a girl," he said.

Trained? Something unfurled low in my belly at the word, something horrible and exciting and confusing.

"But it's not a difficult concept, I don't think. We can—"

"Stretched, you mean?" I suddenly burst out with. "Is that the training?"

His eyes darkened. He nodded. He was still touching my face.

"So, then, you wouldn't... it takes time to work up to..."

"Some centaurs take the stance that women need to be broken, rather like wild fillies," he murmured. "They force it, say that's the only way she's ready to be ridden."

Ridden? I swallowed.

"I don't find that's a particularly intelligent way to go about it, however." He licked his lips. "Especially not if..." He let his hand drop. "But never mind that. Where is your brother? This conversation is not the least bit proper, is it?"

"Don't worry about him," I said, reaching out for him. I

seized his hand and held it in both of mine. "I need to know. I need to know what I'm agreeing to."

"You know what I'm proposing, Miss Llewelyn." He was amused.

"But... but... it *works?*"

He chuckled.

"It fits? It doesn't... injure... and how? Our bodies, I don't even see... a position..."

"Oh, oh, shouldn't there be some surprises in a marriage, Miss Llewelyn?"

I sucked in a sharp breath, letting go of his hands. "I want to see it."

His smile went wide and feral. "You want to see what exactly?"

"You know what," I said, making my voice stern, rather like a scolding matron.

"Do I?" He tossed his head, and his hair — *mane* — sparkled in the golden sunlight.

My body convulsed, all of it, and between my thighs, which I had pressed together on the side saddle, everything felt, well, very warm and sensitive. "You do."

"I'm not sure of that," he said. "I think you'll need to be more specific."

I glanced over my shoulder. Was my brother there, ready to burst through at any moment? I didn't see anything or hear anything. It was silent and still here and we were alone. And Mr. Granville was always unclothed down there, so it was nothing for him, not really. I turned back to him. I licked my lips. I tried to say the word. I couldn't. My face went very, very hot. I drew in a very shaky breath, and I whispered it. "Your prick."

"What was that?" He leaned in closer, his voice deep.

I lifted my chin, and now my voice was strong. "Your prick. Your cock. Your *penis*."

His breath caught and released, and he was so close, I felt it fan out hot on my chin. He shuddered a bit, and that look on his face was back, that wild look, only it was wilder than it had ever been, and I felt that same flush of fear running all through my body, and I yanked on the reins of my horse, pulling away from him.

He started after me, his teeth bared.

Terror rose up my spine, turning my body inside out, and yet somehow my nipples pebbled at the same time—arousal, cold, goosebumps of fear? I couldn't say.

He let out a whinny and rose up on his hind legs, kicking his forelegs into the air, and gave me a brief but clear look at it.

There it was, brown and contained in a dark foreskin, his scrotum hanging brown-black behind it. His prick was huge. But it wasn't erect, either. It was soft and much smaller than it would be when engorged, and...

He settled back down on the ground, tossing his hair again. He gave me an insouciant look, proud of himself. Why are men always so proud of their cocks, really? It's not as if they have done anything to have them. They're just *there*.

I squared my shoulders, clearing my throat. "Well, thank you for that."

He laughed again, another of his deep, booming laughs. "Ah, you're quite welcome. Well? Nothing to say about it?"

"Is there something I should say?" I was prim, trying to keep my composure.

He considered. "You wanted to see it for a reason, I suppose. Was there some sort of criteria you were comparing it to?"

I flushed. "Simply because I have a certain reputation, sir, it doesn't mean that I've been quite free with my favors. Truly, I was tricked, and it was only once—"

"I didn't mean to imply that at all," he said, coming close again, reaching around to retie his hair, smoothing it all into place. "My apologies, my lady. That was rather thoughtless of me, wasn't it?" He left off touching his hair to reach out for me. "Does it frighten you?"

"No," I said very quickly.

He found one of my hands and brought it to his mouth. "Perhaps that was thoughtless as well. How could it not frighten you?"

I shook my head. "I'm not frightened."

He kissed one of my knuckles. "Truthfully, it won't be anything like the prick of that feckless servant boy who had you."

The kiss seemed to travel all the way through me, blooming inside me like springtime. "You know about that?" I whispered.

"I'm sorry you say that was trickery," he said. "That's abominable, that you pay the price for that even now."

"But you'll be different?" I breathed, and there was a current of irony in my tone. "You won't be abominable?"

"I..." He kissed another knuckle. "I shall endeavor—"

"You want to make use of me also, don't you, sir?"

"I'll teach you to take it." There was no bottom to his voice. He kissed another knuckle.

I gasped. "Will you?"

"Slowly and carefully and as gently as possible," he said.

I swallowed.

"Women *like* it, my lady," he murmured. "You'll like it, too."

I shut my eyes.

He kissed another of my knuckles, and I wasn't sure how his mouth there could make my whole body so alert and aroused.

In the distance, the sound of hoofbeats.

Mr. Granville let go of me as my brother galloped into the clearing. He pulled up next to us, patting the neck of his horse.

"Ah, you two look cozy," Laurence said, smiling at us. "What a lovely spot for a proposal. Have you proposed, Mr. Granville?"

"Not yet," said Mr. Granville.

At the same time, I said, "Yes, I suppose."

Laurence looked back and forth between us. "Well, which is it?"

"I suppose I haven't accepted yet," I said.

"I'd like the chance to do this properly, Miss Llewelyn,"

said Mr. Granville. "I've never done it before, and it doesn't seem I'll get another chance."

I smiled, liking that. "Well, all right. Call on me again, then."

He smiled as well, a smile full of the promise of things to come. "Wild horses couldn't keep me away."

"HOW DID YOU know?" I smiled into the bouquet of irises.

"I may have made inquiries," Mr. Granville said, smiling at me. "My servants sent to speak to your maid, that sort of thing."

We were in my sitting room again. It was the following day.

We were alone.

My brother was elsewhere in the house. He had told me that a proposal was the one time that a man and woman were allowed to be alone, after all, and that he was assuming a proposal was finally forthcoming.

"They are lovely," I said. They were my favorite flower, and I didn't think I'd ever been given a whole bouquet of them before. Usually, flower bouquets were other sorts of flowers. Irises weren't the typical shape, but they were beautiful and different and delicate. I adored them. "I should call for a vase."

"You can hold them." Mr. Granville was settled on the floor next to the table that was set up with the tea. I had been holding the flowers, though, and I hadn't served him anything. "I can't say I mind pleasing you, not at all."

"Well, that bodes well," I said. I felt a bit tingly and strange all over.

The previous evening I'd come back from my ride with Mr. Granville in a sort of floating, cloudlike mood. Janet had asked me all manner of questions, and I had answered them, and the two of us had giggled like silly young things, and it had seemed unreal in its goodness.

I couldn't remember being happy like this.

Not...

Well, it sounds awful to say not ever. That couldn't possibly be true. But, well, there was the time after being ruined, which was clearly awful, and there was the time before that, when my parents had just both died of an awful illness and my brother was spending too much money gambling and I was worried all the time about everything—money, whether I'd secure a good marriage, the future. And then before that, well, my parents had been ill. And before that...

I'm sure I was a happy child.

It's only that when I think back on that, I only feel stupid. Happy I may have been, but only because I did not know what was in store for me.

I didn't trust this happiness either, but it had its... well, there was a sordidness to it all, wasn't there? I was being rescued by a rich and handsome gentleman, whisked off to live in a new and enormous town house with white marble and a fresco on the ceiling, and that was all very well.

But it was because my new husband was part animal and because some wild appetite within him was whetted by the sight of me. He wanted to marry me to rut with me in some way that I couldn't even imagine entirely, with some huge member I would need to be trained to even accept and it...

Well, with all of that, perhaps I could trust it.

It was no pretty story.

It was as brutal as life itself.

I wanted it.

I wanted *him*. He was handsome and he made me feel desirable and pretty and I didn't care.

It was the only thing left for me, anyway.

I could have no other husband, and this one... well, this one stirred me in some horrible way, truth be told. I had never been stirred like this by a real, flesh-and-blood man. Perhaps by stories or paintings or imaginings, yes, but a real, breathing creature? No.

I stood up, burying my face in the irises, smiling to myself, still feeling like I was floating. I floated over to the bell pull, and I waited by the door until a servant came. I thrust the bouquet at her and told her I wanted them in my room. "Set them out where I can see them from my bed, so that they are the first things I see when I wake and the last before I go to sleep."

"Very good," said the servant, taking the flowers away.

Mr. Granville was on his feet, coming for me.

I shut the door and turned to him, unable to keep the smile from my face.

"Miss Llewellyn," he very nearly growled.

"Yes," I said—no, I sighed. But I was sighing everything these days. Dash it all, I was swept off my feet by this man.

He advanced on me, crowding me back against the door I'd just shut.

I gasped up at him, craning my neck up to look at his handsome face.

"You..." He reached down to touch my face, my hair. He traced the outline of my ear and it made me moan. "Apologies," he ground out. "I am not doing this properly at all. Do you have any idea how delicate and perfect and beautiful you are?"

I let out a little pleased laugh. "You take my breath away, sir."

"You are less frightened today?"

"Not at all," I said, shaking my head. "But I like the fear, you see. I can't trust it when things are too good. That is not the way life actually is. So, the fear, it assures me it's real."

He drew his eyebrows together. "Oh, Miss Llewellyn," he murmured.

"Is that pity, sir?"

"Never," he said. "How could I pity you, the wealthy and well-connected daughter of an earl?"

"Good," I said.

"You've entirely misplaced the fear, I'm afraid," he said.

"Oh?"

"Yes, you can't be damaged by, erm, my prick. It's the possibility of trampling, you see. That's the danger."

I straightened up, having truly not thought this through.

He lowered himself, down on his hind legs, forelegs stretched, and now he was only as much taller than me than a normal man might be. "Part of it might be... sullying you. That might be why I..."

I shuddered. I thought I might want to be sullied.

"You'll be... This union, it degrades you."

"I am already degraded," I said.

"Yes," he whispered, sighing. "Yes, so you are. And here I am to further cement that for you, am I not?"

"Is this...?" I was confused. "Don't you want to do this anymore?"

"It's not pity, Miss Llewellyn," he said. "But I am... I find myself wishing good things for you. I am not certain that I am..."

"Good?" I supplied.

"There *is* danger," he said. "Danger and humiliation and perversities. There are things I wish to do your body that... things that ought not be done to a lady."

"Yes," I said.

He chuckled. "I haven't asked a question."

"Well, are you ever going to?" I placed my hand on his chest, my palm flat against his tie. "I am no fool, Mr. Granville. I have understood these things from the outset."

"All right, then," he said. He lowered his forelegs as well, and now he was below me, peering up.

I bit down on my lower lip.

"I did not come to town with the intention of ever seeking a wife, I admit, but you have stolen my good sense, I'm afraid. This is..." He shook his head. "No, that's not how I want to go about it. I did practice. You won't believe me, hearing me now, but it's all flown out of my head."

I smiled, charmed. "I make you nervous."

"Terribly."

I laughed. I stepped closer.

He tilted back his head.

I was only a few inches taller than him this way. I could have kissed him if I'd liked. I gazed at him, memorizing his handsome features, wanting to call them up tonight when I lay in the darkness, so that I could look at his flowers and remember his face and live in whatever strange buoyant new world I'd come into. "Yes," I breathed.

He chuckled. "Miss Llewellyn."

"Yes?"

"Will you be my wife?"

"Yes," I said again, and I let out a laugh that was so light and free it must have been a giggle.

"I'm not sure if you should," he said.

"But you want me to?"

"More than anything," he rasped.

I kissed him.

He pulled me down into his arms, and he was frightfully strong and his mouth was hot and soft and intense, and I twined my arms around his neck and groaned against his lips, taken away by all of it.

He somehow got to his feet and pulled me up with him, gathering me against him, holding me in his strong arms and continuing to kiss me.

When he finally, carefully, set me on my feet, I had been kissed quite senseless.

"I think a short engagement," he said.

"I quite agree." I touched my lips with one finger.

CHAPTER FOUR

WHEN THE BANNS were read out at church, the reaction was audible. There was more than one gasp of horror. It was made worse by the fact that my fiancé was nowhere to be seen. He did not attend church.

But then he was some sort of monstrous joining of man and beast, so perhaps that cost him a soul. I did not know, personally.

Laurence ushered me away before anyone could speak to us—not that they would have, for I was roundly shunned, after all. But I knew what people were saying, and I rather imagined they were taking a great deal of delight in how far we had sunk as a family.

Of course, they would also say that if anyone were to marry a centaur, it would be a woman like me, for I was such a loose and horrid woman of low standards.

On the carriage ride home, I asked Laurence where it was that I was going to marry Mr. Granville. If he didn't come to church, would he not marry me there. Would we have to go to some other place for marriage, some arcane place of magic and sorcery?

Laurence didn't know, but he agreed that we must make some sort of plans for it all. "There's usually a reception afterwards, after all, isn't there?"

"Well, no one will come," I said.

"They came to the ball," said Laurence.

He was right. Everyone would come.

I didn't want it.

It was my first argument with my husband-to-be.

We had it in a vast sitting room in his new house. There was a fireplace that dominated the room, but it was empty, for it was not cold enough for a fire to be needed. The floor was white marble. The furniture seemed to be swallowed by the size of the room.

I sat on a chair, but Mr. Granville paced, his hooves echoing sharply on the marble floor.

"Of course there will be a reception," he said. "And we shall marry in the cathedral, exactly where a marriage to the daughter of an earl would typically take place."

Laurence was sitting across from me, and he sputtered at this. "I don't know about that, Granville. You... the cathedral?"

"You don't even come to church," I said.

"I can't fit in the pews," he said. "I must duck and scrape, and it's all very uncomfortable."

I supposed I hadn't thought of that. "Well, I suppose the cathedral is bigger, but it'll be such a spectacle."

"And you don't wish a spectacle?" Mr. Granville smiled at me, but it was a different sort of smile than I had hitherto seen on his face. "Because it will degrade you?"

I squirmed on my chair. "You're the one who said—"

"Yes, and you said you had understood it all from the outset. But if you wish to back out, now, Miss Llewelyn, you are permitted. A gentleman, however, does not break an engagement. I am committed."

"Well, it's nothing for *you*."

"Oh, you think not? They will be whispering *because* of me."

"W-well, yes, but—"

"You're ashamed," said Mr. Granville.

"No, I—"

"Admit it," said Mr. Granville. "It's one thing to accept the idea of me, of all of me and everything I demand of you in private. It's another entirely to parade your curious desires in front of everyone you've ever met and—"

"They already hate me!" I said. "I don't think it's too much to ask simply not to ask to be ridiculed and watched like a *freak*—"

"Well, that is what you will be, Miss Llewellyn, and don't ever question it. I am a freak and you are going to be taken by a freak, and everyone will know whether we parade or not—"

"It will be a triumph for you," I said.

He didn't answer.

Laurence got up from his chair. "Now, see here, Granville, I'm not sure if you're aware of the way of things amongst our sort of people, and I feel as though perhaps I should explain a thing or two about—"

"Not a triumph," said Granville, as if Laurence hadn't spoken. "Nothing so definitive as that. But a win, yes, my lady."

"In some battle you are fighting?" I gestured around at the house. "No, some war. This house, it was a battle, and did you win it? Asking for my hand, it was another—"

"I never intended to take a wife," said Granville. "You were never part of the plan. But now, I have to make it work, yes, and I can't hide things—"

"Why not? What is this war? How do you win it?"

He sighed heavily.

"Is it won when they accept you as one of their own, because they never will, and marrying me is certainly not going to help. Do you *know* how disgraced I am?" My voice echoed against the floors and ceilings. I was yelling this.

"I am quite aware, yes," said Granville. "I did take it into consideration. But you are also a lady. You are a *Llewellyn*, and that means—"

"The only way you could get a woman like me is if I was already tainted, and that is all they will say."

"I am aware of this as well," Granville grunted.

I bit down on my lip. Some part of me wanted him to say I wasn't tainted, not to him. Why had I thought…? When I spoke again, my voice was not nearly as loud. "So, then, why does it matter?"

It was very quiet.

Mr. Granville clopped across the room to stand next to me. I peered up at him. His voice was soft. "I could have simply had you, you know that?"

"What?" I whispered.

"You think your brother would have stopped me?" Granville raised his eyebrows. "I wanted you and I could have kept you that night at the ball. I could have stolen you away and had you well trained and be mounting you five times a day by now."

I choked. Why did that word—mounting—make my whole body go tight and tingly?

"You and I both know there would have been no consequences, not truly."

"That's not true." My voice was shaking. "They would have all thought badly of you. Even though I am not worth anything, they would have thought you a brute."

"Well, that is what I *am*, my lady." His eyes flashed.

I cringed from him. Then I fought it and shook myself. "Well, it's better for you if you marry me, I suppose, but for me—"

"It's better for you, too," he said. He glanced at Laurence. "Better for you, Lord Crisbane, it goes without saying. If you'd simply let her be debauched, they would have thought awful things of you."

I allowed this. "Yes, perhaps for him, but for me—"

"Because I *shall* win this war," Mr. Granville said. "And when I do, you will be entertaining countesses and baronesses in this house, and they will remember your lavish wedding and you will tell them, 'Oh, yes, my husband dotes on me,' and we shall be respectable, my lady."

I shook my head. "You... that will never happen."

He let out a harsh laugh.

"You're dreaming," I said. "I don't mean to be cruel, but if you continue to think that you can have such a thing, you will be crushed, and—"

"I'm aware it won't happen overnight," he said. "But it *will* happen, my lady. I am very stubborn, you see, and I never give up, and I always get what I want."

CHAPTER FIVE

WHITE WAS THE new fashion for wedding dresses.

I had always dreamed of wearing blue or red. Lots of people wore red, or they used to. It seemed a natural color for a wedding dress, I thought.

But white was the fashion, and it didn't really matter what I wanted, because this wedding was not about me. It wasn't about Laurence and it wasn't even really about Mr. Granville. It was about his ridiculous dream, and it was about spectacle.

I had to rein him in from time to time.

Too ostentatious, I would tell him. *There is a point in which it all becomes gaudy. You must show restraint.*

He didn't always listen, but I managed not to make it into a circus, at least I thought not.

The cathedral was procured. There was resistance, but Mr. Granville paved the way with money, which was what he did. The reception was planned. It would take place in his town house, in his great and vast dining room, and there would be dancing in the ballroom afterwards.

It was actually quite well planned in some ways. The first ball had gotten them all there out of curiosity, and this—the wedding of the disgraced woman they had gossiped about so often to a centaur—well, they could hardly miss that, could they?

They would come.

They would all come.

They would watch and they would sneer and they would think of it like the most entertaining thing they had ever seen, a woman married to half a horse.

It was happening.

I couldn't stop it.

I suppose, technically speaking, I could. Mr. Granville kept pointing out that I could refuse him. I could take it all back. I could return to my existence before—to being unwanted and resented by my brother. But it would be worse now. I would be the centaur's jilted almost-bride.

I was singular now.

It felt good, even as it felt horrific. I could not deny it. I could not stop it.

And besides, the dress...

Oh, the *dress*.

Its collar was a wide V that opened nearly to my shoulders. It was trimmed with wide, white lace, frothy and gathered. The sleeves were the puffiest of puffed sleeves, and the bodice cinched me together, making my waist look so very tiny, far tinier than it truly was. It came together in another V, and then the skirt was voluminous—white silk, acres of lace, a dress to twirl in.

Which I did.

Not during the wedding, but when I first tried it on. I twirled and twirled and giggled like a girl, and Janet clapped her splayed fingers over her open mouth and her eyes were shining, and I seized her and pulled her with me, and we twirled together, and we both cried.

She was my friend in some ways—not truly. I'm not an idiot, and I know that a person whose salary one pays can never really be a friend. But she was tied to me in so many ways, and it improved her lot in life too.

I was the one marrying Mr. Granville, but she was my maid, and she would be coming along, going to live in that big, grand house along with me, and we were both caught up in the fairy story aspects of it.

It is like a fairy story to marry a beast, after all.

On my head, I wore a crown of flowers—irises, of course, but tulips and daisies as well—wound through my hair which was braided and twisted intricately around my head. Ribbons threaded through my hair and curled down my back. Over all that I wore my veil, all lace, the edges scalloped. It draped over my face for my bridegroom to pull aside and reveal me to him.

The wedding itself was lovely.

If there were unkind whispers, I didn't hear them. The sound of my own heart beating was too loud. I carried a bouquet of flowers to match the crown on my head and glided up the aisle between the standing members of everyone in the community.

At the front of the cathedral, waiting for me, was my bridegroom. He was resplendent in his finery, and his shining, long hair was down around his face, and he looked at me with that dark, hungry look of his, and I felt special and wanted and beautiful, and it was good.

When he moved the veil away, he tossed it off and it fluttered down on the ground, and he bent at the waist to claim my lips, kissing me front of the gathering, kissing me with that *hunger* of his.

I wouldn't trade it, not for anything.

I was glad he'd insisted on all of it, in the end. It was a magical wedding, and I didn't care that I was a spectacle, not the least bit. Maybe... maybe some part of me *liked* being a spectacle.

Then the reception happened, and this was a bit of a blur for me.

We stood in a receiving line at Mr. Granville's—*our*—house as each and every guest arrived. They reached up to shake my husband's hand and they took mine as well, and every word out of their mouths was polite and proper, but I could see the gleam in their eyes, and I knew they relished this for what it was—it was a mockery of a marriage in their minds, an imitation of what a true and proper joining between our sort of people might be. It was theater. It was sport. We were gladiators and they were here to jeer at our bloody corpses. Everything about it was pretty on the surface and ugly underneath.

I knew it, and it hurt me.

But I didn't let it show. I was good at these sorts of things, at hiding my pain under a veneer of civility.

The reception progressed. Everyone stayed and got very drunk, except my husband, who made sure the wine was flowing and even insisted that my glass be filled again and again but who seemed never to have his own glass of wine. I watched him the entire time. Indeed, I could not seem to tear my gaze from him. And he didn't drink any alcohol at all.

I realized I couldn't remember ever seeing him drink spirits or wine or ale.

The drunker everyone was, the more raucous they got, the more bawdy their horrible jokes about was to occur became. There was discussion of things that still hadn't been made plain to me.

Would my husband take me against a wall? On my back? On my hands and knees? How did it work?

I supposed it wasn't happening at all tonight, because he'd said things about training, and I...

Eventually, Mr. Granville came to me and said softly, "Perhaps you're feeling tired and you might announce that you'll retire?"

I knew he was trying to spare me from the things they were saying, but I knew the minute I disappeared the things they would say would become even worse, and part of me wanted to stay as a shield, to keep them from letting loose entirely.

Still, I *was* tired. I had drunk a great deal of wine.

I nodded, and he had the announcement made.

I went up the steps and hurled my bouquet over my shoulder at the women gathered there. Then I was taken off to my chambers.

Janet was there with the nightdress that had been specially made for my wedding night. It was lacy also, white also, a filmy long sort of piece of fabric. It was barely there. In the mirror, I could see through it, see the darkness of the hair on my sex and the outline of my aureoles. I wondered if this was why wedding dresses were white now—so that everyone could picture the bride in her nightdress, as if the whole gathered assembly could share in her wedding night.

My stomach churned.

There was a rap on the door.

"Yes?" I called.

"I am here to escort you to your husband's chamber," said a voice outside the door.

I motioned for Janet to open the door and a servant was there. He was still dressed for serving at the party. He looked me over, reddened, looked at the floor. Tried to stammer some sort of apology. I cut him off, asking Janet for something to go over the dress and she brought me a wrapper.

Thus covered, I set off down the hallway behind the servant.

There were gas lamps in the hallway—for though my husband insisted on the luxury of a chandelier lit by candles, he had spared no expense putting in modern conveniences in his house—and they shone strong as we made our way down the labyrinthine halls of the place.

We turned corners and went up the stairs.

Finally, we stopped in front of two very ornate double doors. They had been carved with gilded *fleur de lis* designs. The servant knocked on one of the doors and the sound echoed down the hallway.

"Who is that?" It was Mr. Granville's deep voice.

"I bring your wife, sir," said the servant.

"Very good, let her in."

The servant opened the door, but he did not enter. He gestured for me to walk over the threshold.

Mr. Granville was speaking. "All of the food and wine is put up, yes?"

"Yes, sir," said the servant.

I swallowed, taking a step forward.

"Well, the guests will see themselves out soon enough, then," said Mr. Granville. "If there is any trouble, however, you may rouse Mr. Higgins to run them out."

"Very good, sir," said the servant.

I stepped into the room.

It was huge. It was dimly lit.

"Close the door, then," came Mr. Granville's voice. "And we're not to be disturbed, not for any reason, unless the house is on fire. Understood?"

"Yes, quite, sir," said the servant.

I couldn't see my husband. I saw something like a bed against the far wall, except that it wasn't raised. It was sort of like a mattress set on the floor, covered in cushions and pillows. It seemed soft and there were blankets. Hanging over it was a canopy with bed-hanging curtains pulled back presentationally as if this were the bed of a medieval king. But this was all in shadow, and I could not see it clearly.

The door shut behind me.

That echoed too.

My heart picked up speed.

Out of the corner of my eye, I registered light, and I turned toward it.

There was a doorway and through the doorway was light. Not bright light, but perhaps something from an oil lamp, I could not say. "Mr. Granville?" My voice shook.

"Enoch, if you please, when we're alone." I heard the sound of hooves on the marble floor, and then the light in that doorway was blocked, and then he was there, his huge body blocking it. He wasn't dressed, and I could see his bare chest.

Well, I sort of could. It was dark.

My heart went even faster.

"Is it all right if I call you Phoebe?" he said, his voice deep and dark like the hour before dawn.

"Yes, of course." My voice was a squeak.

He stepped back, out of sight, clearing the way. "You're frightened."

I didn't say anything. My heart felt like it was trying to work its way out of my rib cage.

"This way, Phoebe," he rumbled.

I moved on unsteady feet toward that doorway.

When I went through it, he was there, towering over me on the left. "You haven't been frightened in some time." He sounded thoughtful and a little amused. Perhaps affectionate too, in some way. "You've been perturbed with me most of the time, in fact. I've grown accustomed to your faint disapproval."

"I d-don't disapprove, sir," I whispered.

"Enoch," he said again.

But then I'd caught sight of something else out of the corner of my eye, and I jerked around to look at it.

This room was smaller than the other room, which I supposed was his bedchamber. This room, whatever it was, was still large. The ceilings were high. But there was a carpet on the floor on the other side of the room, beneath the… the contraption.

I didn't know what to call it.

It was made of wood. There were hinges and wheels, and it looked as if there was a sort of platform that could swing around, this way and that. It had places that might be hoofholds or footholds or…

"This is for me?" I said.

"This is…" He laughed. "It's adaptable. I had it built according to centaur specifications. Centaurs have a difficult time getting at themselves, if you know what I mean."

I jerked around to look at him. "You're saying…" I thought about that. No, I supposed manually stimulating oneself was not something a centaur was truly capable of. "This is how you… rub yourself off."

"It's truly ridiculous, isn't it?" He laughed softly. "You curse a man to turn him into half a horse, possibly precisely to keep him from sexual pleasure—I can't say who pioneered the curse, truly, but it has been passed down from arcane practitioner to practitioner over the generations and it is currently used as a very nasty bit of revenge. Anyway, what do the men who you've cursed figure out first, but how to build something like this? Rite of passage for a centaur, building your first mount."

I shook my head, reeling from that revelation.

"Men are predictable, are we not?" he whispered.

"Who cursed you?" I said.

"That's a story," he said with a sigh.

"You're not going to tell me?"

"It's not what I wish to speak of on our wedding night, no," he said. "I don't suppose there's any point in keeping it from you forever, however. You can't very well break the engagement anymore."

"I won't like the story?"

He hung his head, laughing again. "I think you're stalling, Phoebe. Is that it?"

I shifted on my feet. I looked at the, er, the mount, and then back at him. "You said... training... so are you going to... tonight?"

"Am I going to put my prick in you tonight, you mean?"

"Yes," I said, nodding. "Yes, perhaps it's best if we're plain about it. I shall endeavor to speak clearly from now on." I folded my arms in front of me and waited.

He just gazed at me, his features shadowed, hulking there in the corner of the room.

"Well?" I breathed.

"No," he said. "No, of course not. Not until you're ready."

"So, if I'm stalling, then, I suppose it's only..." I twisted my hands together, and I turned back to the mount. It was easier to talk in this way if I wasn't looking at him. "All right, well, I have to say I'm unsure about this training anyway. I don't know that there's much in the way of stretching that can really alter, well... Horses are... the length—"

"I'm not a horse."

"No," I said. I still wasn't looking at him.

I heard the clop of his hooves on the floor, and then they were silenced as he stepped onto the carpet. He was close to me. I turned, then, to look up at his shadowed features.

"Touch me," he said in that deep voice of his.

Did he mean touch his...? I bit down on my lower lip and

my breathing went erratic. I touched his stomach instead, touched him in that place where his human body gave way to the horse body. Felt the skin turn to short, smooth fur.

His body jumped at my touch. He let out an audible breath.

I smoothed my hand over him. I rubbed his back and I went down his body, walking as I did so.

Where I touched him, his skin rippled and he made little gasps and grunts. I liked it, affecting him like that.

Then, I was far enough back that I slid my hands over his flank and lower... between...

He let out a very affected noise.

Curious, brave, stupid... I don't know. I knelt down and crawled below him and looked at it.

"Touch me," he said again.

He still wasn't... erect. I didn't know a lot about human men, but when Oscar had deflowered me, I hadn't had to touch him at all. Obviously there was touching when he put it in my quim, but I didn't have to put my hands on it. It got stiff all on its own.

Was Enoch different?

It was big, but it didn't seem so awfully big now, not just hanging there, inside its foreskin.

Tentatively, I reached out and ran a finger over it.

He huffed, and picked up his front hooves and set them down. "Easy," he managed, and I wasn't sure if he was saying that to me or to him.

His cock was suddenly huge though.

It expanded and swelled and broke free of the foreskin and...

Oh, dear, that was enormous.

It was long, yes, but it was thick. It was thicker around than my arm. And the head of it, it was like a human's, I thought, only it was dark—the skin—there was no fur, and it just looked like a very big, very thick human cock, swollen and veined and sort of mushroom-like at the tip. It was maybe proportionate to the horse size of him, but it wasn't... well, I didn't think it was a horse penis exactly.

Could have told me this when I was worried, I thought. Then, *Maybe he doesn't know. I don't suppose he can see it.* Then, *Well, I'm sure he's figured out some way with mirrors —*

"Touch me again," he urged darkly.

"One track mind, haven't you?"

He chuckled. "You're frightened. Don't be frightened of it. I don't think it's particularly threatening in the end. Just… if I tell you to stop, stop."

"Oh, because it's not frightening?" I scoffed.

"Because if I… lose control…" His voice went guttural. "I won't." He sounded very sure of this, but I felt a tendril of worry go through me. What happened if he lost control exactly?

I touched him. I had to use both hands to encircle his girth.

He liked that. He let out a very pleased sound.

It was my turn to chuckle. I squeezed.

He groaned.

Well… well, what did one *do* with a prick? I didn't really know. When Oscar had deflowered me, he'd been stiff at first, and then I'd brought up Rosalind, and he'd wilted. I remembered him seizing himself and rubbing himself in and out of his fist in a frenzy.

Maybe…

I began to use both hands to go up and down on Enoch's big, thick member, quite quickly, squeezing a bit as I did so.

His hooves came up off the floor, *one-two, one-two,* he stamped them.

"*Stop,*" he yelled, his voice strangled.

I let go of him, letting out a little shriek. "Apologies."

"Get *out* of there. Stand *up*." His voice was garbled. "The devil take me, Phoebe, have I hurt you? Did I strike you?"

"No, no, I'm fine." I crawled out from underneath him and got to my feet. "You're worried about the trampling."

"I told you—"

"You did." I nodded. "But you also told me to touch—"

"I meant to explore me, not to frig me like some kind of expert whore," he snapped.

I drew back. I didn't even know what that meant. "A-apologies."

"Oh, no." He groaned. "Hell and damnation. You're... that was... obviously you're..." He let out a helpless laugh. "You can do that again over and over again, and I shall be the luckiest man on the earth. Just when my hooves are secured is all. It was *too* good. I'm sorry. I shouldn't have yelled."

I backed up, hunching up my shoulders. "I..."

"I'm making a hash of this." He ran his hand over his face. "This is not the way to ease your fear."

"I'm not afraid," I said stoutly.

He scratched at the side of his jaw.

"I'm not," I said. "I'm not... you know that I'm not a virgin, and you... well, you could have told me your, er, prick wasn't an animal prick, because that's quite reassuring, and it's all fine. I'm not frightened." I squared my shoulders.

"Mmm," he murmured. "You do seem to know your way around a prick, don't you?"

"Yes, it's fine." I drew myself up. "Well... train me, then."

His features twitched. That wild look went over him again.

My heart went out of rhythm. I regretted it, baiting him. I *was* afraid.

"Take that off," he said, gesturing at what I was wearing.

"A-all of it?"

"Yes." He ran his tongue over his teeth. "I want to see you, wife."

The word made my body tighten. But I was trembling, and I was afraid he could tell. I removed my wrapper and then began to gather up the nightdress beneath, baring my calves and then my knees and then—

"You intend to tease me, wife?" His voice was lilting.

I let go of the nightdress, swallowing.

"Apologies," he said in a raw voice. "I didn't mean for you to stop. That pleases me. Continue. As you were. I am..." He swallowed hard, and I saw his Adam's apple move in his throat.

Dutifully, I gathered up the dress again, pulling it up to expose myself.

He let out a rumbling sort of noise. He stamped his hooves again.

I shivered, pulling the dress up higher. I wasn't wearing anything beneath it. I showed him my hips and the juncture between my thighs and the small swell of my belly and then my breasts and then I pulled it over my head and I was as naked as he.

He lowered his head. He let out a noise, rather like some kind of snort, and he stamped his hooves again, and I felt real fear, certain he was going to simply charge me, plow into me, take me somehow, destroy me.

But he stilled, raising his face again, letting out low, slow, noisy breaths, as though he was panting.

I was trembling all over.

He lifted his hand. He beckoned me with two fingers.

I lurched towards him.

He reached down to cup my face, as he had so many times before. "You're lovely," he whispered. "Can you be mine?"

I shuddered at this.

He tilted my head back. "Answer?" It was a request, but there was iron in it somewhere.

"I am your wife, sir," I breathed.

He searched my gaze, and then his eyes traveled lower, taking in my breasts and my bare skin.

"Enoch," I said.

"Enoch's mount," he said in a small, wondering voice. "Daughter of an earl. With the roundest of eager, rose-tipped teats I think I've ever..." He groaned. He stamped his hooves again.

I jerked backwards, frightened because I was so close, not wanting them to come down on my toes.

"Apologies," he said. "I am... I shall endeavor not to do that with my forelegs, pretty one. It would destroy me to hurt you." He held out his hand to me.

Tentatively, I put my hand in his palm.

"May I put you on the mount, wife?"

Had he just called *me* a mount? Oh, no, he meant... he had called the contraption a mount. Of course, if he mounted me on the mount, then... well, it was confusing. "Y-you said you wouldn't—"

"No, I won't put my prick inside you, I promise," he rumbled. "But you said I could train you, and I'd like to begin. I'd like to look at you as well?"

"All right," I said. "But I don't know if I understand."

"Let me show you." He led me over to the wooden thing, and he pointed to various leather straps and carved bits of smooth wood. "You can face this way or that. You may want to watch, so how about if you face me this time?"

I didn't really understand, even still, but I agreed, and he helped me up into the thing. There were spots for my feet, holding them rather widely apart. He secured leather straps around my wrists and adjusted a sort of padded pillow behind my neck, telling me that it could go elsewhere if I faced the other way.

Once I was secure and off the ground, he eased a lever on one side, and I suddenly swung on something connected at waist level. My legs went backwards and then forwards.

He moved in front of me, grasped my ankles, and swung me so that I was perpendicular, lying flat on my back but quite high in the air.

I let out a little cry of surprise.

He laughed. He tilted me further backwards, so that my head was angled down, my feet in the air, and my pelvis tilting up, right at the level of his *face*. Then he moved the lever so that there was no more swinging, so that I was secure.

"There you are," he said, his breath tickling my inner thighs.

I shivered. "You're not going to—"

He touched me between my legs. His fingers were feather soft, gently parting the lips of me, and it felt nice.

I moaned. Well, I supposed this was all right.

"What a pretty little quim you have, Phoebe," he said. "I

like it very much."

I let out a breath.

"Let's see about this shy little clit here, if we can get her to come a bit out of her hood and say hello," he murmured, and then he touched me, well, *there*. That very good, very sensitive place that I wasn't even supposed to know about, I didn't think.

Oscar certainly had never touched it the whole time he was deflowering me.

I wasn't sure if the fact that I knew about it, that I sometimes quietly rubbed it under the blankets in the darkness, meant that I was heading down the wide road that led to destruction. I thought it was the sort of thing that women weren't supposed to touch, that it was only put there to lead us to sin.

He stroked me there, gentle. "Mmm, how's this?" he crooned, and he licked his finger and rubbed the wetness into me there.

I let out a tattered noise.

"Good?" he said.

"I... what are you... are you sure that's necessary?"

He laughed. "What?"

"It's only, I've done this before, you know, and there was none of... of *that*."

"This is part of the training, pretty mount," he told me. "So, yes, very necessary."

"O-oh," I said.

He licked his smallest finger and wormed it into me, inside my quim. "You'll expand here when you're at your peak arousal. And the arousal happens mostly from your clit. I suppose I should have spent some time with your nipples, shouldn't I? We can do that." He removed his finger from me and worked the lever. I swung down, facing him, gasping, dangling there in front of him.

He kissed me, a wet open mouthed kiss that made me jolt like I'd come alive, and he cupped one of my breasts.

I sighed.

He thumbed the nipple stiff, and it was another jolt.

I cried out.

He deepened the kiss.

I slid my tongue against his as his fingers gentled my nipple into a stiff peak which he gently—so gently—plucked. Then stroked. Then plucked again.

I could not stop making noises.

It was nice, very nice, and I felt like I was swimming in warmth and goodness and pleasure.

He kept kissing me but switched his ministrations to my other nipple, and once he had them both hard and teased, he stepped back and gave me a rakish grin. "Well, let's see how we're doing?" He arched an eyebrow.

"How we're...?"

The lever again, tilting me backwards, putting my pelvis level with his face.

He let out a long, low noise. "There she is, not so shy now." He touched me in my sensitive place again, and it was even better. My entire quim was slippery now, and his fingers slid all over me.

Into me.

His forefinger, thick and long and all the way inside.

"See?" he said. "Much more room now." He slid in another finger and then another.

I gasped.

"Shh," he said. He rotated his fingers and then gently rocked them in and out.

I moaned. That was... that was actually nice, and when Oscar had put his prick inside me, I could swear it felt like nothing at *all*.

"You're very tight and small, actually, wife," he said. "This may take a bit of time."

"How much time?" I said. "Time until what?"

He removed his fingers and rubbed my clit again. Then he... he kissed it.

I let out a strangled, startled sound. His *mouth?*

"I'll be right back, pretty girl," he said to me. He backed away, leaving me strung up in this contraption with my thighs open to the air. I couldn't see him anymore. I tried to twist to make out —

But he was back, and there was something smooth and cold rubbing over my quim. He rubbed it over my lips and gentled it against my clit and then he slipped it into my body.

I let out another little startled cry.

"All right?" It halted, having just breached me. "If you're not quite ready for it, that's just fine."

"What *is* it?"

"It's a training cock," he said. "Nowhere near the size of mine. Much smaller. Just to get you started. Do you want it out?"

Oh. "No, it can... you can... are you going to fuck me with it?"

"Oh, yes, wife. Unless you don't want that."

I tensed a bit. "And if I said I didn't?"

He eased it out of me.

"I didn't *say* that," I said. "I just mean, hypothetically — "

"I won't force it on you," he said. "You want it?"

I hesitated. "Yes," I said in a tiny voice.

It was back. It slid in, cold, hard, smooth. It went in an inch and then another and then another, until I felt his fingers against my skin, and I realized he was holding it and there was no more of it to go, it was all the way in. I tensed again, waiting.

"Relax." His voice was soft. I felt the brush of his cheek on my thigh, the scratch of his stubble.

"It's fine," I said, still tense.

He kissed my clit again.

I moaned.

"That's better," he said, and then he started to *lick* me, his tongue lashing its way over me there and he started to work the training cock in and out of me at the same time.

I made a tiny, strange noise.

I couldn't tell how I felt about that at first.

The thing inside me, it felt... well, the more he moved it, the less cold it felt, as if it was taking heat from my body, and it was very smooth and very hard, and intrusive, a bit...

just... very...

But his tongue, *oh*, his tongue, I *liked* that, and I started to squirm a bit, trying to get my hips to move against his tongue, to rub my sensitive place in just the right way against him.

I tunneled into that, and it was nice.

And then... he moved the training cock to a slightly different angle, and suddenly it hit me, well, differently.

"Oh," I gasped. "*There.*"

"There?" he repeated, and his voice was thick and aroused and full of that wildness I'd heard in him before. The training cock started to hit me there squarely, over and over. "Like that, wife?"

"Yes," I said, shameless, my voice thick too. "Yes, yes, *please.*"

He groaned, licking me again.

I whined. I writhed.

Something inside me started to ache. It was... it might have been bothersome except for the fact that it was so very, very nice. I liked that ache, and I wanted it. "Please, oh, please," I said again and again, my voice strained.

He didn't respond, because his tongue was busy. He just fucked me with the training cock and lapped at me in the filthiest of places and everything felt better and better and better and better and —

Oh.

This. All right, sometimes things like *this* started happening when I touched myself, but it terrified me, and I always stopped. I was afraid of it, afraid it was wrong, afraid it would hurt me, afraid...

So, when I went all tight and I snapped like a violin string, twanging against his mouth, clenching madly on the thick, hard intrusion in my quim, I didn't know quite what to make of it.

What was it? Why had it happened? Why did I like it so very, very much?

He lifted his mouth from me. "Is that it? Are you coming?"

"I... what?" I didn't know what he meant.

"Did you climax?"

"I—I don't know. What's that mean?" I was whimpering again. I was undone. I was embarrassed. What had he *done* to me?

"No," he said in a wondering voice, pulling the training cock out of my body. "No, no, you're not serious." He moved the lever, moving me upright to face him.

I didn't know what he was saying.

He claimed my mouth, ferocious. "You've never had an orgasm before? I've given you your *first?*" He grabbed my chin, digging his fingers into it, looking at me.

"I don't... I don't..." I was out of breath.

He grunted, fumbling at the leather straps that held my wrists. "Fuck, Phoebe, you're so very, very affecting. You make me..." He let out one of those whinnies.

I shied back, worried.

He was up, hind legs kicking out.

I screamed.

His hooves collided with notches in the scaffolding, and he was secure and stretched out in front of me, his big, thick cock pointing straight at me.

"Now," he growled. "Rub me like you did before. Please, wife, please. Hold me tightly with your tiny little hands."

I put my hands on him.

He whinnied again. "Like *that*, Phoebe. Yes." His voice had changed, gone guttural and odd.

I rubbed him, like I had before, frantic up and down motions using both of my hands.

He bellowed. "You're... damnation, that's *good.*"

I kept at it, then, confused, unsure, but sort of, well, *liking* it, because I was pleasing him, and because his cock was hot and pulsing and jerking in my hands, this eager thick trunk of a thing.

"Close your eyes," he said.

I did it. Why?

"Going to bathe you in my seed, I'm afraid. There's going to be a lot. You..." He let off into an extended groan.

I kept rubbing him, and then I felt the first hot eruption on my hands, and then it spattered my chin, my cheeks, my breasts, everywhere.

He bellowed again, moaning something that might have been my name and might have been some kind of praise.

I kept rubbing him.

"Stop," he gasped, "the devil take you, too much."

I let go. "Sorry."

He let out a very loud breath. "Is it on your face?"

"Yes?" My voice was small.

"Don't open your eyes. It'll sting. Give me a moment. I'll get you cleaned up."

So, I waited, eyes closed, as he dismounted, as he came back with a warm, damp cloth, as he gently washed himself from my skin.

When I opened my eyes, he kissed me.

I wrapped my arms around his neck.

He unstrapped me and lifted me off the mount. He carried me back to the other room, and we settled on the mattress on the floor. He wrapped his human torso around me, arranged us semi recumbent on a pile of pillows, tucked his legs beneath him, and was snoring in moments.

I lay awake in the circle of his arms, unsure of anything that had just happened.

CHAPTER SIX

I AWOKE THE next morning to the teasing and prodding fingers of my husband moving over my nude skin.

He was touching my breasts like he had the night before, making my nipples stand at attention and then gently plucking at them before he rubbed them.

I liked it, and I didn't open my eyes, just stretched and arched my back to push my breasts more firmly into his hands.

He chuckled into my ear, hands going to my hips. "There she is. Are you awake, pretty Phoebe?"

"No," I said.

He laughed again, but he used this time to move me, arranging me so that my legs went around his torso, so that I was straddling him, pillows at my back, his chest at my front. Then he went back to teasing my breasts.

I moaned and gloried in it.

I didn't open my eyes. I just sought his mouth with mine.

He obliged me easily with a deep, wet kiss.

When that broke, I let my eyes flutter open to look at him. Oh, he was quite handsome with his hair down and wildly disarrayed from sleep. I let my hands span his broad shoulders. I took in the dark hair that accented his bare chest.

"Are you sore?" he said. "I used the smallest of training cocks, but it's been so long, you're practically virginal there,

I shouldn't wonder."

"What?" I shook my head. "Virginity doesn't come back."

He just smiled at me. "Are you sore?"

"I..." I wriggled my pelvis. Maybe a little. I shrugged. "Why?"

"Well, we need to make a plan for your training, wife," he said, gently tweaking one of my nipples. "I'm obviously eager for you, but if we attempt larger training cocks while you're injured and healing, it will only make everything take *longer*."

"Oh, I see," I said. "I suppose you don't want that."

He just chuckled. He tweaked my other nipple.

I liked that. I squirmed against him. "Well, I must say *I* didn't find the training unpleasant."

His chuckle deepened and he claimed my mouth. He groaned against my lips. "I wouldn't say I found it unpleasant either, wife."

"So, it could go on rather indefinitely as far as I'm concerned," I breathed. "If that enormous cock of yours is going to hurt me—"

"No," he said. "No pain. Not unless you enjoy that."

I furrowed my brow. "*Enjoy* pain? How could anyone—"

The doorknob rattled.

Enoch drew his brows together, perturbed. He raised his voice. "I believe I left strict instructions not to be disturbed."

Muffled noises came from without. Someone was saying something like, "I have told you that you cannot be here."

And then the door burst open.

Enoch stood up, putting his body between mine and the doorway.

I let out a little mew of surprise and scrambled to pull covers over my naked skin.

There was a woman in the doorway.

She was wearing a long cloak. One of her hands was on the door, holding it open. Another hand came out to smooth at her hair. Except, that hand was on the same side as the first hand. Her skin was also a strange color—shimmering nearly purple in the light from the windows, black otherwise—and when her red lips curved into a smile, I could swear that I saw fangs.

I clutched the covers tighter against me and curled up into the pillows behind me, as if they could swallow me whole and save me from whatever that woman was.

She shut the door behind her and tucked that errant hand away inside her cloak. She was wearing a small hat askew on her head and her skirts beneath her cloak were voluminous. "I don't have time to wait for you, Enoch."

Enoch advanced on her. "Arabella. I'm indisposed."

"Well, you're naked, anyway," said the woman, whose name must be Arabella. She looked him over. "Not the first time I've seen you unclothed, though."

I bit down on my bottom lip, and I didn't like that. It didn't matter, of course. Husbands were under no real obligations to be faithful to their marriages in any case. And obviously, whatever had occurred with this strange many-armed woman had occurred before we were married, since we'd barely been married. I didn't have any right to be jealous. I had not come untouched to him myself. He had told me that he knew that he could fit his cock into human women because he'd done it. I didn't know why I cared so much, but it shattered something inside me.

I hunched deeper into the pillows, holding the blankets over me like a shield.

"Hello," said Arabella, leaning around Enoch. "You must be the new Mrs. Granville. So lovely to make your acquaintance. Are you going to be able to sit down today?"

"The devil take you, Arabella," said Enoch. "Quit the room immediately. If you give me but a quarter hour, I shall join you in the sitting room on the first floor and we can speak about whatever it is that—"

"No, I don't have a quarter hour," said Arabella. She closed the distance between them and hands came out of her cloak—how many hands did she *have?*—and she patted him on the chest and the belly and lower, on his horse parts, and I didn't like that either. "Very protective of her, aren't you? You think she can break your curse?"

"No," he said flatly, "and I'll thank you not to speak of that. Not to speak of anything, in fact, because you are going to leave the room now."

"If I go now, you'll never know what I got from Picadon." She gave him another smile. Definitely fangs. And Picadon? Did she mean the Viscount of Picadon?

"Tell me that in the sitting room."

"I shall tell you right here," said Arabella. "But first, you'll sort out my fee?"

Enoch grunted, running a hand through his hair. He glanced at me.

"Don't want your wife to know?" Arabella laughed. "You can tell me in the room with the mount. We can close the door for privacy, if you like."

She'd been *in* here? She knew about the mount?

My throat felt tight and my eyes stung. I hated her. I might also hate my husband.

Enoch glared at her. "You're going to give her ideas, Arabella." He stomped across the room, brushing past her, his hooves clacking loudly on the floor. He went to the wardrobe and opened it and felt around in the pockets of one of his trousers. Coming out with several coins, he held them up to show her. "Now, tell Mrs. Granville that you and I have never been intimate."

Arabella snorted. Dutifully, she turned to me. "I've never fucked your husband."

"Damn you straight to Hades, Arabella," muttered Enoch, coming back towards her. "Picadon?"

"Money first, then the dirt," she said.

"If it's not worth—"

"My labor is the same no matter the quality of the secret," she said.

"Yes, and you were paid by him for your 'labor' already."

Arabella thrust out a palm. She had two extra sets of hands. She was like a spider woman or something. Did Enoch find that attractive? I supposed the extra hands might be, well, useful, but… ugh.

He slapped the coins into it.

65

"He's married," said Arabella.

"No, he's not!" I cried out. Picadon was one of the more eligible men on the marriage market these days, and he was actively seeking a wife.

"Mmm," said Arabella, turning to look at me, nodding. "Yes, married to a woman far beneath him, one to whom he should never have married. He keeps her and their three children in a cottage on his property and he is trying to make it out that it never happened and that she is not his wife. But there are papers, of course, and there are the children themselves, who resemble him quite a good deal."

Enoch drew back. "Truly? You're not making this up?"

"I swear to you," said Arabella.

Enoch let out a delighted chuckle. "I could kiss you."

"I'd settle for an extra coin," she said archly.

"Oh, of course you would," said Enoch, and then he crossed the room to get her more more money.

She took it and smiled up at him, giving him another affectionate pat on the chest.

"Thank you," he said, looking into her eyes, his voice dropping into his deeper register.

Well, that hurt, looking at them together like that. I should have known what was between him and me couldn't be, well, real. I should have known that even though there were elements to it that were distasteful that it was too good. I shouldn't have trusted it.

Now, I was not only going to be married to an upstart half-horse, but I was going to be a laughingstock while he made a fool of me with any number of other women. I wouldn't even be able to keep his interest.

"No need for thanks." Arabella tucked the coin into her bodice. "Just pay me."

"Just find me more secrets," said Enoch. "And never come into my bedchamber again."

She snorted.

"I mean it," said Enoch, his voice going severe. He glanced at me. "You've upset my wife."

"*I've* done that, yes," said Arabella with a laugh. She

winked at me. "Let me tell you something about men, Mrs. Granville, in case you weren't aware. They never make women a priority. We are accents to their real lives and their real ambitions. Meanwhile, we women tend to think of men as the entire point of it all. I assure you, they are easily compartmentalized. Enjoy your husband and find something else to fulfill you."

"Arabella, don't talk to her."

Arabella laughed. "Oh, I think I made a pun. I suppose he is rather fulfilling in a physical sense."

"*Out.*" Enoch's eyes flashed.

She shrugged, using all of her hands to pull her cloak tight. "So sensitive, Enoch. I think I liked you better before you were married." But she left, slipping out of the room, closing her lips to hide her fangs, and he shut the door firmly behind her.

We were alone again.

Enoch glanced at me, looking chagrined. "My deepest apologies. She is... she has no sense of decorum, I'm afraid."

"Oh, no, it's fine," I said, straightening my back and giving him my best I-am-not-affected look. "I assure you, I've been preparing all my life for meeting my husband's former lovers in the bedchamber after my wedding night."

He shook his head. "No. I've never touched that woman."

"Well, *is* she a woman?"

"She's a whore," he said. "She fucks for money. I'm not the sort of... it's not possible for me to simply go into a—" He shook his head again. "Never mind. I assure you, that woman and I have no relationship other than a business one."

"Which is why she's seen you unclothed."

"Oh, for the sake of hell itself, there's..." He gestured. "What is there to see?"

"And this happened because...?"

"Because she has a habit of bursting in places where she doesn't belong and where she isn't welcome. Because she is the way she is." He sighed heavily. "She is useful, and I pay her because she is useful, but she is definitely not someone I would *ever* be intimate with."

I shrugged. "It doesn't matter, I suppose. You are a man. You can do whatever you wish."

"I cannot, and we both know that," he said. "It is complicated to be with me in that way, as has been demonstrated to you. What passed between us, you think that can be attempted casually?"

"I don't know," I said. "It seems easy enough to me. Pay her, bring her up here. She knew all about the mount."

"Don't be jealous, please. Not of…" He groaned, turning away from me. "Not of that."

"I'm not jealous."

"You can't possibly know how I feel about you, anyway. You're *singular*. I told you—"

"What was the thing about breaking the curse?"

"Ah, of course you're going to latch onto that."

"Why were you cursed in the first place?"

He groaned, tilting back his head. "Hell and damnation, yes, *this* is marriage."

"Oh, well, if that's how you wish it," I said, "we shan't talk of anything." I gathered up handfuls of the blankets in fists.

He came back to the bed—well, to the cushion on the floor. He settled down next to me, tucking his legs under his body. Even so, he towered over me. He sighed again. When he spoke, his voice was very soft. "It's not a difficult thing to guess, truly. I'm sure you've worked out the broad strokes, even if you don't know the details, but I don't suppose the details much matter."

"Broad strokes of what?"

"Of why I was cursed."

I licked my lips. Well, he had a point about that. "You angered a woman?"

"My fiancée."

"You… with another woman?"

"Well, there you go." He was sardonic. "Not difficult at all to guess, was it? Yes, I went to bed with her dearest and closest friend, in fact, and her friend was already married, and I got her with child, and when she realized that, she threw herself out of a window rather than let her husband know, and... well, that was how it was all discovered, and then my intended... she... then the curse and..." He was not looking at me. He was looking out the window. "So, yes, that's what you've married. My apologies. You are quite lovely, Phoebe. You deserve better."

I wasn't sure what to do with any of that. "You killed her," I breathed.

He let out a sharp, pained noise, almost like a sob. "Quite. Indeed, yes." He was up off the bed now, away, going for that window. He yanked the curtains out of the way, clinging to them for dear life as he looked down at the street.

"I'm sorry." I repented of having said that. "That's not really true. She did it, and it wasn't as if you wished her—"

"I murdered her and murdered my unborn child. And then I was cursed like this, so there's no real hope for offspring, ever. You have no idea how often I've thought on it, how often I've wished with everything in my being to go back and not to do it. To stop my idiotic, stupid self from destroying everything."

"Murder is a very strong word," I said.

He didn't say anything. He only stared out the window.

"Why *did* you do it?"

He laughed softly. "Why does anyone fuck anything, wife?"

I flinched.

"Why did you let that servant boy under your skirts?"

I hunched into the pillows. "He got me very drunk. He made it into a game, who could drink the fastest. But he wasn't trying very hard to win. And I was quite smaller than him, so it went straight to my head. Everything was spinning. I hardly knew what was happening, truly. I simply wasn't in my right mind, and—"

"Sorry," he said. He hadn't turned from the window. "Sorry, it's not the same, not at all. You... you're just another in the list of people—women—I've trespassed against, I suppose. I'd like to say I'd stop, and I'll leave you be, but I can't do that. I want you too badly. Couldn't possibly stop." He put his palm against the window pane. "So, wife, are you sore?"

I let out a noise of disbelief.

"We'll continue the training this evening unless you say otherwise." He dragged his fingers over the glass. "Do you know the way back to your room, or shall I ring for a servant to take you?"

"I'm dismissed, then?"

"Yes," he said tightly. "You're far too distracting, and I have business to see to."

CHAPTER SEVEN

JANET HOVERED AT the edges of the room while I soaked in the bath in my room, eyes closed, submerged to my shoulders in the water. The water was growing cold, and I only opened my eyes to ask if someone could bring another bucket of hot water.

Finally, after the bath had been refreshed and warmed, Janet approached, sitting down next to me to ask if I was all right. "Look, I know I'm not supposed to know about things," she said, "but I do a bit. I have married sisters and sometimes, when they get together, their lips start flapping and I sit and listen. So, it's not as if I don't know whatever it is that you and the centaur were... are you all right?"

"He didn't," I sighed. "Not with his... body, anyway."

"Oh," she said, rocking back, staring at me.

I shut my eyes again.

"You can tell me," said Janet. "You don't have to protect my innocence or anything, you see, that's all I'm saying. I think you need someone to talk to."

I opened my eyes. "That part of it, Janet, is... well, I have really no complaints about that part of it. I suppose it's shocking. However, it is not... I do not mind... he did a thing with his tongue that was, well, very nice."

"His tongue?"

"Oh, dash it all, Janet, I cannot talk to you about that." I straightened up in the tub.

"The other servants say he has something built in his room for it."

"Yes," I said. "But that's... it's quite useful, and I think it only improves safety, and..." I groaned. "But the thing is, I'm not sure he's..." I let out a breath. "I think he may *be* a monster."

"A monster?"

"Or, if not a monster, then at the very least, *not* a good man."

"Oh," she said softly.

"Why has he built this house, Janet? What is his reason for doing this? Why has he married me?"

"I think he wishes to rise in station, Miss Llewel—Mrs. Granville."

"Yes," I said. "I think he wishes that more than anything. I think there is very little he is not willing to attempt in the service of making that happen. I think he is willing to do, well, bad things in order to achieve it." The secrets of the viscount? What was he going to do with that? How many other secrets had he amassed? And certainly, he expressed regret for what he'd done to be cursed, but was it because other people had been hurt or because he had been punished? Would he have cared if he had not been cursed?

"Oh, dear," said Janet. "And we are bound to him, for life."

"*I* am bound to him," I said. "You—"

"Well, you know what I mean," she said. "Of course... maybe that's just how it goes, though? In the stories, when a woman is wedded to some creature, and he is cursed, doesn't he have to change? Doesn't she help him by making him fall in love with her?"

"How does one *make* anyone fall in love?" I said. "He doesn't love me. He wants to fuck me, but he doesn't..." I shook my head. And then, my voice full of tears, I slipped down into the bathwater, letting it cover my face, which was now too hot and too wet anyway.

ENOCH LAID THEM all out in front of me on a table in the room with the mount. They were all made with black glass, thick and solid through, and they were all shaped like cocks. I'd heard the word before, of course, whispered.

Dildo.

It was an old word. Once, I'd found a book hidden in the back of the library in my family's country house with a very naughty poem addressed to such things, from a chagrined man whose lover preferred fakes to the real thing.

The dildos started small and grew gradually thicker and longer. There were six of them. The biggest one seemed insanely big, too big. I looked at it for a long time, chewing nervously on my lower lip. "Is that... your own..."

"Yes, that's bigger than me," he said, touching the biggest of them. "If you can take that, you'll have no problem with me, though."

I nodded. "Yes, I suppose that makes sense. But that... I don't see how..." I writhed under my nightdress, revolted and intrigued at once somehow.

"I only wanted you to see where we're headed," he said. "We won't get anywhere near this one tonight."

"How long... do you train me?"

"It depends on various things," he said, running his fingers over the array of black phalluses. "Your comfort. How easily you take to it all. Whether or not I get too distracted and spent to continue a session." He gave me a wicked smile. "You *are* distracting, wife."

"But there must be an... an average. When you've done this before—"

"I've never trained a woman, I told you," he said.

"But you've..." I didn't want to know. I needed to know. I looked at the mount. "You've been with women."

He didn't respond.

I looked away from the mount and back to him.

He was rubbing at his chin with one hand. "All right, I spent some time with a herd."

"A herd? Of centaurs?"

"They are... they can be... there is a brutishness to them with women." His nostrils flared.

I knew there was more to this. I waited.

"You won't like it," he said finally.

"It doesn't seem there is much you have to tell me that I do like," I managed.

He laughed bitterly. "I let her out. I let them all out. But first I... well, I have told you that centaurs lose their heads around women who... trigger..."

"I don't understand any of that," I said, folding my arms over my chest. "There are a number of things I don't understand, in fact."

"They scented the women out and kidnapped them," he said. "They corralled them in pens, kept them in stalls, and they strapped them to mounts and... *broke* them. It wasn't always... it was confusing. Sometimes, some of the women seemed to be... I don't know. Not all of them left, at any rate, when I freed them."

Well, then. I simply blinked at him. "You did that. To a woman who'd been captured. You..."

"It was a long time ago, Phoebe," he whispered. "At the beginning of it all, right after the curse, I was angry."

"You ravished her."

"I suppose," he said with a nod.

"You suppose?" I drew back. "And then, because you think you rescued her, you think that makes it better?"

"Sometimes the mounts become..." He gestured with his hands as if he was searching for words he couldn't find. "There were the ones that were common property, for any of the herd to mount, and then there were... I told you women enjoy it."

I shook my head. "But you also—

"I don't think it's quite like that anymore, anyway," he said. "It was a long time ago, and then Nescuss, who was the chief of the herd, his curse broke, and he made rules, and then... if I thought they were still stealing women like that—"

"A long time ago?" I looked him over. "How long could it have possibly been?"

"I'm probably older than you think I am, Phoebe," he said softly. "We don't age after we're cursed. And I was cursed nearly eighty years ago."

I drew back. "So, what? You're... over a hundred years old?"

He nodded. "Indeed."

I backed away. I turned my back on him and walked several paces off. But there was nothing in this part of the room except the mount, and so I went there. I touched it, hand against the wood.

"Perhaps we don't do any training tonight," he said with a sigh.

"I don't understand you," I said.

"Perhaps you do," he said. "Perhaps you understand me perfectly, and you are simply horrified by what you keep uncovering about me."

Perhaps he was right.

I rounded on him. "How does the curse break?"

"How do you think?" he said, spreading his hands. "True love, of course. Is there another way?"

This was like a dart to my heart. He had said he didn't want the curse to break when Arabella was here. And I knew he didn't feel anything like love for me, only lust.

"I find it perverse," he said, picking up the largest of the dildos. He turned it this way and that. "I can't understand why anyone would construct the curse in this manner. But here it is: I shall never lose these legs or this tail. I shall live out my life as a centaur, regardless. But there are certain women and when I come in contact with them, they make me mad with lust for them. The *way* I want them... the way *all* centaurs want them... And if, in the course of doing whatever it is one does with a woman one wants to fuck like an animal, somehow this turns to love? Then I stop aging, and I can sire human children on her and live happily ever after." He laughed. "Like a fairy story or something, I don't know. I have plans, though, and they tend to hinge on my living forever, so..." He shrugged.

I gripped the mount for balance, too stunned to speak. This... this was more horrible than I had imagined.

He groaned. "Oh, look at you. I suppose it's better in the end, really." He set down the phallus and came for me.

I wanted to back away, but there was nowhere to go, unless I climbed inside the mount, so I didn't go anywhere. I just stood there.

And he came for me. He was shirtless, and his hair was down, and he was the most handsome thing I had ever seen in my life, and just the look of him made my heart become the fluttering wings of a trapped bird, and I wanted to scream and sob and beat his chest and kiss him and beg him to put his mouth back between my legs again.

Then he was practically on top of me, and he reached down to caress my cheek in that way of his.

I tilted my head back and looked up at him and he peered down at me.

His voice was as deep as the depths of hell and as horrifyingly enticing. "The true love must go both ways, you see, so it's best if you're repulsed. Because, pretty Phoebe, I feel my danger. I think I could fall for you. I think I might already be half in love with you. You must hold strong for us both. Hate me. Can you do that?"

I shook my head. "No."

"No?" He smiled. "You can't hate me? Are you some sort of—"

"No, you're not," I said. "Not half in love with me. You don't love me at all."

His smile widened. "Ah, indeed not. Not at *all*."

I shoved his hand away from my face, angry.

He took a step back.

I seized handfuls of my nightdress and hurled it over my head.

He let out an audible gasp. "What are you...?"

I climbed up into the mount. "Train me," I said in a strangled voice.

He let out another noise, this one tinged with desire. He

came closer. "That's what you want?"

I was bending down to secure my ankles. "Perhaps you should do it the way you did with the girls who were captured and ravished and just keep me in a stall and pen me up. If you want me to hate you, that is."

"Ah," he said, coming closer, grasping one of my hands and tying it with a strap as well. "You'd look quite pretty bridled, I imagine." He touched my face. "Bit in your mouth." He shoved his finger there.

I convulsed. That aroused me, the devil take me. I *was* on the broad path to destruction. Perhaps *I* was cursed. I sucked on his thick finger.

He groaned. "Maybe this needs trained too?"

I spat him out. "You can't be serious."

He pushed his finger back in, and then another and then another, stretching my mouth until I had half his fist in there.

I made noises of protest, and I scrabbled at his arm with my free hand, and my quim clenched again and again and my whole body felt heavy and ready and eager and I *did* hate him.

"Just the head, I think. You could definitely suck me, wife."

I groaned, horrified, excited, disturbed. He *was* a monster.

He moved his hand out of my mouth, letting out a sigh. His hand went to cup one of my breasts. "I've heard it said that it helps with the training, that a belly full of centaur seed loosens a mount's cunt, but I think that sounds ridiculous, don't you?"

"You mean... swallow..." I shuddered. "But that sounds—"

"You liked it when I used my mouth on you, didn't you?" He crooned this, teasing my nipple.

I moaned. "I do hate you."

"Good," he breathed, and then he kissed me.

I held onto him with the hand that wasn't strapped down, tangling it in his mane.

He groaned.

I tugged, pulling his head back.

He let out a noise that sounded as if he liked that, and I remembered what he said about enjoying pain—

I let go of him with a horrified whine.

He kissed the inside of my palm. "You're beautiful and fierce and perfect, wife." Then he tugged my hand down and secured a leather strap around my wrist.

I groaned. "So, your plan is to live forever, while I grow old and die."

"I suppose," he said. "But you needn't worry, because you... it won't matter. I'll want you regardless."

"What?" That was horrifying.

"You're mine," he said to me. "I have you now. I couldn't dream of letting you go. I couldn't bear to be separated from you. My Phoebe." He cupped my cheek again. Then he adjusted the lever and swung me back into the position I'd been in last night, with my pelvis angled up.

I cried out in surprise.

He secured me so that I wasn't swinging anymore, planted a quick kiss against my mound, and then went over to the laid-out dildos. He came back with three of them.

I tensed. I had sort of thought, well, that it would be one at a time?

He rubbed at me there, gentle, eager. "Already so very wet, Phoebe. What a good wife you are. I'd like you to always get this wet for me. What if I tell you to do that? What if I make that a request?" He licked me, right in the most sensitive of places.

I moaned.

"An order?" he said. "How do you feel about *that?*"

I whined.

"And if you don't get this wet," he said, "then I'd have to take a riding crop to your arse, of course." He reached back and squeezed me there.

"No," I said, shaking my head. "No, you said you wouldn't hurt me."

"So I did," he said. He rubbed my clitoris. "There, there, then, don't worry, Phoebe. I'll be very careful with you. You can trust me."

Oh, I definitely couldn't do that.

He rubbed me until I was senseless though, stopping to check every so often, fingers inside me to feel if I was opening for him. When he was satisfied, he went to get the dildos.

"This," he said to me, "is the training cock you took last night." He jammed it into me.

I cried out.

He pulled it out. "And this," he said, "is a bigger one." He pushed that into me, slower, but it slipped right in, and it wasn't even difficult. It even felt good.

I moaned.

He rubbed my clitoris and rutted the training cock in and out of me, searching around for that spot he'd found inside me the night before. "There?" he said.

"Uh unh," I managed.

He adjusted. "There?"

I let out something that sounded like a sob. "Yes, yes, *oh* yes."

He groaned. "Good girl," he breathed, and then he made me climax.

It seemed to happen more easily tonight, as if my body had needed to be taught to do it, and now it knew its way around it. But perhaps it wasn't quite as shattering as before? I didn't know. It was very good, and I felt as if some bright wondrous pleasure had crashed through me like an ocean wave.

But right on the heels of it, he was shoving the even larger training cock into me.

It went in easily too, no pain, slipping in there as if it had been made to fit inside my body. But surely it filled me with no space to spare. Surely I couldn't take more than this.

"How's that, wife?" he murmured.

"Big," I said.

"Bad?"

"N-no," I whimpered.

He began to move it inside me. "Good?"

I let out mangled noises, moving my hips with it, against it. I was so very sensitive now, and it was good, but it was also, oh... it sort of hurt but it was good, and I suddenly understood it, the enjoyment of pain, because when they blended together like this, it became confusing in its intensity.

"Tell me to stop and I shall," said Enoch, thumb on my clitoris.

"Don't stop, don't stop," I said.

"Good, that's very good," he said. "I want you to come again for me. Can you do that?"

"I..." I was falling apart. "I don't know."

"Yes, you can," he said, his thumb making tiny, tantalizing circles on my clitoris. "You're quite good at having orgasms, my pretty wife, and if you just let yourself, you can squeeze nice and hard on this big, big training cock."

I just let out a series of tiny noises, no words.

"Phoebe," he said in an even and deep voice, very serious. "I need you to tell me that you'll come for me. Say it, pretty girl."

"I-I'll come," I moaned.

"Say that you'll be a very good girl for your centaur husband and you'll come just like he wants you to."

I couldn't possibly say all that. Damn him, I was close again already.

"Say that you're a very obedient, sweet little mount who takes cock very well, who comes and comes, because she's *such* a good a girl, such a very, very—"

I didn't hear anything else he said. I was banging against the ceiling of the room, jostled in and around the rafters that held the roof onto his huge house. I was raining down over all of the city streets in gold shimmers of intense pleasure. I was shattering again.

He pushed the training cock home, piercing me somewhere deep and wondrous, and I hit another peak and the gold shimmers went white, like frost, and I was crystallized, and I *screamed*.

He held it there, deep in me, as I rode the rest of it out. Then he removed his hand. "Keep it inside you, wife. Hold that there."

I clutched it with my cunt.

He moved the lever, adjusting me as he had the night before. His hooves went up into the grooves. His cock was huge and hard and pointing at me.

But he hadn't unstrapped my hands this time.

"Just the head," he wheezed. "You can do it. I won't last. I'm ready to burst."

I hesitated.

"Phoebe?"

"Yes, husband," I breathed.

"It's an order." His voice was like music. "Suck my cock. Swallow my seed. Are you refusing me?"

"No, husband," I said, and I moved forward and went eye level with his huge, huge prick.

I licked it.

It was smooth and salty, and I liked it.

He let out a noise above me, such a noise.

I sucked him into my mouth. He was girthy, but I could fit him between my lips, more than the head, I thought, though he was too long to really fit in my mouth truly. I only took the tip of him though, and I barely suckled him at all before he let out a shout above me, and my mouth was suddenly flooded with his salty, thick seed.

I choked trying to swallow it.

It dribbled out of my mouth, and I struggled at it, barely noticing whether it was unpleasant or not, so intent I was in completing the task he'd set for me.

When he settled back in front of me, he kissed me and then touched the places he decorated my chin. "Sloppy," he breathed, but he liked it. He caught it on his finger and offered it to me.

I licked it clean.

His eyes went cloudy, and he kissed me, fierce and hard. He pulled away, panting. "If I wasn't... if you hadn't just drained me, wife, I wouldn't be able to stop. Lever you back and have you now. Damn everything, the way I want you." His mouth was on mine again, hungry and desperate. He smoothed his hands over my bare skin. "You're the prettiest woman in the whole of the city," he groaned. "You're everything I ever wanted. You're so lovely, *so* lovely, wife." He pulled away, gazing at me, shaking his head. "How? How are you mine?"

I swallowed. I didn't... when he said those things, the emotion I felt wasn't hate.

He rubbed his thumb over my lower lip. "I don't deserve you."

CHAPTER EIGHT

I DIDN'T TELL Janet about the curse, or about falling in love, or about anything he'd told me.

I wasn't sure how I felt about it.

Well, no, that wasn't exactly it.

I suppose I was ashamed of myself for feeling conflicted. It was clear how I should feel about him. Pure hatred. But... well...

He was horrid in many ways, but there were compensations. The pleasure he gave me. How pleasing I found looking upon him. The sheer intensity of our couplings. And, after all, he had gotten me out of my brother's house and brought me here, to this new and splendid place.

That day, a dressmaker came to take my measurements and drape all manner of pretty fabrics over me. More compensations, the promise of dresses and pretty things. I was not shallow in that way, at least I did not think that I was.

However, the truth was that life was a series of compromises, one after the other.

This was my new life.

It was not so bad in the end, truly.

He didn't love me, and he only wanted to use my body, and he had some plan to live on forever while I withered away, and I couldn't think of that without some sort of dread that nearly choked me.

What would that be? He would be perpetually young? Meanwhile, I would be old and childless and he claimed he'd still lust after me, which I didn't think that I was going to welcome forever and ever. Wasn't there a point in time when interest in that waned?

Why had he married me at all? That didn't make sense. But, then, I supposed that his desire for me was all-encompassing and nonsensical and he couldn't bear it otherwise. That was a compensation, too, I had to admit. Being wanted in that way by a powerful man-beast, it was heady in its way.

He came into the room where I was with the dressmaker, and he was somehow so quiet I didn't notice. It wasn't an easy thing for him to be there unnoticed, because he was no small creature. He had hitherto shown no interest in the dresses, as men tend not to do. But now, his voice drew my attention. "I like her in blue. What about that one?"

The dressmaker looked up, startled. She was frightened of him, and I had seen it in the way she shied away in his presence. "Oh, yes, of course," she said, gathering up the blue fabric. She bustled over and began to drape it over me. "We could do this with something off the shoulders."

"Yes, quite," said Enoch, his voice gentle, looking at me in a way that made my stomach flip over.

"We shall save this one then," said the dressmaker, smiling at me.

"You'll have callers today, wife." Enoch was still holding my gaze, a small, affectionate smile playing on his lips.

"What?" Who would call on me? How did he know?

"The Countess of Headon and Lady Nixby, I believe," he said. "They'll be coming for tea in the afternoon. I need you to be pleasant, if you don't mind. And lively. I want them to enjoy themselves. I want you to receive them in the sitting room on the west wing."

My lips parted and I shook my head. "Lady Headon? Lady Nixby? How?"

His smile deepened. "I have ways, wife. Can you promise

to be everything a truly well-bred young hostess should be?"

"You have secrets about them?" I said in a tiny voice. "You've blackmailed them into it."

Enoch glanced at the seamstress. "What a thing to say, Mrs. Granville. I'm appalled at the very thought of it. Of *course* not."

I looked at the seamstress too. Fine. We weren't going to discuss such things unless we were alone, I supposed.

"Well?" he said. "You haven't promised to be a pleasant and proper hostess."

"You think I'd be otherwise?"

He chuckled. "It would be wonderful if you had some use, wife. Some use besides my other appetites, that is. Make me seem respectable, do you understand?"

I lifted my chin. "Well, is that some sort of threat, husband?"

He only chuckled. "No, no, I could never truly punish you, Mrs. Granville, not in a way that you wouldn't also enjoy."

I thought of his discussion of using a riding crop on my rear end. I went hot all over and the fabric draped over me felt far too heavy.

His nostrils flared. His jaw twitched. "I'd best go, then. I'd hate to interrupt your fitting." He left the room, but he watched me on his way out, and I felt trapped in his dark gaze.

When he was finally gone, it was as though all the air had gone out of the room. I let out a noisy breath and clutched at my chest.

The seamstress's eyes were very wide. "Well, he's quite something, your husband."

"He is that," I said. I flushed again. "You mustn't... whatever it was he said about..." Punishment. Enjoyment.

"There, there, dear," said the seamstress, and she looked amused now. "I was a newlywed once too."

It was my turn for my eyes to widen.

She laughed softly under her breath. "He is rather taken with you, so that bodes well for you, I think."

He is not, I wanted to say, but I didn't. I didn't really want those words spoken aloud to her. I was afraid they might seem too final if I did and perhaps make it so that I could not appreciate my compensations.

Later that afternoon, Lady Headon and Lady Nixby arrived.

Lady Headon was the wife of a marquess and Lady Nixby was married to Sir Nixby, a knight. They would never have been caught dead calling on me before, not when I was ruined and unmarried at my family home.

It wasn't quite fair, I didn't think. Lady Headon had courted scandal herself. Why, two young dukes had nearly gotten into some sort of duel over her honor. But in the wake of it, she'd ended up with neither and married to the aging Marquess of Headon. Now, she was respectable, all the scandal somehow purged away.

Could mine be thus now that I was married as well, even if I had married a centaur? Best not to set my hopes too high, I thought.

Lady Headon looked all over the sitting room in the west wing. It was too large for a sitting room, of course, but at least it was tastefully decorated. It was one of my husband's white rooms—white marble, white walls, white pillars along the walls—I said it was too much. The furniture was dark, however, and I liked the contrast. There was a deep, luxurious fur rug and imposing leather chairs. My husband had a tendency to add too many accents and too many colors, but at least here, we were limited to dark brown and white and there was not an excess of anything. Because the room was so big, it almost seemed sparse, in fact.

"Well, isn't this charming," Lady Headon said to Lady Nixby.

"Charming," agreed Lady Nixby.

Lady Headon sat down and smiled perfunctorily at me. "Honey in my tea and just a touch of cream."

"Of course." The tea service was set on a wooden table, stained dark to match the leather furniture. I made the tea for Lady Headon and for Lady Nixby, and we spoke of the weather, how hot it was and how unfortunate it was that spring was ceding to summer with no interval in between and how it might be likely to simply go cold at a moment's notice.

Then I attempted to engage them in conversation about Lady Nixby's dress, which I complimented. I went on too long, asking too many questions about it. Who had made it? Who had commissioned the style? Had Lady Nixby selected it herself or had the dressmaker suggested it?

When this subject was well and truly exhausted, I fell silent.

They did too.

We all stared at each other.

Lady Headon set down her tea and smirked. "Well, let's be honest, Mrs. Granville, we all know why we're here."

"We do," I said, not quite a question, because I wasn't sure if I was curious about this, truly. I did not wish to be insulted if I could help it.

"Does it fit?" She raised her eyebrows.

Lady Nixby giggled, covering her mouth with one gloved hand. "Sybil!"

Lady Headon lifted a shoulder. "Oh, it's just us girls, isn't it? We're all married. Everyone spent the entire wedding trying to get a look between his hind legs. How big *is* it?"

I looked into my tea, my face heating up. "I can't say my husband would approve of this conversation."

"Yes, well, your husband cannot get ahead on the cache of his, um, unusualness and then expect to be treated just like everyone else, can he?" said Lady Headon.

"I think that's exactly what he wishes," I said.

"He..." Lady Headon gestured around at the room.

I inclined my head, agreeing tacitly.

"If it doesn't fit, perhaps you could get it annulled," said Lady Headon. "Come now, Mrs. Granville, it's only a question of legalities. Is your marriage consummated? Such things are important to know. Is it *possible* for your marriage to be consummated, that's what we're all wondering."

"And this is why you've come today?" I said.

Lady Headon lifted that shoulder again. She sipped at her tea. "Would you like to call on me?"

I drew in a sharp breath. Here she was, dangling that in front of my face, the idea that I would be so accepted into her society that I could make a return visit which she would accept, and this might turn into invitations on either end, in mixed company, an end to my imposed loneliness. I had thought myself well beyond caring about such things, but I was surprised at the yearning that welled up in me. "And there is a price for such things? The price is secrets about the bedchamber between me and my husband? Who will you tell? Everyone?"

"No one, dear," said Lady Headon. She glanced at Lady Nixby. "And it's no transaction. It's just girls talking, after all. We share secrets. I shall tell you about the Duke of Montague if you're interested." She smiled a wicked smile. "Should I go first? Should I relay the sorts of things he says to divest a girl of her clothing?"

"So that did happen," I said. "But then, the duel, why didn't he—"

"Oh, Montague is a scoundrel," said Lady Headon, waving this away. "But you are no stranger to the ways of men, are you?"

"I suppose not," I said.

"You'll call on me in three days," said Lady Headon. "The Duchess of Rells will be there then. All right?"

"Not yet," I said.

"Not yet?" said Lady Headon.

"It doesn't fit... yet," I said, raising my eyebrows. "But he seems confident he'll get it in there eventually."

Lady Headon's expression went shocked then quite, quite pleased. She gulped tea, and then gave me the most brilliant of smiles. "Is it... like a horse?"

I shook my head. "Well, I don't know exactly. I've not gone around examining horses, truly, but I don't think so."

"Like a man?"

I nodded.

"But larger?" Lady Nixby's voice was a bit breathy.

I let out a giggle. "Well, yes."

"It likely has to be large," said Lady Headon. "Proportionately speaking."

"But is it thick or is it simply long?" said Lady Nixby.

"Both," I said.

They both let out wild titters.

"Am I going to have to relay this information to Her Grace in three days' time?" I said.

"Oh, heavens, no," said Lady Headon with a guffaw. "No, she'd be scandalized. Can you imagine, Gertrude?"

"I can't, I can't." Lady Nixby was wheezing, because she was laughing so hard.

"No, no, dear, don't be foolish," said Lady Headon. "There are some people with whom we can speak of such things and others with whom it is impossible." She held my gaze, smiling. "Let's be friends, Mrs. Granville."

Well, I couldn't say I quite trusted that. But of course, I acquiesced, smiling.

LATER THAT EVENING, my husband was quite curious about the tea, and I didn't know what to say. I felt as if I'd betrayed him in some way. He'd asked me to be respectable, and I'd used his penis as a calling card to get myself an invitation to tea with a duchess.

It was shameful, really, and I'd done it for myself. I wanted it. I wanted friends. It was pathetic, really.

I should know better by now.

Someone like me did not have friends.

"Did she like the sitting room?" he said. We were at the dinner table. He did not sit at a chair but folded up his legs and settled on the floor to be roughly at the same height as a table might be, though I thought that the table and chairs we sat on were a bit high. Someone shorter than me might find that her feet would not touch the floor.

"Like it?"

"I take it that's a no," he muttered. "But I removed all of

the fancy draperies and the entire set of paintings from the far wall and I feel the whole room looks—"

"It is as good as it could get," I said. "Truly. Much more subdued and controlled than your normal sense of style. But it is far too large a room for a sitting room. And why are there pillars? Who puts pillars inside a room?"

"I like the pillars," he said, almost sulkily. He sighed heavily. "Well, we'll keep trying. Have a look around while I'm gone, then. I want you to point out the best rooms you think that could be sitting rooms, even if they are used for some other purpose currently. And we shall have them redone entirely to your specifications."

"But that's... the money..." I was agog. Redone entirely? How many rooms? And I had never decorated an entire room in my life. My spirits surged at the thought of it. "Are you certain?"

"Oh, this pleases you?" He chuckled, smiling at me. "I always forget how much I like it when you're pleased, wife. I want you to make a list, also, of things you like, foods and flowers and colors and books and anything you can think of, yes? When I return, I shall ask for it."

Return. Wait, I'd missed that. He'd said, *Have a look around while I'm gone.* "Where are you going?"

"Never mind that," he said. "It's nothing for you to worry about, just business. I shan't be gone too long. I don't think I can bear it. While I'm gone, you'll also work on your training yourself, but I'll instruct you on that later."

My body jolted at that.

"Now, did you get an invitation to tea with the Duchess of Rells?" said Enoch.

"You knew she was going to ask that?"

"Sybil can be an infuriating woman," said Enoch. "I'm sure she extracted it at a price I won't be entirely pleased about. She seems abundantly too interested in certain aspects of me." He rolled his eyes.

"Did you bed her, too?" I said. Then I realized, no, or she wouldn't have asked questions about his penis. "Sorry, I suppose it's obvious you didn't. Why are you calling Lady

Headon by her first name?"

"Right, that was improper of me." He shook his head at me. "I likely shouldn't enjoy your jealousy as much as I do, wife." He smiled at me, a wild, eager smile, and my heart picked up speed. His voice dropped in pitch. "But know it's been fifty years since I've coupled with a woman, all right? No need of your concern, truly. You are singular, never doubt it."

"Who was she? This woman fifty years ago?"

He threw back his head and laughed. "Of course that's what you'd say. Of course. I told you about her already. She was the one I freed from the herd."

"You said that was right after you'd been cursed."

"Did I?" He shrugged.

Oh, perhaps he was lying to me. Lying about *everything*. I hated that. I clenched my hands into fists, feeling impossibly helpless against this man.

He reached across the table and caressed my cheek. "Tell me about your servant boy, then."

"He wasn't really a boy," I said. "He was two and twenty. He was the age of my brother. And it wasn't really about me, what he did. It was about my brother."

"Was it." Enoch's face went thoughtful. There was a long pause. "He wasn't yours at all, then. It seems to me, the more you talk about it, that it was a sort of violence done to you, wasn't it? Ravishment in its way."

I pulled out of his grasp. "I don't wish to speak of it."

"Of course not," he said. He let out a shaky breath, clenching and unclenching his hands. "I had never felt it when I did it, the pull of a woman like you on a centaur. I don't want to say I'm helpless against it, because I obviously... look at us. I have been admirably restrained with you."

"*Have* you?"

He let out another laugh. "You have no idea what I could be doing with you, do you, Phoebe?"

"I'm not sure this is an appropriate dinner conversation," I huffed.

He laughed again. "We are the only ones here."

"Even so."

"Your rules, Phoebe, every part of your ridiculous class, all of the rules, it is exhausting."

"You're the one who thinks he can rise inside my class," I said. "You're the one who wants such things."

"True," he said. "If it were easy, it wouldn't be worth anything." He paused. "Look, what I'm trying to say is that... yes, I suppose whatever I did with that woman, it was ravishment, but for me it felt as if I was also ravished. It didn't feel like a choice. It felt like instinct, like my body took over, like the curse forced... forced us *both*, I suppose, me and her. And after, it felt... it was quite a bad feeling, that's all."

"Oh, 'that's all.' Really, we don't have to—"

"I don't mean to equate them, obviously, our experiences. They're nothing the same. But it's possible I might understand if you wanted to talk to me about it."

I gaped at him, horrified.

His face shuttered at that look. "Never mind, obviously. That was quite stupid of me."

I leaned forward, and I hissed at him, "You tie me to a mount and give me orders and you think—"

"It's not the same thing," he said.

"Nothing is the same, is it?" My voice went sour.

"It's *not* the same, is it?" He looked concerned.

"Does it matter? You have told me plainly you have no ability to stop yourself with me."

"I obviously do, though. I haven't actually had you, or are we forgetting that?"

"I have a headache," I said, tossing my napkin on the table. "I'm afraid I need to be excused."

He blinked at me. "All right. Well, I quite hope you feel better, Phoebe."

I stood up very straight and walked in slow, measured steps out of the room. When I had cleared the door, I fled.

CHAPTER NINE

I SNAPPED AT Janet and wouldn't speak to her when she tried to help me. After she made a few more soft attempts at conversation, I told her to leave me be.

I had hitherto not slept in the bed in my room. I had not even lain on it. I did that now, throwing myself face down on the thing and beating my fists against it.

Ravishment.

It might not have mattered if anyone had bothered to call it that.

I supposed the way that Laurence had dealt with Oscar was in line with that.

But maybe… maybe if I hadn't been blamed for it all, maybe…

I rolled back over and looked at the ceiling. No, it wouldn't have mattered. Not in the end, because it would have all been the same, regardless. Still no husband, still shunned from society —

Well, *would* I have been?

Maybe there would have been pity, and people would have included me only out of some sense of charity, and it is true that to be charitable, one must look down upon those they are being charitable towards, and that this would have been difficult for me to bear, but overall, I would have preferred it to…

I didn't even want to think of it, though.

I did my best not to.

Some time afterward, a servant came to summon me to my husband's bedchamber and I declined it. I assumed that would be the end of it, but quite soon afterwards, my room was crowded by my centaur husband, who came in the doorway — all of the doorways in his house were tall enough that he didn't have to duck through them — and then stood over the foot of my bed.

"I know you don't have a headache," he said. "I am leaving in the morning. I'll be gone for days. I'd like to..."

"I know what you'd like," I said to him. I was curled around a pillow, my skirts askew. I scrambled up the bed, pulling down my skirts to cover myself, bringing the pillow with me to hide behind.

"But I angered you tonight," he said.

"No," I said.

"I'd kill that boy if he weren't already dead," Enoch said matter-of-factly. "What was his name? Oscar Smithy? I made inquiries."

"His being dead did nothing to help me," I said.

"No, I realize," said Enoch.

"*Do* you?"

"It seems quite a foolish thing for him to have done," said Enoch. "He seemed to wish for the both of you to be caught. He had you right out on that table in the servants' dining room."

"You know, I was there. You don't need to replay it for me," I said. "And if you wish to... to do things with me tonight, it's certainly not the sort of thing that we should talk about."

"Why was it about your brother?" said Enoch.

"Why can't you let it be?"

"I don't know," said Enoch. "But I need you to tell me everything."

"If you're jealous, you should know—"

"Not jealous," he said. "Sort of... I don't know... a kind of strange helpless outrage, I think. It makes me feel a bit like vomiting. Why did he want caught?"

"It was about my brother," I said. "It was never about me. Because Oscar worked next door at the house where he took me, where we were discovered, and he loved Rosalind, who worked in our kitchen, and who... my brother..."

"What did your brother do to your kitchen maid?"

"Got her with child," I muttered.

"Oh, so it was revenge," said Enoch quietly. "This Oscar person wanted to take your brother's woman from him the way your brother took his."

"She died trying to birth the babe and it died too," I said. "Oscar married her anyway, even though he knew..."

"I see," said Enoch, rubbing at his chin. "I see."

I burrowed into the bed, feeling dull now that I had said it.

"Well," Enoch finally said in a rumbling voice, "you're mine now—"

"Yes, and you are the *same* as him."

"As the Smithy boy?"

"As my brother!"

Enoch tilted his head back. "Ah. Because of how I got myself cursed, you mean. Because your brother lusted after that maid and wasn't the least bit careful, and because of what I did to Deborah."

"That was her name?"

"Yes."

"You're not wrong," said Enoch. He sighed, looking me over. "Do you want me to kill your brother anyway?"

I sat up straight. "*What?*"

He shrugged, elegant and careless. "It was his fault, what happened to you, and he let you bear all the consequences. He killed that maid, his own child, he shot Oscar Smithy, and then you... this... everything. I think he deserves to die. I'd enjoy killing him."

"Killing him won't fix anything."

"It'd make me feel better," said Enoch.

"Oh, yes, well, I'd forgotten it was all about you."

He laughed. "Let me know if you change your mind." He started for the door.

I climbed out of the bed. "Why are you horrible?"

"Old and bitter, I suspect." He paused, glancing down over his shoulder at me. "What are you doing, coming after me?"

"What if I say I only want to sleep? But that I wish to do it in your arms?"

"All right," he said.

"That won't tempt you to distraction?"

"Of course it will." He smiled at me. He reached down then, and caught me under my armpits. He lifted me, hauling me up, even as I screeched in surprise, and then he set me on his back.

I gasped, legs astride either side of him. I scooted forward, pressing into his back, and wrapped my arms around his chest.

He leaned back into me, sighing a pleased sigh. He nuzzled back his head for a kiss, and I gave it to him. Then he covered my hands with his own. "Hold on, wife."

But he went very slowly up the stairs, and I liked it, riding him. It seemed absurdly intimate in some way that I couldn't even quantify. Maybe it was because there was only the thin fabric of my drawers between his back and my thighs, but I didn't think so, because it didn't feel like that sort of intimacy.

It felt like something else, something deeper and more real, and it was sweeter for that. Sweet and yet bitter, too, for I felt it and knew I couldn't trust it, knew it was all on my side, and that I was feeling close to some man who was brutal and awful and who only wished to use me.

But later, in bed, burrowed into the pillows like I usually was, my legs on either side of his horse body, his torso pressed tight against mine, both of us holding onto the other, I felt safe and cherished in a way I didn't think I'd ever felt.

He slid down, resting his head on one of my breasts, as if I was his pillow, and he made a little humming noise that spoke of happiness and satisfaction. I put my hands into his mane, shut my eyes, and clutched him to my breast.

We slept.

In the morning, he was up and moving as dawn split the sky, barely lighting the room. I rolled over, pulling blankets over my head, making noises of protest.

"You must continue the training," he said to me.

"Mmmph," I said.

"I'm serious, wife. You come up here and use the training cocks, as big as you can manage, every night while I'm gone. I want you to make yourself come as well. Around the cocks, if you please."

I moved down the blankets. "Where are you going?"

"Don't worry your pretty little head about that," he purred.

I narrowed my eyes. "Would I not like it if I knew where you were going?"

He only laughed. "I shall get back to you as quickly as possible. I won't have any way to relieve myself, of course, so I'll spend each night restless, with my prick so hard it'll likely hurt—"

"Oh." I sat up. "I'm sorry about last night. I didn't do anything for you. Should I help you now?"

His lips parted and he gazed at me with one of his wild, hungry looks. "No time, I'm afraid," he managed.

"Couldn't I quickly, though?" I crawled out of the bedcovers and went for him. I climbed under him to tease him free of his foreskin.

"Fuck," he said in a tattered voice. "No, no, it's not safe. If I—"

I put my mouth on him.

He let out a groan. "Phoebe, that's not a good idea."

I put both of my hands on him and began to rub him back and forth as if I had before.

His hooves came up. His front hooves, his back hooves. He stamped and bellowed. He whinnied.

And then he erupted in my mouth again, and I was better at swallowing every bit of him this time.

In the wake of it, he tackled me back onto the bed and he was all smiles as he kissed me senseless into the pillows, breathing my name over and over again. "Ah, Phoebe," he said, lips against my jaw. "You take me apart. If I ever manage to get inside your cunt, I shall likely not manage to last long enough to please you. Perhaps *I* need training."

I touched his face, smiling up at him, pleased with myself, and very happy, though I wasn't really sure why. I wasn't sure if I should be so gratified by drinking his seed, by suckling his prick. It seemed to me that to enjoy such things likely meant that I was damaged in some way. They didn't seem as though they *should* be enjoyable.

He kissed my nose. "Have I told you lately that you're perfect?"

I squirmed.

He pulled away and gazed into my eyes, smiling a lazy little smile. "Oh, damnation, how do I leave you?"

The door opened, and Enoch's valet poked his head in. "Sir? Are you ready for me?"

Enoch turned to look at him. "No, no, not quite, Mr. Stevens."

"Very good." The door closed.

Enoch groaned. "Damn us both, Phoebe, how quickly can you come?"

I shook my head. "Couldn't you stay?"

"No." He was still smiling at me. "No, I could not. But I shan't reward my pretty, perfect wife for putting her small, wet mouth on me in such a lovely way by telling her to get out so that my valet can dress me."

I supposed I didn't want to be here while the valet was here. I wasn't really dressed, after all, and it seemed frightful for the valet to witness me in bed.

Enoch kissed me quickly and then got up. He was back in moments with one of the black glass phalluses and he lifted the skirts of my nightdress to bare my quim to him. "There's my pretty, wet little wife." He handed the phallus to me. "There, then, show me how you'll train yourself while I'm gone."

I hesitated for a minute and then I did as he asked and penetrated myself.

"Good Phoebe," he said. "Now, you need to come as quickly as you possibly can."

"I'm not quick," I said as I wriggled the thing around. I didn't know how to find that spot he found, I—*oh*. I let out a gasp.

"Touch your clit," he said.

I did, and once I started that, it was a bit easier. I did know how to touch myself here, even if I always stopped when it felt too good. I supposed, this time, I'd just... keep going until...

"You *are* quick," he said in a deep, reassuring voice. "You are my perfect Phoebe, my very obedient wife, and you are a good girl who comes for her husband whenever he wants her to."

I did like it when he talked that way to me.

"What arouses you, Phoebe?" he said. "Does being strapped to the mount arouse you?"

I shook my head. "No, j-just your fingers, the way you can—"

"Does being mine arouse you, being a vessel of my pleasure?"

"I..." I whimpered, and I closed my eyes, pumping the training cock with one hand, moving my finger on my clitoris with the other.

"You were aroused by sucking me, weren't you?"

I gasped.

"Say it, Phoebe," he said.

"Yes," I managed.

"Yes, what? What did you like?"

"I like your prick in my mouth," I said. My voice wasn't strong, but it was a little bit throaty.

"Good," he said. "Very good girl." A pause. "And you'd be very, very aroused if I did keep you like my own mount, like nothing more than a pleasure filly I used. That's why you brought it up. You'd like it if I built a little stall for you right there, and you were made to stay in it all day, naked, for me to look at whenever I wanted, and if you only came out of it for our daily rides, morning, noon, and night, when

I'd mount you and ride you hard."

I came in a crashing clench, gasping, surprised by its speed and force, terrified by how much that had aroused me, terrified because I had positively no interest in living in a stall, and that was—

"Good girl," he breathed. "Good get it all out, just like that, every last bit of that pleasure. I knew you'd come quickly for me."

I yanked the training cock out, going up on my knees, shaking my head at him. "You won't *do* that."

"What?" he said. "Keep you in a stall?" He chuckled. He pulled me up so that I was standing, and he was still down, so that our torsos almost lined up. I was just a tiny bit taller than him. He looked up at me, grinning rakishly. "Would you keep *me* in one? Put a saddle on me? A *side* saddle?"

"You said you couldn't bear saddles," I gasped.

"Would you give me orders, Phoebe, command me? Or strap me to a carriage?" His voice had gotten positively gravelly.

My mouth was dry. Why was that…? What?

He laughed. "It's just pretend. Sex is like that, though. It's quite arousing for most people to be subjugated. Probably because sex makes you vulnerable, don't you think? The vulnerability is part of it. I just said it to make you come." He kissed me. "But if I had a bridle made for you, would you wear it for me?"

I choked.

He laughed, letting go of me. "Shall I make sure Stevens is gone, then?" He got up and crossed the room.

I struggled to catch my breath, to gather myself. He badly disrupted everything about me. I called out, "I want to sleep here while you're gone."

He turned, smiling. "Oh, yes, please do. And fuck yourself with the training cocks in the bed?"

I nodded.

"Perfect." His smile widened.

CHAPTER TEN

THE TEA WITH the duchess was like most teas I'd attended. Staid, stuffy, and a bit uncomfortable, but there was something reassuring about everything returning to form and about being accepted there. The duchess seemed quite interested in the house my husband had built, and I found it easy to invite her to come.

"Oh, a tea would be lovely," she said. "Won't His Grace be jealous when he hears that I've been inside and he hasn't."

Of course, she and her husband had been invited to the ball and to the wedding reception, but they hadn't come, apparently. Not everyone had come, of course. Some people had held to their principles and steered clear of something so terribly gauche. The fact she would come now, though, it was promising.

"Well, you could both come," I said. "I'm certain Mr. Granville would love it if we hosted you for dinner."

The duchess eyed me, thinking that through, and then inclined her head. "You're too kind. We would be honored."

And just like that, I'd secured the Rells.

I thought that Enoch would be pleased.

I wished he'd come home so that I could tell him about it.

But he didn't come home, of course. He'd said he'd be gone for days, and he was.

I had called out to him, before he left, that I wanted to

sleep in his room, in his bed, but the first two nights, I didn't. I'd said it in the heat of the moment, still in a state of arousal after whatever we'd done together. Then, it had seemed frightfully exciting and quite erotic to come up to his room, roll around in his bed and touch myself.

But afterwards, with him gone, all of that was dimmed.

I was embarrassed about it. I didn't want to tell the servants that I'd sleep up there — definitely didn't want to take Janet up to his room to help me undress in the evenings or dress in the mornings. And I had always been a bit reticent about touching myself.

Now, especially with the added wrinkle of shoving those smooth black phalluses into my body...

It seemed sordid, disgusting, and mortifying.

No, before being married, I had rarely explored my own nether regions. The urge would come on me somewhat often, I supposed, but usually, I was able to argue myself out of it.

I would tell myself it was a shameful and unladylike thing to do, a sin against nature, and that I must control myself.

Usually, that worked.

Occasionally, I would give in to it, but I never took it all the way to its end, of course, because the pleasure became too intense and too frightening.

Now, my husband had educated me in the most awful of ways about what my body was capable of feeling, and now, it was much harder to resist.

The third night, I rolled around in my bed, unable to sleep, pressing my thighs together and then releasing them — both seemed equally miserable, the pressure and the lack of it. I finally slipped off into a fitful sleep but I had strange and erotic dreams about riding naked on my husband's back through a field of flowers, my bare breasts brushing against his back, the warmth of his body scalding me between my legs, even as the up and down of his steady gait urged me toward heights of sweetness.

But I woke up before I could climax, and I was now

frustrated.

It was the middle of the night.

Everyone was asleep.

I threw on a wrapper over my nightdress and opened the door to my room. Peering out into the dark and empty hallway, I determined no one would notice if I left. I scampered quietly down the hallway, up the steps, and to the door of my husband's room.

I was afraid it would be locked.

It wasn't.

I went inside, taking in the dark and shadowy outlines of the room. I moved through it by feel, because I had not bothered to bring a light. I could have turned on the gas lamps. There was a chain by the door, I knew. But I didn't want the room bathed in light. I didn't want to be seen. If I were up here in the dark, perhaps I could pretend it wasn't entirely real.

So, it was by feel that I found the training cocks. I ran my hands over them and selected two. One that seemed a reasonable thickness and length and one that seemed too big. I wasn't sure why I did that. It was only that it seemed exciting to push myself.

When I settled into my husband's bed, it smelled like him, and I basked in that, rolling my head over to put my nose in the pillow and breathe him in. The scent of him made me feel even more aroused.

I took off everything.

I picked up the huge training cock and rubbed it all over my body. I rubbed the tip against my breasts, swirling it around my nipples until they hardened, and then against my sex, running it back and forth over the seam until I fell open. I teased it against my opening.

It was too big.

I laughed softly, thinking there was no way I could get such a thing inside me. I set the thing down, rolled over, tucked my hand between my legs, and rubbed myself to a quick climax.

Then I knew I should get up and go back to my bed,

because otherwise everyone would know I had slept up here last night, and they would wonder what I was up to, and they would probably have all sorts of dreadful imaginings, considering I was married to a centaur.

So, yes, I needed to go.

In a moment. For now, it was so comfortable here, and it smelled so good, and I was wondrously sleepy.

I'd just snuggle in and be still for a few moments.

I awoke to the sun streaming in the windows.

I hurriedly dressed and went down to my own room where Janet greeted me with obvious relief, having been worried about my whereabouts.

MY BROTHER CAME to visit me that day.

He hadn't been invited, but he was simply there, in one of the sitting rooms, and I was obliged to receive him and provide tea and sweets. I tried to remain polite, but he was agitated.

He paced, not taking any tea, and he began asking me questions. Had the centaur given me any jewels as presents? Necklaces, bracelets, earrings or the like?

I said that he hadn't.

This made him angry for some reason, and he railed for some time about how he thought I was being mistreated by my monstrous husband.

I tried to hint that I had a prior engagement and I was going to have to leave soon.

"Do you know where he keeps any jewels or any coin or anything like that?" said Laurence.

"What?" I said.

"I am in need of a loan to cover a recent gambling debt," said my brother. "Otherwise, I am going to have to sell our carriage."

I shook my head, unable to quite believe that he could be so audacious. He had come to take my jewels for a gambling debt? He had thought I would give them over? He thought himself entitled to my husband's money? I stood up, trembling, glaring at him. "Get out."

He gave me a funny look. "What did you just say to me?"

"Get out and don't come back. You are not welcome in this house."

He snorted. "I shall do no such thing." He settled himself into one of the chairs in the sitting room and began helping himself to biscuits.

I clenched my hands into fists and shook. I ran at him. I snatched the biscuit from his hand and I took him by the collar and shook him. I screamed in his face, "Why? Why are you so selfish and horrible? Why could you never have cared about me? Why — ?"

He shoved me off and I fell backwards into a couch, and I cried out.

At that point, the door opened and Mr. Higgins stood there. Mr. Higgins was not young and he was not tidy. He had a grizzled gray beard and a chest like a barrel and arms nearly as thick. He wore a suit, but the suit always looked shabby, and he was constantly sneering.

He marched over to my brother, seized a handful of his shirt, and yanked him to his feet. "I believe the mistress of the house asked you to leave," he snarled.

"Unhand me, you brute," sputtered my brother.

"What did you call me?" said Mr. Higgins. "Let's try that again, and you call me sir."

My brother laughed in Mr. Higgins' face.

Mr. Higgins hit him.

I think he broke my brother's nose. There was blood. My brother howled. He said "sir" over and over again, and he apologized and blubbered and moaned.

Mr. Higgins threw him bleeding out the front door.

I was still shaking.

Mr. Higgins brushed his hands together and came to me. He was not sneering now. His expression looked nearly gentle. "Are you all right, Mrs. Granville?"

I swallowed, nodding. There were unshed tears in my eyes.

"If you're willing to take advice on this, and I don't know if you are, I wouldn't let that man darken this door again."

I licked my lips. "I... well, he's my brother." My voice wasn't strong.

"Family being family, I understand," said Mr. Higgins. "But that one—" He jerked his finger at the door where my brother had been summarily thrown out. "He's no good, and I can tell, being no good myself."

I raised my eyebrows. "Oh, I'm sure that's not true. About you, I mean."

Mr. Higgins chuckled softly. "More than that, you're good for him."

"For...?"

"For Granville," said Higgins. "His equine master himself." He laughed again. Then he sobered, looking down. "Wish he wouldn't have left, of course. Hoped he wouldn't, not with you here."

"Where did he go?" I said.

"Ah, I like my head attached to my neck, Mrs. Granville," said Mr. Higgins. "He'd lop it right off if I told you that."

"Because I wouldn't like knowing where he is," I said softly.

Mr. Higgins looked down at his feet.

It was quiet.

He reached out and patted my arm. "Perhaps he needs to work it out of his system. Perhaps just work it out and make enough room for you, that's all. He's never been this way before, I can tell you that, not the way he is about you, and I've known him a long time."

"I don't care where he is," I said, squaring my shoulders. "He said it was business, and husbands never involve their wives in such things."

"Business," repeated Mr. Higgins.

A tendril of cold went through me. "Isn't it business?"

"Does he seem like the sort to lie to you, Mrs. Granville?"

He did, yes. Oh, he very much did.

But I found myself back in the room again that night, and this time, I did get one of those training cocks inside me, not the too-big one, but one bigger than he had ever used on me, one that I thought would be too big, but which slid snugly into my wetness, filling me all the way up. And when I clenched around it, I thought of him, my lying husband, and I missed him.

CHAPTER ELEVEN

HE CAME HOME the next night.

His first words, the minute that he was inside the door, were that he'd be indisposed upstairs with his wife, and that anything anyone had to say to him could wait. And then he swept me up and deposited me on his back, and I rode astride to the top of the house to his bedroom.

I climbed off of him and resolved I would confront him. "I know your trip was not about business."

"Did you make your list of things that please you as I asked?" He was gazing at me with that hunger of his in his eyes.

"No, I sort of forgot about that," I said. "Anyway, don't change the subject. You lied to me about your trip."

He laughed. "What do you mean?"

"You did," I said stoutly. "I overheard some of the servants talking, and I know."

"Overheard who? What?" He shook his head at me. "You don't know anything, Phoebe. None of the servants know anything."

I didn't want to say that Mr. Higgins was the one who'd hinted it to me. I wouldn't say that I liked Mr. Higgins, exactly. I was frightened of him, but he also seemed to have a soft underbelly, and he had been gentle with me, concerned for me, kind. I wouldn't repay that by babbling to my husband and exposing him.

"Just tell me what it was about."

"Business is a bit of a vague word, is it not?" he said. He shrugged. "Was the trip about my investments, about money? No. But it was about business, about my own business."

"We are married," I said. "So, it is my business as well."

He only shook his head. "Is this what you've been doing while I was gone? I thought I left strict instructions how to occupy yourself. Have you been fucking yourself and training your sweet, small quim as I asked, wife?" His voice went darker and deeper.

I squared my shoulders. "What if I said I hadn't?"

His eyes narrowed. "Are you trying to make me angry on purpose? Are you asking for punishment?"

My eyes widened. "No. And you said you would never do anything to me that I didn't want, and—"

"All right," he said. He looked me over, sighing. "So, we are back to this, then. I go away, and I lose all the ground I had gained with you."

"We're not back to anything," I said. "I don't know where you were. You left me all alone and lied about your whereabouts. You have some strange, awful plan which you won't share with me. You are not a good man, I don't think, and I am stuck with you, and I am simply trying to protect myself, and I want the truth."

"Wife," he said, with a groan. "I've rushed home as quickly as I could, and every night I was away from you, I dreamed of you, and all I wanted when I arrived is to touch you, and be close to you, and… I had thought… perhaps… if you had trained…" He shook his head. "But no. We'll have to wait."

I swallowed. "You wanted to… fuck me."

"It was silly of me to think you'd be ready," he said, closing the distance between us, reaching down to feather a thumb over my cheekbone.

I almost wanted to say yes to being fucked. I wasn't sure entirely why. Maybe it was some hope that if we were joined in that way, I would have some sort of hold on him, though I well knew it did not work that way for men.

Well. I *did* have a hold on him, some kind of magical hold. He was obsessed with me.

"I got you something," he said.

I straightened up.

"But I have a feeling you aren't going to like it." The grin he gave me was wicked.

"Why say anything, then?" I felt trepidation.

He reached into the inside pocket of his jacket and drew out something delicate — leather and metal clasps, jewel encrusted.

My lips parted.

"You know what it is," he whispered.

He'd threatened to bridle me, and there it was. I was horrified. I was aroused. My body went taut. My nipples tightened. There was a tiny jerk between my thighs.

"Will you wear it for me, wife?"

I bit down on my lower lip. My voice was hoarse. "Only if you tell me where you were."

He laughed. "I was in Milluxe."

"Where in Milluxe?"

"I was at an estate called Leddings," he said.

"With whom?"

"With the current resident who is letting the place," he said, laughing.

"That is not an answer."

"No one you know or have ever heard of," he said.

"But why were you there?"

"Personal business."

"Which you won't share with me."

"No." This was flat. "I'd like to see you in nothing but this bridle, wife. It has a bit here." He gestured to the metal rod that was attached. "It can be removed if I want to make use of your tongue, of course. But I thought you might like the feel of the metal in your mouth?"

My core clenched hard, and I whimpered, and I didn't know why that was so arousing. It shouldn't be. Maybe *because* it shouldn't be.

"Will you wear it?" He raised his eyebrows.

Damn me to hell, I nodded.

"Everything else off, then," he said. And he began to undress too.

For several moments, I simply watched him removing his clothes. He unbuttoned his jacket and peeled it off and then he went to work on his waistcoat.

"Phoebe, you're just standing there."

"I need help with my buttons," I said.

"Come here."

I gave him my back. He unbuttoned my dress. When he was done, I was able to step out of it, and then I was able to undo the front grommets of the corset I was wearing. I could remove the elements of my undergarments myself also.

By the time I was entirely naked, he had been so for some time. The remnants of his suit lay scattered on the floor with my clothing.

He was holding the bridle.

I stood there, looking up at him, waiting, my breathing going erratic, my body going taut all over again.

He looked me over approvingly. "My beautiful, beautiful mount," he murmured appreciatively. "How I missed you. How I went mad without the sight of you." He stepped closer, bending at the waist to put his face in my hair. "The scent of you."

I gasped at this, remembering the way it had felt to climb into his bed, to be wrapped in his scent.

He ran an appraising hand down over my clavicle and found a breast. He squeezed it—gentle.

I gasped again.

He pulled my hair back from my face and began to put the bridle on me. It wasn't tight or heavy. It didn't hurt anywhere. Even the flat metal piece in my mouth, which held down my tongue, was not unpleasant. He was right that I liked it there, that the sensation of the cold metal in my warm mouth was erotic.

He fastened it onto my face, touching the places where it lay over my features. Then he reached down to fondle my breasts again.

"How do you like it, Phoebe?" he murmured.

I couldn't speak with the bit in my mouth, and he knew it.

He teased one of my nipples absently. "Nod if you like being bridled for your husband."

I nodded, letting out a little breathy gasp.

"Nod if you like being mine."

I nodded. Another gasp.

"Nod if you like being subservient for my pleasure," he said, his voice going gravelly.

I moaned, nodding again.

"Very good," he murmured. Both of his hands were reaching down to tease my nipples now. He had them both extremely stiff and he was brushing the hard peaks back and forth with his fingers and thumbs.

Moans ripped out of my throat with every breath now.

He smiled down at me, a feral sort of smile, a smile of possession. "I almost bought reins as well, but I thought it might be too much. But you'd like it as much as I would, them draped down here, between your pert breasts. We'll get them long enough that I can direct your head when you're pleasuring my prick with your mouth, hmm?"

I choked, a little mini-explosion going through me. I hated that I responded to this in some ways, because it made me feel so helpless. But I *was* helpless, and I also loved it, and I was eager and willing to surrender to him.

He pinched both of my nipples—hard.

I cried out, because it hurt and also felt divine. It sent shocks to my quim, and my clit stuttered in a sympathetic response.

Then he was touching my face again, stroking my bridle straps, stroking the place where the bit went into my mouth. "Would you like to be tied to the mount in there with the reins, sweet Phoebe? Perhaps while I'm out in the other room, conducting some conversation with someone else, the door cracked, you naked and bound and unable to speak with the bit holding down your tongue, just waiting there for me to use whenever I get around to wanting you.

Existing only for my gratification."

I pressed my thighs together and leaned into his touches, feeling embarrassed and very aroused and also feeling that edge of horror out on the edge of my consciousness. He said things like this to me, and he claimed that he didn't mean them, but... but... well, I suppose some part of me didn't believe him. What was more, I thought the danger was part of the reason that my body was so responsive to the threat.

"Nod if you'd like that, wife."

I nodded, whimpering again. I tried to say please. But I couldn't really move my tongue, and it didn't sound like a word.

He stuck his thumb in my mouth. "Don't try to talk, pretty mount," he said softly.

I pressed my thighs closer together.

He noticed. "Would you like to touch yourself, Phoebe?"

I made a high-pitched noise.

He reached down with one hand and danced his finger back and forth between my nipples again. He was pinching and then rubbing, back and forth, sometimes two pinches in a row, a little tweak for each one, sometimes, a pinch then a rub, then another rub. Sometimes he pinched hard, sometimes he was gentle, a barely-there brush of his thumb and finger.

"Nod, mount, if you'd like to put your fingers between your pretty, shapely thighs."

I nodded quickly, sucking on his thumb.

He began to thrust his thumb against my tongue, against the bit, finger fucking my mouth.

I groaned, sucking harder.

"Cup your own cunt, wife, but just put pressure there," he said to me and gave one of my nipples a nearly vicious pinch.

I gasped around the thumb that was rutting my mouth. I cupped myself between my thighs. I let out a noise of utter and sheer relief, something guttural.

"You like that?" he said.

I nodded.

"Should I let you come, wife?"

I nodded.

"Will you be very, very grateful if I let you tease your pretty clit to a climax, sweet one?"

I nodded.

"Will you do whatever I ask of you?"

I nodded, vigorous, a little frightened, and my quim crested in response to this. The devil take me, I was already that close.

"I think you will." He eased his thumb out of my mouth and painted my lower lip with my own saliva. "I think you are the most obedient and eager of mounts. You've been waiting around for years in that house with that horrid brother of yours, ready for me to corrupt you. My Phoebe. I can *smell* your arousal."

This should have embarrassed me. It didn't. I crested again. I clutched my mound and I tried to say please again.

"Nod if you wish to be corrupted by your centaur husband."

I nodded, whimpering again.

"Touch yourself, pretty wife. Make yourself come," he told me.

I slid a finger between the lips of my very swollen cunt and found my clitoris, which was a tongue of flame ready to leap toward the ceiling. I cried out.

He sighed. "Nod if you're dripping wet, wife."

I didn't nod. I was concentrating on climbing the pinnacle that my body wanted to climb. I was halfway up the mountain, rushing towards the summit and I couldn't move or breathe or nod, or—

I whimpered.

I peaked, like the sun rising above clouds and splintering through them, light filling me and I came violently. It felt as if my whole body was racked with the tremors of my climax.

Afterwards, I sagged into him, spent, out of breath, a little sweaty.

He brushed my hair back from my face, away from the bridle, murmuring soft little noises of approval, saying my name in whispers.

He sank slowly down to tuck in his legs, so that he could line up our faces. He pulled me down to kiss me thoroughly.

I couldn't move my tongue with the bit. He dragged his own tongue over the metal, and I strained mine, and I liked that.

Then—without breaking the kiss—he fumbled at the bridle and freed the bit, letting my tongue free.

We kissed in a fury.

He pulled away, giving me a breathless smile. "So? Grateful?"

"Yes, husband, yes," I managed, reaching for him.

"Good," he said, getting back up on his hooves. "Go to the mount. Strap your feet in and one of your wrists. I'll get the other when I get to you."

I didn't even hesitate. I went to the mount, and I strapped myself into it, and then I waited.

I could hear his hooves on the floor in the other room, but I couldn't see him.

He appeared in the doorway with his hands full of black phalluses.

I tensed.

He sauntered across the room. "Did you use them at all?"

"O-once," I gasped. "Last night."

"How big did you manage?"

"That one."

He stopped in front of me, holding them out.

I touched the phallus with my free hand.

He smiled, pleased by this. "Truly?"

I nodded.

"How did it fit? Any pain?"

I shook my head.

"Good wife." He kissed me again. And then he set down all of the phalluses except one, which was two sizes up from the big one I'd put in myself. It was the one I'd gotten before—the one I had determined was never going to fit.

"That—Enoch, I don't think so. That one's too big."

"You said you'd do whatever I asked of you."

"I was on the edge of my climax!"

"Taking it back?" He tilted his chin back.

"What happens if I say yes?"

"Nothing," he said, voice going flat.

I surveyed him. Did I believe him? "You won't be angry with me?" My voice was far too breathy.

"Do you wish to court my anger, wife?" He rubbed the very big phallus against my lower lip.

I shook my head. "I don't know."

He smiled at me. "Open your mouth."

I hesitated, and then I did.

He eased the training cock's head into my mouth. It was big enough that the girth of it stretched my lips.

I made a muffled noise.

"Get it very, very wet, wife," he said, pushing it gently deeper into my mouth.

Oh. So that was what he wanted me to do. I obliged him.

He pulled it away from my lips and it gleamed. He dragged it down my body between my breasts, over my belly, through the curls on my mound and swirled it around my clit.

I cried out. I was very sensitive there.

He tried to put it in my opening.

It slid in a little and then hit resistance. And it *stretched*.

I bit down on my lip, making a noise.

"Pain?" he asked.

"A little," I breathed.

"Hmm," he said thoughtfully. He pulled it out and stuck it back in my mouth again.

I made another noise around it.

"Hold that, wife," he said, busying himself with strapping my wrist down. That done, he touched my face, tracing my bridle. "I'm going to need you to take a little pain for me tonight, wife," he whispered. "You said you'd do whatever I wished, remember? I promise, I'll give you another orgasm, though, and it won't be all pain."

I shivered. I instinctively sucked on the fat phallus in my mouth.

116

"If it's too much, you should say 'mercy,' do you understand? Nod if you do, pretty bridled wife."

I nodded.

He removed the phallus. "Will you let me hurt you a little, then?"

The devil take me, I wanted to. I didn't understand why, because I was nervous about the pain, but submitting to him, my pain for his pleasure, it aroused me. I nodded, biting down on my bottom lip.

"Say it, Phoebe," he said.

"Yes," I breathed.

"Yes, what?"

"Yes." I choked again. I found my voice. "Yes, you can hurt me, husband." My body gave another mighty clench at this.

"Very good," he breathed. He kissed me. "Very brave." Then he moved me on the mount, swinging me around so that he could stand between my spread legs, just as he had when he'd used his mouth on me. He spread my legs even further this time, using the mount to make me very wide open to him. He gave my clit a few kisses and then concentrated his mouth on my opening, adding to my natural wetness with his saliva.

He licked the phallus. Then he put it inside me again.

He wasn't too hurried about it.

The tip fit again, of course. It had fit before. He worked that in, got some of the wetness from inside me on it, and then pulled it out, transferring it to the outside of me. Then on his next thrust, he pushed it in further. It stung.

But I didn't react. I just breathed.

He continued this process, occasionally adding more of his own saliva to ease the process, crooning praise to me as he penetrated me. "That's a good wife taking all that jammed into her cunt," and variations of that. He planted lots of soft kisses on my clitoris.

It took a while, but eventually, he'd gotten the entire thing into me, and it wasn't stinging anymore.

He slid the huge phallus in and out of me, again and

again. "That's all of it, Phoebe," he told me. "You're taking the whole thing. You're a very, very good girl. I'm quite pleased."

I gasped.

And then he pulled it out.

I felt achingly empty. Cold.

He moved away, leaving me on the mount, splayed open.

When he came back, he had another phallus, but I couldn't see it clearly.

He put his mouth to my split-open, wet cunt. He licked me there, kissed me, thrust his tongue inside me. Then he petted me as he told me, "You're going to take a bigger training cock now, Phoebe."

I mewed.

He licked my clit. "Shh, that's all right. You'll do very well, I know you will. Trust me, my pretty wife. You were meant for a centaur, meant for me. Don't be frightened."

I was frightened, but in a breathless sort of way. I couldn't tell how big the training cock was that he was going to use on me, and I shivered a little, tensing.

He tried to breach me with the phallus then. It didn't work at all.

Maybe because I had tensed. I didn't know.

He stepped back and petted me again. "All right, wait here. One moment." He left me again.

I hung there, the cold air tickling the insides of my thighs, drying out my wetness.

When he was back, he had a small tin. He got something out and began to rub it into me. "Grease," he told me. "Just need a little help this time." He greased the training cock as well.

When he tried to breach me with it this time, the head slid in easily.

I let out a little noise.

"Good girl, Phoebe," he said, pausing. "Pain?"

"I..." I wasn't sure. There was a lot of pressure. I felt very, very stretched. "No."

He pushed it a little further. "Now?"

"Yes," I whispered.

"Good girl," he said. "Take a little more, now. You can do that for me, can't you?"

I nodded. Then realized he couldn't see me, but I guessed it didn't matter, because he was pushing it deeper and deeper within me.

It stung like the last one had, stretching me very, very wide. But I had to admit that it also felt good in an intense way, because I was so very filled up, and I *liked* being that filled. It felt right in a way I couldn't quite describe, as if I'd been an aching cavern all my life and now I was finally just filled, *really* filled, crammed full to the brim.

When he stopped pushing it in and it was seated all the way inside, I let out a long, soft, moan.

"You like it, don't you, wife?"

"Yes," I admitted.

"How bad is the pain?"

"Not... I..."

"You can bear it," he said.

"I..." I wasn't sure.

"You can, sweet one," he murmured. He was kissing my clit again.

I cried out. That felt.... Oh, damnation, the walls of my passage rippled around the huge intrusion, and I'd never felt anything quite like the explosion of different sensations that was. Then he began to slowly thrust the phallus inside me and it was if my clitoris was being prodded from all angles, even as he gently licked and suckled it in an alternating pattern.

I began to make strangled noises, noises that didn't even sound human, but I didn't care. I had never experienced that kind of pleasure. It was the edge of pain, but that edge made it more intense, and I enjoyed it.

He licked and sucked and fucked me, and I came for him again, an overwhelming orgasm that seemed to come from all directions, that seemed to make my entire pelvis tremble, that undid me.

Then he lowered me, leaving the cock in me, filling me

up, so that I was lower, stretched out flat on my back. He reared up, secured his hooves, and lined his prick up with my spread lips. He rubbed it against my clit, against the place where the training cock was tucked inside. He coated himself in my wetness as I gasped up at his belly above me, and then he exploded on *my* belly, covering my naked flesh in ropes and ropes of his white seed.

He used the pulleys to lift me up so that I was upright. He stood in front of me, dragging his fingers through the mess he'd made, shoving his fingers into my mouth, and telling me to lick them clean.

I did it. He pulled the phallus out, coated it in his seed and rutted it back inside me, muttering something about the seed making me more ready. I remembered he'd said something like that before, but he'd also said he thought it was ludicrous.

Eventually, he cleaned us both up, removed my bridle, and we went to bed.

It was the same as before. I was propped up on pillows, straddling him, our torsos pressed together. He kissed me all over, muttering that he'd missed me like I was a missing part of him, telling me that I had the most perfect set of breasts he'd ever touched, and that he wanted to sleep pillowed on them every night.

I liked hearing it, I had to admit.

I liked his head lying against one of my breasts, his hand resting gently and possessively on the other, as we fell asleep.

I tangled up my hands in his hair and said stupid things back, that I'd missed him too, that I wanted his head resting on me like this every night, that I wanted to sleep with my thighs wrapped around him, that I'd been lost with him gone. I knew I shouldn't admit these things. I shouldn't allow myself to feel them at all, let alone voice them. But he'd stretched me wide open and invaded every part of me. I was helpless now. I'd surrendered too much already.

He sighed and claimed my lips again and again. "I shan't be able to wait, I'm afraid. I'm going to mount you tomorrow."

I gasped, surprised at that. "But—"

"You had the largest training cock in you tonight, Phoebe," he murmured into my breast. "If I were less mad for you, I'd want to get you accustomed to it over several sessions, perhaps for three or four days, but I..."

"That was the biggest one?" I could hardly believe that. I'd taken *that* one?

"Yes," he said in a gravelly, affected voice.

"Well, all right," I said.

He chuckled into my skin. "You were perfect tonight, lovely wife. I know it was uncomfortable for you, but you enjoyed it also." It wasn't a question. "It was torturous for me too, going that long with my cock so hard and swollen I thought it was going to burst and split open. You have no idea how badly you affect me."

I supposed he had only touched me. I hadn't given him any relief throughout the entire evening. Torturous, though? He had been in charge of it all.

"My prick will fit just fine in your sweet, tight quim," he assured me. "We'll both enjoy that. You'll like being mounted and rutted and being completely taken. And I must do it soon or lose control."

He'd said things like that before, about how centaurs were driven mad by their desires for women like me. But he'd also said he was not badly affected by it.

I felt another trill of fear.

This husband of mine, he terrified me in some ways. Why did that also excite me so badly?

CHAPTER TWELVE

THE NEXT MORNING, I awoke alone.

This surprised me. There had been a promise of mounting today, and I assumed he'd be eager for it. I hadn't been sure if he'd wait until night for it. I had thought it was possible I'd be strapped to the mount first thing.

But he was gone.

I asked servants about it, and no one knew where he'd gone, just that he'd taken the carriage and that he'd been speaking to Mr. Higgins on his way out. They didn't know when he'd be back either.

It was common for my husband to speak to Mr. Higgins as he was leaving. Mr. Higgins was sort of the enforcer of my husband's household (something I don't think the butler was pleased about, being subjugated to the muscle) and my husband often gave Mr. Higgins all his orders, and Mr. Higgins delegated the responsibilities.

I went to find Mr. Higgins to ask him when my husband was coming back and where he had gone.

Mr. Higgins wagged a thick finger at me. His knuckles were covered in dark hair. It was peppered with gray. "You, missy, have been speaking out of turn, have you not?"

"I didn't tell him that it was you," I said, wincing. "And you didn't tell me anything anyway."

He harrumphed, folding his massive arms over his massive chest.

I ducked down my head.

"Don't do that!" he exclaimed. "I'm not going to strike you, child."

I lifted my head. I hadn't thought he was!

He sighed.

I sighed. I folded *my* arms over *my* chest. "You're not going to tell me anything."

"Afraid I can't risk it, Mrs. Granville. He can be fearsome, you see. And I have hitched my harness to his star. Nothing for it now. He gets my loyalty. But I think he's a right fool, and I told him so when he went off this morning."

"A fool?" I bit down on my bottom lip. "Where did he go?"

He only shook his head.

"Do you know when he'll be back?"

"He did not say, Mrs. Granville."

How could this be?

He indicated he was going to go out of his head if he didn't have me, and now he'd run off to who-knows-where and would be back who-knows-when, and how could that be?

You thought you were the most important thing to him? spoke up a knowing, oily voice in the back of my head.

I suddenly felt like crying.

"I didn't even get a chance to tell him that I had secured the Rells for dinner," I said. "He distracted me so very badly, and if I do not follow up with the duchess and set a secure date, it is all going to fall through."

"As to that," said Mr. Higgins, "I think I can be of assistance. Come with me."

He led me through the house and we went into my husband's study. It was a vast room—were any of the rooms in this house *not* vast?—dominated by a huge fireplace and a massive oaken desk. On the desk, he showed me a calendar.

Mr. Higgins informed me that he wrote things into this calendar with my husband's permission. "Anything on this calendar, Mr. Granville treats as law. So, if you need to use it to secure a dinner, please do. I know that will be important to Mr. Granville."

So, I found a date and drafted an invitation to the duchess. I sent a servant off to carry it to her and to wait for a response.

If the duchess did not respond, I would know I had left it too long. It would also be a blow if she denied it. She would say she was busy whether she was busy or not. I would be obliged to offer an alternate date. If she was "busy" for that one too, I would have to give up the entire enterprise.

I waited with my stomach in knots.

I was purportedly doing this for my husband, of course, but I realized I wanted it for me. I wanted to be accepted into society again. I wanted to be respectable.

But I had spent last night bridled and denigrated and it had gotten me frightfully wet, and I'd had two orgasms, and I was not even remotely respectable anymore.

The response came back in the affirmative, however, and I sought out Mr. Higgins to enter it into the calendar.

He said that I could do it myself, and I demurred, saying that I didn't know if my husband would see it as law if I wrote it.

He gave me a look of sympathy that made me feel like crying again.

To hell with Enoch Granville. Some part of me despised him.

THE DOOR TO my bedchamber opened.

I stirred, turning toward the door, fear filling me, cowering beneath the blankets. It was very dark outside. I didn't know how long I'd been asleep, but I knew it was the middle of the night.

The hulking form of my centaur husband stood in the doorway. "Phoebe, I thought you would sleep in my bed when I was gone."

"No," I said.

"But you indicated to me—"

"I didn't mean it," I said. "It would only be pain to do that."

He sighed heavily. "I'm sorry I left. Something came up, and I had to see to it. It couldn't be helped."

"All right," I said. "Is there anything else? You've disturbed my rest."

"You're angry with me."

"No," I said. "No, I am a foolish, foolish girl who keeps thinking that you care about me when there is a mountain of evidence to the contrary. I shall endeavor to cease at once. Forgive me." I rolled over, giving him my back, and I waited for him to go.

There was no sound except the faint echo of his breath.

All was still.

I tried to close my eyes, but I kept opening them. I could see the shadow of him against the far wall—not clearly, but just the basic shape of him. I saw him move a bit, but he didn't leave the room.

I waited.

He spoke. "Phoebe…"

I didn't respond.

"I *am* sorry."

I still didn't respond.

"I suppose you can't forgive me?"

Still, I was silent.

"What if I order you to come upstairs with me now anyway? What if I say that I have been waiting all day and half the night for you, and that I intend to have you now, and that I don't care if you don't want it?"

"So, you'll force yourself on me, then? Like that woman you spoke of before, the one who was being held captive by the centaur herd?"

He sighed heavily. "No, obviously, of course not." Then he did leave. He shut the door carefully, and I heard the sound of his hooves going down the hall. They were dejected hoofbeats.

I almost got up and went after him. I wanted to. I wanted him. I wanted to be *wanted* by him. I had grown rather fond of the way that made me feel. His hunger for me was gratifying.

But if I did, I would lose all self-respect, and I was going to be married to this man for a very long time.

I managed to keep myself in check and stayed in bed.

CHAPTER THIRTEEN

IT WAS MY favorite breakfast the next day—waffles with cinnamon and pear butter and dollops of clotted cream. I had never told this to Enoch, but he seemed to have rooted the information out from someone, likely Janet. I resolved to corner her and tell her not to give any more of my secrets to my husband.

Then I resolved against it.

What did I care?

It was my favorite breakfast and my husband was eager to make amends. He cared about making me happy. That was pleasing.

He didn't apologize at breakfast, though. He didn't grovel or make any indication that he'd gone to trouble.

I didn't say anything about it. I didn't mention that it was my favorite breakfast or ask how he knew or any such thing. I was stonily silent, tucking into my waffles with gusto.

He could have asked if I liked the breakfast or something of that manner. He didn't.

Instead, he said, "I have you to thank for this dinner two weeks hence with the Duke and Duchess?"

I inclined my head, smiling. Then I stuffed my mouth full of more waffles.

"It's quite well done, Phoebe." He smiled at me. "You're a wonder. My wife." He looked me over as if I was stunning and rare and he was privileged to have me.

I nearly choked on my waffle.

"I repay you badly," he said, nodding. "I see that. You are well within your rights to be angry with me."

I waited for the apology to come.

It didn't.

If it hadn't been waffles, I would have simply excused myself from the breakfast table. But I was hungry, and waffles were wondrous. So, I stayed, and I ate.

He began to talk of what this would mean, how we might leverage the dinner with the Rells into other invitations and how this might go very well for us. This was the first step, and he was quite excited. He complimented me more and more. He asked me how I'd managed it.

I thought about swallowing the waffle and saying that I had traded a description of his penis for the invitation to see the duchess. I thought it would wound him, but then I wasn't sure it would.

Besides, I was determined not to speak to him.

So, I remained silent.

He surveyed me, shaking his head. "It has to be tonight, you know."

I lifted my chin, staring him down, utterly quiet.

"Please, Phoebe," he murmured. "I know I don't deserve it. I know you likely haven't even been adequately trained. But I am going to literally go mad if I don't have you."

"Literally mad?" The words ripped out of my mouth. "You have told me you have control of yourself."

"It's slipping. The madness is not entirely predictable."

"Well, let me finish my waffles," I said in a nasty voice. "Then I'll meet you in your bedchamber and you can strap me to the mount. I suppose we *do* need to consummate our marriage, after all. For legal purposes."

"I'm not saying right now," he said. "Tonight is adequate."

"I'm perfectly willing to do it right now." My eyes flashed. "And you have made out that you're on the brink of utter insanity, so—"

"All right, *fine*," he said. "We'll continue this conversation later." He got up from the table and excused himself.

The devil take that man!

With breakfast over, however, I was steeped in boredom. I had nothing to do with myself today, and I couldn't help but think of him. He was *all* I could think of.

I determined I would distract myself, and thus set about finding a book to read. I went into the library of the house—which was poorly stocked, truly, and I would have to have a conversation with Enoch about getting more books—and tried and discarded three books.

The first was something I had always wanted to read, and the second was something I had thought about reading, and the third was something I had read before and always enjoyed.

But they were all pointless, for none of them could hold my interest, and I could not stop thinking about Enoch.

Eventually, I found myself seeking him out, which was undoubtedly his plan.

However, I couldn't find him.

Had he left again?

I inquired of the servants, but they assured me he was here and that the carriage was here.

However, he didn't appear to be in the house anywhere. He was not in his study. He was not in his bedchamber. He was not in any of the sitting rooms.

I even checked all of the guest rooms, and no one was in them.

Finally, I went looking for Mr. Higgins, but I couldn't find him either.

Eventually, I saw Mr. Higgins coming up from a door that led down to the basement of the house, which was where the kitchens and the offices for the butler and housekeeper were located. He was red in the face, wearing only the remnants of a suit, his shirt sleeves rolled up. He had been sweating.

"Where is my husband?" I demanded.

"Left it too long, he says," said Mr. Higgins.

"Left what too long?" I said.

Mr. Higgins cleared his throat and looked away. He might have been blushing, but his face was already so red that I couldn't tell.

"What?" I said. "Where is he?"

"He's down there." Mr. Higgins pointed his thumb back at the door.

"Well, all right," I said, going for the door. "Then I shall simply go down and—"

"Mrs. Granville, I can't advise that," said Mr. Higgins. "I don't think the sight of you is going to calm him."

I stopped, door halfway open. I looked at Mr. Higgins and then I looked down the long row of steps into the basement. I wondered about my husband descending these steps with his hooves. The other staircases in the house were wider than this. These were frightfully narrow.

From below, I heard a wild and desperate whinny.

"Is he... all right?" I whispered.

Mr. Higgins sighed. "He's gone wild. I've never seen it before, though he warned me it happened to centaurs. Said it was possible when he married you, that you were the type of woman to drive him out of his head."

"What does that mean?" I said.

Mr. Higgins spread his hands. "He came to me mid-morning and said he was worried it was coming on. He told me why it was coming on, because he hadn't..." He grimaced. "Right fool, I told him. But at any rate, missus, he seemed to have lost all sense of speech by the time I had him tied down."

"Tied down?" I whispered.

"He could cause a lot of damage. Trample people to death, destroy all manner of priceless art in the house," said Mr. Higgins.

"I see," I said. "And what can we do about it? How long will it last?"

"That I don't know," said Mr. Higgins. "I've never seen him like this. I tried to ask him if he's going to come out of it, but he was too far gone to answer at that point."

"He needs me, then," I said. "He needs to..." I twisted my

hands together. "He needs me on the mount."

Mr. Higgins was definitely blushing. "W-well, Mrs. Granville, that is none of my affair, I must say, and I don't wish to—"

"If I can get myself onto it, strapped and secure and... ready? Can you get him up into the room and make sure his hooves are secure?"

"Me?" Mr. Higgins coughed. "I have no desire to watch—"

"Please, Mr. Higgins," I said. "I have no desire for you to watch either, and I'm certain my husband doesn't wish it, for that matter. You said you are loyal to him above all, however, so will you do it?"

He let out a long, whistling breath, looking vaguely ill. "Aye, Mrs. Granville. I shall do my best."

"All right," I said. "I shall engage my maid to assist me. Have him there in fifteen to twenty minutes?"

He gave me a stiff nod. "As you wish, Mrs. Granville."

I HAD ALWAYS faced Enoch on the mount, but this time, I wasn't sure that was the best way to go about this. I had seen horses mount other horses, and I thought—if Enoch was wild and out of his head, pure instinct—then I should mimic that sort of posture.

So, with Janet's help, I was able to secure myself on the mount bent over, legs spread, elevated into the air at a level that seemed to be the right height for Enoch. I was able to keep my hands free, and after Janet left, I spent all my time reaching back and rubbing as much grease into myself as I could.

I was terrified of this.

It was going to be brutal, and he wasn't going to be easy with me at all, and I didn't *want* to do it.

Perhaps I should have waited to see if he returned to himself, but I was frightened that if I waited, he would only grow more wild and out of control and that this would still be necessary, only that it would be worse.

I supposed I could have... well, if my husband was essentially a rabid animal, then he could be... put down? If centaurs lived forever, could they be killed?

I didn't want that.

Being a centaur's widow did not appeal to me.

No, I wanted him alive. I wanted that stupid dinner with the duke and duchess. I wanted...

I wanted him back.

If this was the way I got him back, so be it.

I heard my husband and Mr. Higgins approaching far before I could see them. There were all manner of loud huffs and whinnies and maddened cries. When they did come into sight, my husband was bound and muzzled, his arms tied tightly behind his back and some sort of contraption over his mouth that was a horrible version of the bridle he'd put on me. How he was making such noises through that thing, I could not even understand! His legs could move but they were chained, so he could not move them too quickly.

When he saw me, he started for the mount, but the chains caught him and he staggered and nearly fell down.

Mr. Higgins spoke to him in a calm and commanding voice, keeping his gaze only on my husband, never even looking at the mount. He pulled on the chains, keeping Enoch from moving too quickly.

I shivered, feeling debased and disgusted.

Was this what it had all come to?

I was being taken by an animal in the end.

Tears formed in my eyes, and I took several shaking breaths.

Don't think about it, I told myself. *He is not an animal. He is your husband. You must give him back his humanity, and you must get through this.*

Enoch strained for the mount, and Mr. Higgins kept him moving slowly, but eventually they got there.

"He needs to be unchained to get his hooves up," I said.

Mr. Higgins wouldn't look at me. "But what if he kicks you?"

"He can't mount otherwise," I said.

Mr. Higgins seemed to be considering this. I realized that for him to unchain Enoch, it would also endanger him, for he would be risking the trampling of Enoch's hooves.

"Just the front ones perhaps?" I said. "I don't mean for you to take your life into your hands—"

"I do what I must for him," said Mr. Higgins, and he bent over. From the angle where I was strapped into the mount, I couldn't see anything, but I heard the clattering of chains.

I shivered again. I was likely cold. I wasn't wearing clothes, and I suppose that should have felt very shameful, but something about being in the mount made me feel oddly covered in a strange way. And anyway, I suppose it all seemed so mechanical at this point, a sort of problem to be solved, nothing more.

Enoch let out a whinny, his front legs kicking up.

Mr. Higgins swore and jumped back. He landed on his backside, clutching his side, gazing up at the ceiling, letting out a string of swears.

Enoch's hooves came down.

I screamed.

But he lodged them in the grooves above my head, lodged them on the mount, and I felt the brush of his belly against my back and then—

His prick.

It prodded its way over my backside, and Enoch whined.

A jangle of chains as he moved his hind feet and tried again.

But this time, his thick, hot, stiffness only slid against my greased opening, slid through my lips, not penetrating me.

I had my hands free, so I reached back.

I found him and guided him.

I lined him up.

He pushed inside.

My eyes widened and I couldn't breathe.

It was nothing like the training cock the night before, because then, I had been aroused and ready and eager, and he had been touching my clit, and adding to my wetness however he could.

It hurt.

I tried not to tense, afraid that would make it worse.

I tried to stay loose and relaxed.

Enoch rutted into me, stabbing me, stretching me, rooting around in me, too huge for words.

I managed one noise, a sort of mewling sound, and then I fell silent.

He stroked into me, his movements jerky and erratic.

Every few moments, I remembered to breathe and sucked in air.

Suddenly, I was flooded with hot, wet liquid and he withdrew.

"Hell's bells," came the sound of Enoch's voice above me.

I let out a sob of relief.

Enoch scrambled off the mount. He nearly tripped over the chains on his hind legs. He struggled against the ropes that bound his arms. He could barely move his jaw through the muzzle. "Higgins." He was livid.

Higgins was standing with his back to the mount. He hadn't been watching, but he'd stayed, I supposed, in case something had gone wrong.

"Did I ask you to do this?"

Higgins glanced at him, sidelong. "No, sir."

"But you did it anyway?"

"Your wife—"

"My wife is *bleeding*."

Was I? I whimpered.

"This is not the way this should have..." Enoch's voice broke.

"She set it up, sir," said Mr. Higgins. "I only followed her orders. Shall I remove..." Higgins gestured.

"Quickly," said Enoch. "My wife needs—"

"I shall leave her to you," said Mr. Higgins, who was busying himself untying Enoch's arms.

Enoch, arms free, clawed the muzzle off his face.

Mr. Higgins knelt and freed Enoch's hind legs of chains. He hauled them up and carried them out, chains spilling out of his massive arms. He shut the door behind him.

Enoch was unfastening me from the mount. I could feel that his fingers were shaking when they brushed my ankles. He had to lift me higher to get to them and then lower me. It was a bit of a production to get me out of it.

When he was done, he stepped backwards and let me climb out of the mount.

I looked up at him, free now.

His face was screwed up in a strange expression. His eyes were shining. I watched as he reached up and wiped his cheek with the heel of his hand. He was crying?

I tried to think of when I'd seen a man cry.

I looked away.

He was moving across the room.

I looked up to watch him leave the room.

Where was he going? Was he embarrassed that he was crying? Or trying to be proper and hide it from me?

But he came right back with a blanket and he wrapped me up in it.

I wanted him to embrace me.

He didn't. He backed away again. "I don't suppose you wish to be near me now. I can ring for your maid."

"Do you wish to be near me?" I said in a tiny voice.

"Always," he rasped.

"Can we...?" My voice cracked. "Can we lie down in the bed together?"

He let out a noisy breath, and tears spilled out of his eyes. "You would... with me, after...?"

I reached out for him.

He pulled me into his arms and carried me out to the bed. He arranged us, and I was worried that I was bleeding and I would sully the blankets, or him, and he was adamant that didn't matter, and so we ended up tangled up together, pressed close.

But instead of his cheek pillowed on my breast, he held my head against his chest and stroked my hair, raking his fingers down and down and down.

We were quiet for some time.

He was the one who spoke. "Apologies seem pointless after that," he said.

"I don't think it was your fault," I said.

"How can you say that?"

"I was being peevish," I said. "You told me that it you would lose your mind, and I didn't take you at your word—"

"You had every right to deny to speak to me—"

"I didn't realize it would make you into a maddened beast, or I would have—"

"It's not fair. It's wrong to demand of you. You can't be forced to submit to me for the fear of my going crazy and hurting other people!"

"Is that how it is then?" I breathed. "Can it happen again if we don't do it regularly?"

His silence was answer enough.

I submitted to the steady flow of his fingers through my hair.

"I've never lost it like that before," he said finally. "I've seen it happen to other centaurs, and I perhaps recognized the signs, but I was too certain of myself, and I thought I could keep it in check. I never meant to be so brutal with you, my sweet one."

"Do you remember it?" I said. "Or is it like a rage that descends and robs you of your senses?"

"I was aware," he said. "But out of control. A torment. I wish I had not remembered. That would have been a relief of some kind, I think."

"Oh," I said. "W-well, it wasn't so bad."

He snorted.

I fought out of his arms to look up at him. "No, truly, I think that bleeding is... well, it's supposed to happen, although it didn't with me, not the first time. But perhaps there was simply something left of my maidenhead—"

"I don't think it actually works that way," he said. "If there's tearing, it's because you weren't ready to accommodate me."

"Well, I did think that," I said. "I should have tried to get myself, um, aroused, I suppose, but I was so afraid, and I couldn't quite get into the right, er, mood for it."

"Of course," he said.

"I'm sorry."

"Don't you dare apologize," he said.

"It was my idea," I said. "I know you were angry with Mr. Higgins, but I thought we had to do it."

"We likely did," he said, and his voice wasn't strong, as if he was going to cry again. "But I have never despised myself as much as I do in this moment, Phoebe. Not even after I was told Deborah had killed herself did I feel like *this*." He considered. "Perhaps that's only a sign that I deserved to be cursed, for I'm not sure I knew what it was to feel self-hatred. This, hurting you, however, I—"

"I don't need you to hate yourself," I said. "What does that do for me?"

"*Why* did you do it?" He was agonized.

"The last time we were intimate, husband, you demanded I give into pain."

"Not like this," he said.

"No," I admitted. "No, not like this."

"You enjoyed that. But this—you weren't aroused, you just offered yourself up as a sacrificial lamb—"

"Well, what would have happened if I hadn't? Would you have come out of it?"

"No," he said. "Well, not until I got free and mauled some woman—any woman. That is what happens with centaurs, anyway. I've seen it. Without the mount… the women don't always survive."

I let out a horrified breath. "Well, then, you see, I had to."

"I was locked up," he said. "Mr. Higgins has orders not to leave me in that condition for too long, you see. He would have put a bullet in my skull."

"And you can die?"

"From violence? Oh, yes. Many a centaur puts an end to themselves after they rut some woman to death, you know. I wonder if I would have." He sighed.

"No!" I said.

"No? Why did you allow it? Why not be free of me? We had a bargain, Phoebe, and you are supposed to stay strong in your hatred of me—"

"I have! I do!" I jerked away from him, my lips peeled back from my teeth.

His nostrils flared.

I licked my lips. "I need you, I suppose. And you... we want the same things. I want that dinner with the Rells. I want to be part of society again. I want... A centaur's widow is not the same thing as a centaur's wife."

He nodded slowly. "All right, then."

I sagged backwards, into the cushioned headboard of his bed, ashamed of myself for admitting this. Between my legs, it throbbed.

"So, you hate me?" he breathed.

I nodded.

"I am... I would..." He looked up at the ceiling. "I can't bear to hurt you again, all right? Don't ever do something like that again. Promise me that. Promise to have me killed first?"

"I can't promise that," I protested.

"I love you, Phoebe," he whispered.

"You don't." I dismissed this.

He looked back at me. "I think I do," he said, and he sounded terrified at the prospect.

CHAPTER FOURTEEN

BY THE MORNING, I was barely tender between my thighs.

Enoch asked me about the pain, worried, agonized, and I told him this, and he said, wonderingly, that perhaps what they said about centaur seed was true. He had spent inside me, of course, and that had been dribbling out of me all night. It had actually woken me several times and I'd been worried it was blood, but it never had been, just his seed, so much of his seed.

It was annoying and a bit repellent, and yet... oh, I didn't know, I sort of like it, because it made me feel claimed and his.

It hadn't been the way either of us would have liked it to be, but it had happened.

Something had shifted between us.

We stayed in bed that morning. He had breakfast brought up to us—more waffles and cinnamon and pear butter, in fact. I was naked, and there was something erotic about my beautiful husband with his long mane of hair feeding me in bed, but he wouldn't allow anything of that nature between us, he said, not until I was entirely healed.

"We must be careful with you, Phoebe," he whispered, kissing the crown of my head. "You are very precious to me."

I liked that, in spite of myself.

Oh, I hated him.

I did.

It was horrible, really, truly disgusting, that I could submit to such a thing, that he could have me in the most vicious of ways, and that he could rip my skin and make me bleed, and yet... I felt more tender towards him than ever.

I wondered if it was some sort of horrible wrongness within a woman's soul, to feel tenderness for a man whose prick had been inside her no matter what he had done.

But no.

I'd never felt anything like this for Oscar, after all. I'd never felt anything for him at all. Admittedly, he'd been dead within twelve hours after the deed had been done. If he hadn't been dead, maybe I would have hated him more fiercely. But as dead as he was, he seemed only pathetic.

I did not like what he'd done to me, but I supposed I recognized his pain and helplessness.

I'd never blamed him.

I'd always blamed my brother, for better or worse.

I wondered if Mr. Higgins had told Enoch about the visit Laurence had made while Enoch was gone. I didn't think Enoch would like it, and I thought it would not be a good thing if Enoch really did kill my brother. It would not give me any kind of peace, I didn't think, and it might go badly for Enoch and then for me.

Perhaps I should tell Mr. Higgins not to bring it up at all.

But Mr. Higgins had been ordered to stay clear of me, and I couldn't get close to him.

The afternoon after my marriage was consummated, I began bleeding again, which was alarming at first until I got the requisite cramps and realized it was simply my monthly bleeding, coming rather right on schedule.

This was relieving, for it meant that at least one of us—or perhaps both of us—still hated the other. My husband's curse had not been broken. I was not with child.

He was very, very pleased with the news, though.

This tended to sour my relief, I had to admit.

I must want him to fall in love with me. I couldn't be sure why, but maybe it was just because any woman would want her husband to be in love with her, wouldn't she?

Besides, he'd *said* it.

I'd denied it, but...

And children? Well, I'd despaired a long time ago of becoming a mother, but I thought I might like it. Certainly, motherhood was difficult, but there was something wondrous about it — the idea of a small bundle of tiny limbs and coos? Planting kisses on the tip of a tiny little nose?

I would like to love, truly.

I couldn't have loved my brother, not after what he'd done to me, and my parents were gone. I was not able to love my husband either.

But a child...?

Ah, there were no restrictions on that. I had love to give. I knew I did. It was all down buried inside of me, and it wanted to come out.

But thinking thoughts like this made me teary, and I sat sniffling until Janet came and offered me a handkerchief and reminded me that I was likely only teary because it was the time of my monthly bleeding, no other reason required.

I BLED FOR six days, and my husband wanted me in his bed all those nights anyway. I tried to protest, saying that he couldn't possibly be serious, but he said, if he had his way, we'd never sleep apart, and that affected me too.

Damn that awful centaur.

So, we slept in each other's arms, curled around and into each other, and I liked it.

And when my bleeding ended, he inquired how my quim had healed, and it was not even a little sore anymore.

I considered lying.

Perhaps I should put him off.

Not because I didn't want him. Quite the opposite. We already seemed so very close, and what would happen to me if I joined with him truly in that manner? What if it burst through the last of my defenses, and I did fall in love with him?

But then I wondered at myself.

Would it be bad if the curse broke? If he loved me, and if we had children, and if we lived out a normal lifespan?

I didn't think it would be bad.

Of course, he'd be angry. I knew he would. He had his plans, after all, whatever they were, and his curse being broken would end them. But maybe, if he loved me, maybe he'd find a way to make peace with that. Maybe he could be happy. Maybe we could both be happy.

So, I told him I was his and he could have me however he wanted.

His gaze went dark and eager.

Still, he was shy with me that night. He stripped me of my nightgown and traced my breasts with reverent fingers and there was no discussion of bridles or of reins or of keeping me in a stall.

He put me in the mount and we kissed for quite a long time.

I was curious, because I was facing him. Could he mount me this way? I asked, and he seemed even more shy.

"Of course, it can be done," he said. "You'd wrap your thighs around me and I'd have my hooves up here." He gestured. "You'd be staring up at my belly, of course, but we might... maybe we could catch each other's gazes. It seems frightful that we can't be face to face when we are joined." He touched my cheek.

"That does seem frightful," I whispered.

"Would it bother you, looking up at my horse body?"

"No, your horse body doesn't bother me," I said, laughing gently. "How could you think it did?"

He let out a rueful laugh and kissed my forehead. "You don't have to say such things, pretty wife."

"I'm not making it up," I insisted. I had my hands free, though my ankles were strapped into the mount, and I reached down to brush against the place where the skin of his waist gave way to short, glistening fur.

He sucked in a breath, goosebumps appearing on his

belly. He shut his eyes.

"I don't simply tolerate your body, you know, husband. I am quite affected by it." It was true. He stirred me, and he always had.

He claimed my mouth, desperate, hard, a little sloppy.

I clung to him.

When he broke the kiss, he was a little out of breath, and so was I. He feathered his fingers over my cheekbone. "I don't deserve you."

"You don't," I said with a little shake of my head.

He chuckled and kissed me again. He put our foreheads together, and his voice was a soft rumble. "Shall we do it that way, then, facing each other?"

"Yes," I whispered.

"We need to make sure you are very, very wet," he said.

I nodded.

He touched my breasts again. "And we'll need to be clever with the straps on the mount. Your legs can't be fastened down if you are going to wrap your legs around me, so you'll need to be secured at your waist and your arms only."

"Arms?" I was disappointed. "I want to touch you."

"Maybe one arm free?" His voice was husky as he teased my nipples stiff.

"I think I'll be secure enough with the straps at my waist," I said. "If I'm holding onto you with my arms and legs, Enoch, I won't fall off."

"I think we might need some extra straps," he said. "They could go here." He reached down to trace a line around me, in the sensitive crease between my leg and my sex. "One one each side, to hold you in place."

"Mmm," I said. "That's good."

"For now, you'll need to have your arms restrained—"

"But—"

"No, no arguments, Phoebe," he rumbled. "Submit to your husband like a good wife."

I shivered at this, because I was always aroused by submitting to him. And besides, he was doing it for my safety, and I liked that too. I felt very close to him. I tangled my hands up in his hair and kissed his mouth.

He went back to teasing my nipples, giving them the clever pinches that he was so good at.

I began to be distracted from kissing him by the moans that were tearing their way from my lips.

He gently extricated my hands from his hair and put them into the straps above my head, kissing the inside of my palm, the sensitive underside of my wrist as he secured me.

Then he had to lift me to get to my ankles, using the pulleys on the mount to raise my body. While he had me like that, I was treated to his mouth between my thighs. He kissed my mound all over and then delved in to gentle his tongue against my sensitive spots, moaning my name into my trembling sex.

"Can you come for me, pretty wife?" he asked me. "I'd like you as wet and eager and ready as we can manage."

"I can try," I said.

And then he went back to licking me. It felt lovely, and I shut my eyes and basked it in, biting down on my lower lip. I was concentrating on trying to find the thread of my pleasure, to bear down on it and follow it to its end. But, well, I couldn't find it. Or when I did find it, I couldn't get it to go anywhere.

Finally, frustrated, embarrassed, I said, "I don't think it's going to happen."

He kissed the inside of my thigh. "You're nervous?"

"No," I said. I considered. "Yes," I admitted.

"I put too much pressure on you," he said. "Usually, I help you along with some erotic imagining, but they're all so… I wanted it different between us for this, I suppose."

"It's not your fault, it's mine," I protested. "And I want it different too."

"How about this?" he murmured, going back to lick me. "Shall I tell you how much I like your quim?"

"Why don't we just get on with it?" I said. "Just have me already. It's not as if it hasn't happened before."

"I can't bear the idea of hurting you, sweet one," he said.

"I don't mind waiting. It only makes me more aroused, truly. Do you have any idea how hard I am now?"

I had a tiny tremor between my legs. "Tell me how hard you are, husband," I ordered in a throaty voice.

"Oh?" He was pleased. "That is what you want?"

"Are you very stiff?"

"Very, very stiff, yes." He licked me again.

"And…" I panted. "Huge?"

"You like my hugeness?" This was unsure.

"I like being able to take all of you, yes. I like being yours, stretched perfectly for you, torn wide open to make room for your thick, fat cock. As if my quim has been remade just to fit you."

He grunted against me. "Phoebe," he panted. "*Phoebe.*"

"Suck my clit," I breathed, frantic.

Obediently, he took it into his mouth and gently suckled.

I exploded against him in an ecstasy of clenches. I bowed out, the pleasure like being submerged in a hot bath, water over one's head, water everywhere, buoying one up, overwhelming, steaming, suffocating—too much and exactly enough, all at once.

The aftermath was a fumbling of rearranging me—unstrapping my ankles, adjusting the mount, lining us up. His hooves were secure overhead as I slid my thighs against his body, against the powerful muscles of his upper legs and flank.

He was there—hot, enormous, very hard—and he was prodding away at me in all the wrong spots.

My hips were strapped down. I strained to move them to accept him.

He struggled to find the right spot.

And then…

There.

He let out a mangled gasp.

I echoed it.

He thrust—one long stroke—and he was inside me to his hilt. "Fuck," he breathed.

He stung, my quim stretching for him, but I could feel the

sting was fading as he began to work himself within me.

I had my eyes closed, concentrating on relaxing, on accepting him, on accommodating his girth and length.

He was breathing noisily, every breath coming out a wheeze.

I opened my eyes, and I could see his horse belly over me, see the muscles under his skin constricting and releasing as he pushed his way in and out of me. But further up, I could see his human body. He was bracing his hands against a cross beam on the mount and gazing down at me.

The expression on his face was fierce, as if he was concentrating very hard, too.

But then our gazes caught, and his expression went impossibly gentle and affectionate.

This went through me like a rippling stream.

Suddenly, the sting was gone entirely, and I was assailed by intensity and pleasure.

I had the sensation of my clitoris being battered from within again. It was so sensitive from having already climaxed that this sensation was very pleasantly bothersome, a sort of insistent nudge that began to wake little tremors inside my body.

I groaned.

"Fuck," he whispered again. "Are you all right?"

"Oh, yes," I told him, my voice destroyed. "Please, Enoch, you feel so good."

"You feel like heaven on earth," he informed me.

My quim convulsed around him.

He grunted. "Hell and damnation, wife."

I managed a laugh.

"I wish I could kiss you," he breathed.

"Enoch." My wrists strained at the straps. I wanted to touch him. I tightened my thighs around him instead.

He sighed. "So, so good." He began to fuck me harder, as if he'd been holding back before, trying to be careful with me.

I let out a scream, because it was as if my battered clitoris had been urged to a small flame and now, he was turning it into a burning inferno. I began to moan as my whole cunt twitched and clenched around him.

My pleasure built as I looked up at him, built and *built*. He was so very, very large, I felt as if his cock was touching me everywhere, touching every sensitive part of my body.

And my quim seemed to relinquish my orgasm grudgingly, as if it had been forced upon me instead of coaxed. It happened in wild, uncontrollable jerks, and it was so much that I couldn't even make noise. I gaped up at his face, mouth wide open, barely able to breathe.

But he felt it and he slammed all the way home and let go as well. I felt his orgasm, so similar to the tremors of mine. I felt the hot, wet rush of his seed.

I wrapped my legs tightly around him, wanting to keep us together like this for as long as I could.

But he retreated, taking down his hooves, unstrapping me from the mount, kissing me all over, murmuring little sweet nonsense words to me, kissing me in affectionate places like the tip of my nose and the end of my chin.

I was boneless and very relaxed in his arms. "So, that's being mounted?"

"That was like nothing I've ever felt," he told me. "You are the most perfect and wonderful woman to ever exist."

I giggled. "Am I?"

"Mmm." He kissed my throat as he pulled me into his arms to carry me to our bed. "You're the ideal of what a mount should be. You're too lovely for words, wife."

I rubbed into him like a satisfied cat.

We arranged ourself on the bed and there was more kissing, our hands roaming over each other as we sighed and basked in each other.

I felt a little like I was floating, I thought. I liked him, and I liked the pleasure, and I liked having him inside my body, and I liked this—now—very little distance between us, as if he'd left enough of himself inside my body that we were still connected even after.

I threw my arms above my head into the pillows I was propped up on. I shut my eyes. "Are we going to do that all the time now?"

He laughed. "I think so."

"Good." I snuggled into the covers. "Regular rides, you said. You mount me and ride me several times a day."

"You think you can handle that?"

"I *know* I can." I was sultry. That orgasm around his cock? I liked it. It wasn't better than the other orgasms I'd had with him, not exactly, but it was different. It was intense and insistent and impossible to deny, an inevitability. I wanted to feel that sort of pleasure again.

"You're not sore?"

"No." This was a lie. I *was* sore.

He rubbed my bottom lip. "Maybe we can make use of your mouth for a few of the riding sessions."

I opened my eyes in slits and licked his thumb. "Mmm," I said appreciatively.

He thrust his thumb into my mouth.

I sucked it.

He groaned, pulling it free. "Wicked, tempting thing."

"You started it," I said, undulating there—against him, against the pillows, against everything. I was awash in sensation, even now.

He kissed me. "I *don't* deserve you," he whispered.

I ran a hand through his hair, my voice quiet too. "Can't you be better, then, husband? Try to please me?"

"I don't please you?" He kissed my forehead.

"You please my body," I said. "You are a master of all my pleasure. But... what is the thing you are doing that I won't like?"

"No, Phoebe." He pulled away. "No, we shan't discuss this."

"Could you stop doing it?" I stroked a hand down his chest. "Don't tell me about it if you really don't want to, but... could you stop?"

He sighed heavily. "I don't know," he murmured.

That wasn't no.

I pulled him down against me, tucked his head down to my breast.

He sighed again, but this was a happy sigh.

"Let's sleep," I told him.

He turned to plant a small, sweet kiss on my nipple and then put his cheek against my breast. He rested his other hand possessively over my other breast. "I can't imagine how I slept before I could lie on your beautiful breasts, wife."

I tangled my hands into his mane. "Better together," I said.

"Yes," he breathed.

We slept.

CHAPTER FIFTEEN

WE SLEPT LATE and woke together, pressed close, because someone was banging on the door.

Mr. Higgins's voice boomed from without. "Begging your pardon, sir, but I'm coming in."

"Don't," cried Enoch. He glared down at me. "The amount of times we're interrupted in the mornings is criminal."

I nodded. "It truly is."

"I want you this morning," he said to me, the bottom having gone out of his voice.

I let out a shaky breath, nodding.

The door opened and Mr. Higgins came inside.

Enoch turned, but only his neck. He was still in bed with me, and he blocked my bare body from view with his torso. "Mr. Higgins, get out of this room."

"I can't, sir, I'm afraid. You see, she's here. Mrs. Gwendolyn Marsh is in your sitting room downstairs."

All of the blood drained out of Enoch's face.

"I know what you're going to say, sir," said Mr. Higgins. "You're going to tell me to get rid of her. But if I could have done so, I would have, don't you think? She is threatening to go to gossip sheets with a number of accusations about you, most of which are either true or have a thread of truth, and if you think your reputation will survive such a thing—"

"Devil of a woman." Enoch got out of bed all at once,

leaving me to scramble for covers. He stalked out of the room, hooves banging on the floor, not even bothering to get dressed. He went straight past Mr. Higgins and disappeared.

I clutched the blankets against me. "Who is Gwendolyn Marsh?"

"I shall have to let Mr. Granville explain that to you," said Mr. Higgins. "Shall I send your maid to you to help you dress?"

"Have her meet me in my room," I said, tugging up the blankets and wrapping myself up in them. Then, covered entirely, I went past Mr. Higgins and stalked out of the room.

I didn't know who this woman was, but I also *did* know.

I didn't know the specifics, but…

He was fucking her.

I tried to argue myself out of that, because… well, he had told me it had been a very long time since he'd had sex with a woman, and the mount—it wasn't easy to accomplish—but I couldn't make myself quite believe it.

Janet wanted to chat with me, but I wasn't in the mood.

I had her dress me and asked questions about Mrs. Marsh.

"I haven't seen her," Janet said. "She arrived about a half hour ago, I think, and I wasn't there when she came to the door."

I hurried down and asked to be directed to the sitting room where this woman was waiting for my husband.

The servant I asked looked nervous, but I said that I was the mistress of this house and I demanded to be obeyed, and the servant told me.

Inside the room, I found them.

Enoch stood there, naked, chest bare, gesturing wildly with his hands as he spoke.

She faced him, hands on her hips, face red.

At first, I was too stunned to even understand what was being said.

Slowly, I began to hear Enoch's words here and there.

Promises. Patient. Must go.

But then he saw me, and he stopped talking. "Mrs. Granville," he said in a low, destroyed voice.

Gwendolyn Marsh turned and looked me over. She was not young. I thought she must have been in her late forties, maybe her early fifties. There was gray in her hair, lines on her face. Her figure was no longer girlish. She had a stately, commanding beauty to her, even so. Her clothing was well made but out of fashion, something that wasn't entirely out of the norm for women of her age, as if they could not be bothered to keep up with trends. "So, this is her. Not much to look at, is she? But I suppose it doesn't matter. It's a magical connection. You keep telling me you have no control over it."

I swallowed hard, tears coming to my eyes.

"Please quit the room, Mrs. Granville, if you don't mind," said my husband. "This conversation is not meant for your ears."

I shook my head. I meant to stay.

"I suppose she makes you happy. You swore to me that you couldn't *feel* happiness." Mrs. Marsh laughed, and it wasn't a nice laugh. "So much for your promises, Enoch. *Any* of your promises."

"Gwendolyn, I have already gone out of my head once from this woman, do you realize? It's not within my control. I must have her at regular intervals, or everything is ruined. Everything. And have I not suffered enough, truly?"

"It's never enough," said Gwendolyn.

I was confused. *Was* he fucking her?

He came across the room to me, then. He turned me forcibly and nudged me toward the door.

"I'm staying," I managed, but my voice wasn't strong.

"I shall carry you out if I have to," he said. "Is that what you want? Thrown kicking and screaming over my shoulder?"

I gaped up at him, hatred zinging through my body. "I despise you."

"I know," he said. "It is all I deserve, after all. I shall

explain, Phoebe, but I need you out of this room now."
I was going to start crying.
I left.
I didn't want to give him the satisfaction of watching me fall apart.

CHAPTER SIXTEEN

I GATHERED THAT Mrs. Gwendolyn Marsh was being given a *room* in our house, as our *guest*.

I was livid.

Part of me wished never to speak to my husband ever again. Part of me wished to wring his stupid neck.

I settled for screaming at him.

He was in his study, slumped over his desk, legs tucked under his horse body, looking disheveled even though he'd finally dressed, and he wouldn't look at me.

"You told me there hadn't been a woman in fifty years," I said.

"There hasn't," he said.

"You expect me to believe you're not fucking her?"

"I'm not," he said. "She would never agree to such a thing. I am an abomination, after all, and she specifically made sure I was this way so that I couldn't fuck anything."

She made sure? I drew back. Wait, did that mean…? "What way? Made you what way?"

"Made me into a centaur," said Enoch. "You see she's—"

"She's too young. You said you are over a hundred years old." That woman would not have been born when he was cursed! It *couldn't* be.

He sighed. "Yes, well, that's… it's all complicated. There are things that can be done with centaur blood, arcane rituals… It requires animal sacrifice. But she has not aged in some time, it's true."

My jaw dropped. There were so many awful, awful realizations that were going through me now, but the most important was this. "She's the one. The one you betrayed. The one who cursed you. You were going to *marry* her. You were in love with her then, and you're *still* in love with her."

"No," he said.

"Yes," I said, and my voice broke.

"She hates me."

"You love her," I said. "And this is what? All some elaborate penance to her? Giving her eternal life and... and what else?"

"Whatever she wants, I suppose," he said. "Riches, land, an estate. I have been supporting her for some time. She never married, you see. She's adopted the name Mrs. Marsh, but only because people assume a woman her age must have been married. But that's not her original surname, and she's never had a husband. She's never had children. When I found her, she was miserable, and it was all my fault. I ruined her life."

"You ruined her...? She cursed *you* and turned you into a *centaur*."

"Well, that only made things worse for her. Everyone knew what she had done to me, and it made her seem vindictive and horrid. Men were afraid to cross her. They were not interested in her. And she had every right to be angry with me. I did deserve to—"

"You are in love with another woman," I said. "You've been in love with her for nearly a hundred years. And you married me *anyway*. I... I..." I shook my head in disgust. I could not explain how horrifying this was.

"I'm not in love with her," he muttered.

I hugged myself. "But you owe her, you think. You wish her forgiveness. You do endless penance for her. You do whatever she wants. You suffer for her enjoyment."

He shrugged. "I suppose."

"Well, she has more power over you than I ever shall, regardless of how you feel."

"I suppose," he said softly.

That *hurt*.

"You never offered to keep *me* from aging," I said.

"You don't want to grow old?" He looked up at me.

"Well, not if you're not going to." My voice shook. "Except... that was before. Before I knew that I would always be the interloper into your love affair with Gwendolyn fucking Marsh."

"It's not like that," he said, wincing.

"So, is this why you wish to climb in status? For her?"

"No." He shook his head, looking sheepish. "No, she... that's always been for me. I've always wanted it. My father, you see, he was a wealthy merchant. He could have bought and sold the upper class during our time. But they wouldn't speak to him. He didn't care, of course. He laughed it off, said he wouldn't be part of their snobbery anyway. But it bothered me. I always wanted... I don't know. Just to be *acknowledged*."

"Well, Enoch, I have told you it's impossible," I said.

"I know," he said. "She... she was the daughter of a knight. I secured her hand in marriage. I thought it would have been a foot in the door. I'm not saying I didn't love her, but I loved her for what she represented more than for who she was, do you see? Deborah, on the other hand... she was funny and witty and bright."

"So, all of this is to prove that you truly love her now."

"It is not."

"Stop treating me like I'm an idiot, Enoch."

"I..." He got to his feet and came around the desk. He came for me. "What I feel for *you*, Phoebe—"

"Is some strange magical pull and part of the curse and not even real." I was backing up. If he touched me, so *help* me.

"It might have started that way, but surely you felt it between us last night. That joining, it wasn't about sex, it was about... it was something deeper, some ephemeral part of both of us, and I don't feel things like that for her. I never have. You mustn't—"

"It's not real for *either* of us," I said.

"You're lying," he snapped. "It was real, and I know you felt it."

"So, what? You love me?"

"I do. I love you."

"No, you *don't*," I said. "You don't even know what love *is*."

He flinched at this.

I held up both of my hands. "All you know of love is whatever twisted bit of devotion and guilt you have for her. What is the arrangement between you? That she torments you for all eternity? That you submit to her and keep her alive so that she can watch you suffer until the end of time?"

"Something like that," he muttered.

"And this, all along, this was your plan."

"You knew you wouldn't like it," he said.

"I thought it was... I thought you wanted to destroy *other* people, not to revel in your own pain."

"It's not exactly like that," he said with a sigh.

"No?"

"Well, you know what it can be like with another person, when you surrender to them, when you let them hurt you to... to gratify them."

I let out an anguished noise, because I did know. I remembered how it felt to give that to him, to surrender my pain for his pleasure, how much power there had been in it. Power taken from me, yes, but power given to me, too, power over him because I could grant that to him. I knew the bond it had created between us. I knew it, and I knew he had all that with *her*.

Decades upon decades of that.

With her.

"It's not love with her, Phoebe," he said.

"Stop," I whispered.

His shoulders sagged. "Maybe it's something like love, though," he allowed.

Hearing it out of his mouth was too much. I knew it, of course, but his *admitting* it?

I was going to vomit.
I fled from the room as fast as I could tear out of there.

CHAPTER SEVENTEEN

IF I STILL had parents, I would have packed up my belongings and gone to them. I would have sought solace from people who actually cared about me. I would have severed whatever ties I could from this man. I would have had to remain his wife, of course, but it would have been in name only, and I would have seen to it we never resided under the same roof again.

Of course, I didn't have any parents.

The idea of going to my brother was ridiculous. Impossible. Abhorrent.

And anyway, I couldn't sever anything with Enoch, because his sanity was reliant on regularly inserting his prick into my quim.

If I stopped letting him fuck me, he'd go crazy again, and then... then I supposed what eventually happened to him was that Mr. Higgins put a bullet in his skull.

So, by withholding sex from him, I essentially killed him.

I sat down on the bed in my room and let that thought wash through me, let it penetrate very spare bit of my consciousness, and let it sink deep down into my very being.

He deserved it.

He had been alive too long as it was. He was an awful man. Truly, the *things* he had done. His infidelity to Gwendolyn was a betrayal that had ruined that woman. It had led to the death of Deborah and her unborn child. Then, he had ravished some woman in the woods with the other centaurs. So he was a cheater, a murderer, and a rapist.

Yes, he deserved to die.

However, I didn't want to be the person to do it.

I still had all these confusing tender feelings towards him.

The thing that hurt the most was just... not being as important to him as he was to me.

He had quickly become the center of my world, and the person who was really the kindest to me. Maybe that wasn't saying much, but he had seen to my comfort, made my pleasure a priority, and had cherished and enjoyed me. There was no one else who had made me half as important, truly. So, I couldn't help but think of him as, well, my husband.

A wife was supposed to prioritize her husband, after all.

The only people who she might ever put ahead of him would be their children, and we didn't have any.

He was the most important person in my life.

But in his life, in his long and awful life, there was another important person, and that was Gwendolyn Marsh.

I believed him when he said he wasn't fucking her.

It was still infidelity.

I supposed, however, since she'd been there first, our relationship was the betrayal. Yet again, he had betrayed Gwendolyn with another woman. That was my role in this little vignette. I was just another of Enoch Granville's whores.

Anyway, I didn't know what to do.

I went to Mr. Higgins and asked him how long we would have until Enoch lost his head again.

Mr. Higgins didn't know, but he said he'd try to find out. "I told him I thought he was a right fool," he said. "But I've never held with that woman of his. Mrs. Marsh, she is poisoned and twisted, a withered hag of a woman who has traded all her sweetness for vitriol. He did her no favors keeping her alive like this either."

"You don't think so?"

"I know," said Mr. Higgins. "How old do you think I

am?"

My lips parted. "He does it to you, too?"

"Wouldn't be parted from his best and most loyal man, would he?" Mr. Higgins gave me a mirthless smile.

"B-but you don't like it?"

"How could a body like it, Mrs. Granville? Watching everyone you ever knew wrinkle up and die right in front of your eyes? If you go to them, they look at you with horror and envy, seeing how you haven't succumbed to the ravages of time. You can't do that to them, so you stay away. You're all alone, and you don't get close to anyone. He's all you have. You..."

"Well, then, leave," I said.

"Dying is still so terrifying," said Mr. Higgins with a grimace. "I haven't the strength to embrace it, not when I know... but if he stopped, if he ever asked me if I wanted it, if he gave me the choice, I feel as if I might have just enough strength to resist."

I swallowed hard. "Oh, dear. Oh, dear. Are there others?"

"Just me and Mrs. Marsh, I think," said Mr. Higgins. "Maybe you, though, if you'd consent to it. I was hoping, however, you were going to break the curse and then we could all age together."

"I..." I wanted to cry. "Well, maybe I hoped it, too, but all that is ruined now. I don't know how to feel about him, truly. Maybe a part of me still cares, but mostly I am just hurt and disgusted and angry. I hate him ever so much."

Mr. Higgins nodded. "Of course you do. I hate him as well."

We were quiet.

"So, he is all she has left as well?"

"Mrs. Marsh? Aye, she's nothing now but her concentrated obsession with him. She loved him once, you know. But he is good at turning women's love to hatred. He is quite good at that."

I nodded. "I see that now."

Another silence overtook us both.

I spoke up once again. "If I don't... if he loses his wits

again, he has told me that you have been instructed to… to… well, put him down."

"Aye," said Mr. Higgins in a grim voice.

"Perhaps…" I hesitated. "Is he pure evil, Mr. Higgins? Would we all be better off if he…?"

"Nay, missus," he whispered. "He's not pure evil. I'd venture to say he's not evil at all. No one really is, you know. Most of the evil done in the world is done with the best of intentions."

MR. HIGGINS CAME back with good news.

Well, sort of, I supposed.

It turned out that my husband's madness was rather contingent on one important aspect of everything — proximity.

I drove him mad, yes, but only if I was there, near him, and he could see and smell me and refused to take me. As long as I was gone, I would have no effect on him at all.

Mr. Higgins said that arrangements were being made even now for me to go to my husband's country estate, which he had spoken of to me before. It hurt, thinking of those little erotic imaginings, of my riding him bareback all over the countryside. It reminded me of being half in love with him. I missed the way that had felt, despite everything.

But I sent Mr. Higgins back to say that we had a dinner planned with the Rells and I wasn't missing it for the world. Indeed, my retiring to the country estate would put quite a wrench in our plans to integrate into society. People would want to know why I had left. They would make unflattering assumptions.

Mr. Higgins delivered my message and came back with the following: My husband would leave until the dinner, and then we would see each other only for that night.

On the next morning, I would go off to the country estate, and the word that we would put out was that I was with child and wished to relax there for my pregnancy. It was good. It made sense for me to say, and it was a reason that would not make it look as if there was any strife between us.

Of course, it would also mean that at some point, I would have to have lost the child, because I was not pregnant. That was impossible, considering how much I hated my husband. The curse could never have been broken. Furthermore, he could never really have loved me, not while he was still so intertwined with Gwendolyn Marsh.

It was acceptable, however, and thus put an end to any communication between my husband and myself whatsoever.

He left before luncheon that day; I watched him from the window of my bedchamber.

Gwendolyn Marsh was still under our roof.

I forbade her entry to the dining room. I said all of her meals must be taken in her room. I said that she must stay to her room and to the sitting room that was closest to her there. I said that if I saw her, I would claw her eyes out, and I would severely punish any servant who did not keep the woman from me.

So, I didn't see her at all.

I threw myself into preparations for the dinner with the Rells. I had the cook try out a number of different dishes, and I tried each and every one and found fault with them all.

I knew it wasn't the poor cook's fault. It was me. I was broken and unable to enjoy anything anymore. I had never truly had a broken heart before, that was the thing. I supposed it was likely time. It was only unfortunate that it had to be my husband who broke my heart.

But Janet said it was often the same for many women. She said that there seemed to be a great number of women who were unhappy in their marriages, a great number of husbands who betrayed their wives. She was not wrong.

I was perhaps simply a cliche.

It wasn't as if it wasn't a common story, to marry a man who already was devoted to some mistress or other, who could never replace that woman in his affections? It happened.

Oddly, this wasn't much comfort.

Eventually, I told the cook to prepare whatever he thought was appropriate for the dinner and I told Janet to pick out my dress, and I left the servants to see to the decorations on the table—the flowers and centerpiece and the like.

I went to bed and stayed there.

CHAPTER EIGHTEEN

I WAS ROUSED from bed five days before the dinner with the duke and duchess because there was a constabulary who had come to pay me a visit, I was told, and he was waiting in a sitting room downstairs.

I dressed and met with him, confused as to why he was there.

The first thing he said to me was, "When was the last time you heard from your brother?"

"My brother?" I said. "It's been weeks. What has happened?"

"Well, I hate to be the one to inform you of this, but we suspect foul play."

"What do you mean?" I had not heard this phrase before.

The constabulary wore a uniform and carried a whistle. He strode back and forth in front of me, hands clasped behind his back, his tone matter-of-fact. "We likely would not have known a thing about your brother's disappearance. An earl's business is his own, of course, even if—as it seems—your brother has not been conducting business well for some time. We were only alerted to the idea that anything was wrong because one of the men I work with is the brother of a footman who works at your brother's household."

"Oh," I said. "Which footman?"

"Mr. Whitman."

"Mr. Whitman," I said. "Yes, he's quite an agreeable fellow." Handsome, too, for no one wanted to be served by footmen who weren't pleasant to look upon. Wouldn't do for guests either, not that we ever had any guests.

"He is," said the constabulary, furrowing his brow. "Well, I only know his brother, truly. I say, Mrs. Granville, are you not the least bit concerned that your brother is missing?"

"Have you said so, sir?" I bit down on my bottom lip.

"Yes." He glared at me.

"Well, my brother could have gone to our country estate," I said. "It's in Brent. Perhaps if someone sends a letter there to see if—"

"Your brother is not in Brent," said the constabulary, looking me over now with what I might term suspicion.

"Oh," I said, folding my hands into my lap. "Well, he must be somewhere. Perhaps he is visiting someone else. Perhaps he has gone with one of the other men to one of their estates. He's fond of those sorts of trips, truly. Hunting and gambling, those are his favorite pastimes."

"No one knows where he is, madam," said the constabulary. "We have inquired with everyone who he typically associates with. As I said, we typically wouldn't have done such a thing, but it came out that he was not paying his staff."

"Oh," I said. "Well, that's hardly atypical, I'm afraid. There have been a number of incidents in which he has been unable to raise the coin for salaries. He always sorts it out, though."

"Yes, this is what your Mr. Whitman told my Mr. Whitman," said the constabulary. "However, he said, this time, it was very curious, because Lord Crisbane left one afternoon on horseback and never returned, though he was supposed to be there for supper. Indeed, the horse came back the following morning but without Lord Crisbane."

"Truly?" I said, sitting up straighter. "So, something has happened to my brother?"

"You are just now gathering this, madam?" He glared at me.

I blinked at him, slowly putting all of this together. "You think someone did him harm." And I thought I knew who. Was this some attempt to win me back or to pacify me? Because it was ill-conceived, if so. My husband should realize I would not look kindly on his killing my only blood relative, no matter how I felt about my brother.

"We have spoken to everyone who he might have associated with and none have seen him. In fact, they all said that your brother owed them money from gambling debts and had been avoiding them all."

"Well, that sounds like my brother," I admitted.

"Where were you on the afternoon and evening of Thursday two weeks past, madam?" said the constabulary.

"Me?" I touched my chest. "Well, here. I don't go anywhere else. I suppose I did go to a tea with the Duchess of Rells but that was... no, that was at least three weeks ago." Then I realized why he was asking. "You suspect me of being the one to hurt my brother?"

"No, no," said the constabulary. "It is routine, however, you see. We call these inquiries, 'establishing alibis.'"

"Alibi?" I said, startled. "Am I on trial?" I had not heard the word used in any other context.

"No, no, of course not, madam," said the constabulary. "But, you see, this is what constabularies *do.*"

In all truth, the police force here in town was a very new thing. Many people of my class were not pleased with the idea of it, for we had all always solved our own problems and had not needed the interference of others.

Admittedly, the general way that gentlemen solved problems was dueling.

Dueling had been illegal for some time, because it was brutal and it was also a terrible way to solve a conflict. It left everything up to chance and one person ended up wounded or dead at the end of it.

So, the idea of going to a constabulary to punish those who had done wrong, I could see the reasoning behind it.

But we were proud people, and having men of a lower class take up airs, hold power over us...

Well, people did not like it.

I did not like it.

This man had come into my sitting room and was demanding to know my whereabouts. My whereabouts were none of his concern!

"I would never hurt my brother," I said.

"The servants at your old home say that he treated you badly."

I gasped at that. "How dare they gossip to anyone about what went on in my private life!" But, well, *obviously* servants gossiped. I was being ridiculous.

"Of course, he was stronger than you, madam. So, it would have been difficult for you to have hurt him. But you did sometimes join your brother shooting at clay pigeons?"

My eyes widened. "What?"

"Would you say you're a good shot?"

"Dreadful," I said. "Quite a dreadful shot, in fact, and I hated the activity and my brother didn't like having me along, and I can't believe you would suggest that I would *shoot my brother!*" My voice steadily rose until it was exceedingly high pitched.

"Apologies, madam."

I shot out of my chair and walked across the sitting room to stand next to the window. I clutched the window sill. I stared out at the street, trying to get my breathing under control. "He may be all right. You say he has simply disappeared?"

"That is true, Mrs. Granville," said the constabulary. "I hope that is the case. I am sorry for bringing you such upsetting news."

I nodded but didn't say anything.

"What was the content of your conversation with your brother the last time you saw him?"

I hesitated. I wanted to lie, but I wondered if I should. Clearly, the constabulary had access to the network of servant gossip. I felt I had to tell the truth. "I'm afraid it was not civil, sir. You see, he came to ask me for money. He wanted me to give him any jewelry I had been given by my husband and barring that, to steal any money I could get my hands on from the house and give it to him."

"For gambling debts?"

"Indeed, sir," I said.

"Gambling brings out the demon in a man," said the constabulary.

I nodded.

"So, you refused him?"

"I did."

"And he did not take that well?"

"He did not." I decided not to say that I had grown angry at my brother's demands.

"Well, such behavior is truly beneath a man of his status, coming to his married sister for funds," said the constabulary. "In all truth, Mrs. Granville, I cannot say your brother was, er, well-liked. If he did indeed come to some harm by another's hand, I'm afraid that there are a number of possibilities. He could have quarreled with any number of men to whom he owed money, and many of them may have... well, anyway..." He cleared his throat.

Then it was quiet for some time.

Finally, I said, "Is there anything else I can help you with, sir?"

"It matters not, I suppose, madam," he said.

"It doesn't matter whether I can help you?"

"No, I mean, whether or not your brother was well-liked, whether or not, perhaps, the world is not made overly worse by his passing, whether there might be some who might feel his absence as a relief, the truth is... Murder is a crime against the crown, madam. If he has been killed by someone, that person will be hanged."

I turned to look at him. "Yes, of course. That is what is done to criminals of that nature."

"And we are rather good at rooting out the truth, you see, madam." He nodded at me. "So, well, do that with information what you will. I shall say that we do not have jurisdiction outside of town, so if you were to be, er, in the country, well... do you see what I am saying?"

"I do," I said. "But I assure you, sir, I would never have hurt my brother."

He cleared his throat. "No, of course not."

THE NEXT DAY, I went to my old house to speak to the servants there and to see what had been left in my brother's wake.

They told me that my brother had left with no warning and that they were certain he had not meant to leave. He was expected home, two weeks ago, but had never come home. It was not new information, of course, but seeing his book left out on his bedside table, his letters left out unfinished, it did make it very obvious that he had intended to come home, likely within an hour or two.

I went through my brother's ledgers, which were in horrific shape, not kept up with, mostly useless. I did find a list, on a piece of loose paper, of what I thought must have been all of my brother's debts. At the bottom of the sheet was the full amount, circled with an unsteady hand, and it was enough to beggar him.

Where could he have gone to get enough money for such a thing?

I sorted through some of the other papers on the desk and I found a letter that had been crossed through. It was addressed my husband, asking if they might meet later that week.

My stomach turned over.

I had thought this — but finding evidence —

No.

I needed to find other evidence, of someone else, not of my husband being the killer.

What happened if one hung a centaur?

I thought of the heaviness of my husband's horse body dangling down while his neck was in a noose and...

Well, I stopped thinking about that immediately because it made my stomach churn in horror.

I spoke to my brother's valet. "I suppose the constabulary talked to you?" I said to him.

"Oh, I didn't tell him anything, my lady," he told me.

I was no longer 'my lady,' but that was all right. I didn't correct him. "It would be understandable if you did."

"No, no," said my brother's valet. "Your brother, he..." He squared his shoulders. "I'm not saying he and I are as close as some valets are with their masters, true. He can be short and a bit cruel when he wants, but you don't undress and dress a man and shave him without closeness forming, my lady."

"Yes, that's true," I said.

"I wouldn't betray him," said the valet. "Not to some bobby, that's for certain."

I nodded. "All right, then. Is there something you know, then? Something you would tell me? Do you know where he was headed that afternoon?"

The valet nodded.

"Where?" I waited, holding my breath. *Don't say that he was meeting with Mr. Granville.*

"He was headed into the Serpentines, my lady."

I drew back. "Oh, dear." The Serpentines were a set of streets in the southern part of town that curved like a snake. It was a dangerous part of town, full of bawdyhouses, taverns, and it also happened to be where the self-styled crime lords of the city kept their headquarters. "Did he go to secure a loan?"

"It wouldn't have been the first time, I'm afraid," said the valet. "So, like as not, my lady, when he appeared, they weren't pleased with him."

"He already owed them money?" I touched my lips, but inside, I was relieved. The crime lords had a reputation for making examples of people who couldn't pay their debts in rather awful ways. It wasn't uncommon for them to send thugs to break people's legs or smash in their noses.

I always thought it was stupid, of course. If a man couldn't get the money together, then being laid up for months with two broken legs seemed to only ensure he'd *never* get the money together.

But I supposed it was done for the purpose of scaring other people who owed money. They would think to themselves that they must pay to avoid the same fate.

"He did." The valet nodded.

"Do you know to whom?" I said.

The valet sighed. "Well, what are you going to do with that information, my lady?"

"I don't know," I said. "I suppose, perhaps, try to talk to them..." I considered. "No, that's foolish. If they did hurt him, if they broke his legs, and he lay out on the street and could not get help and... and... well, whoever did that, that man is hardly likely to admit it to me, is he?"

"You can't go to the Serpentines. It wouldn't be safe."

"Of course not," I said, with a sigh.

"I have gone myself, of course."

"What?" I exclaimed. "William!" That was the valet's name. "You can't put yourself in danger like that. You wouldn't be safe in such a place either."

"I don't always dress this way, my lady," he said, with a small smile. "I can make myself a bit grimey, you know, and I don't always put on this accent either." As he said that, his vowels slid and broadened.

I smiled at him. "I meant no offense, William."

"I know you didn't, my lady," he said. "I'm only saying..."

"I'm only saying that you can't know how I appreciate such a thing. How much I'm sure that Lord Crisbane appreciates it as well. Well, would appreciate, I suppose, if..." I swallowed. "If he knew," I finished, instead of saying *if he's alive.*

"I didn't find anything out, I'm afraid. People saw him cross the threshold of The Red Bloom." That was a tavern that was owned by the Strattera crime family. "He would have gone there instead of to the Collinses, because he had already gone into debt with them."

"I see," I said.

"But it's common knowledge they work together in some

ways, and that they would have known he wasn't good for it," said William. He shrugged. "Anyway, that's the last anyone saw of him. If the Stratteras know a thing about it, mum's the word."

I sighed. "But they... he went in and never came out?"

"Didn't come out a way anyone saw."

"And his horse came back without him," I said. "They did something to him."

"Maybe," he said. "Maybe they just turned him over to the Collinses."

"How much did he owe them?"

"Difficult to say. They start adding ten percent every day you're late with a payment, so it adds up quick."

"But if they killed him, they would never get their money," I said.

"True," he said.

I turned this over and over in my head. I was pleased with it, pleased that it didn't implicate my husband. "You should tell the constabulary what you've told me, I suppose."

"No, my lady, I can't do that. Tell the police about the Collinses? You want me to end up disappeared as well?"

"Oh," I said softly. "No, I suppose that wouldn't be wise."

"I keep thinking he's got to turn up," said William. "And first thing he'll do is send for me. He can't manage without me, you know?"

"He can't," I said. Which made it only more likely that my brother was never coming back. A lump rose in my throat and I ducked down my face, trying to get myself under control. My brother didn't deserve my sobbing over him, but I could not help the grief.

Perhaps it was as much for the pain of all he'd caused me as it was for his loss.

Family was complicated.

CHAPTER NINETEEN

I CHECKED WITH Mr. Higgins anyway when I got back home that day.

Had my husband met with my brother, to Mr. Higgins's knowledge? Where had my husband been the day my brother had gone missing?

Unfortunately, the response was that Mr. Higgins did know that my husband received a letter from my brother, but that Mr. Higgins did not know what my husband did about that letter. My husband was not at home, but he had been in and out of town, even at Brakestills on occasion, conducting business and the like. So, there was no reassurance there.

My husband could not account for his whereabouts.

I considered asking Mr. Higgins to escort me to the Serpentines, but I decided it would be a pointless trip. There was nothing that was going to make anyone admit murder to me. At any rate, the fact that my brother had gone there should be enough to deflect suspicion if the police came after my husband.

And I would protect him, of course, because if my husband were hung for murder, my reputation would never recover.

It didn't have anything to do with my feelings for my husband.

Because, of course, I hated him.

Now, having been roused from bed and from feeling sorry for myself, I began to wonder what it was I was going to do.

If I left for the country house, I supposed I was going to accept the fact that Mrs. Marsh would be taking up residence here with my husband. I supposed I would be ceding him to her.

I wasn't sure how well that sat with me.

No, I wanted her gone.

I might not wish to touch the man again, and I might be willing to wash my hands of him. But that didn't mean he could continue on in his twisted little sadistic affair with her. I knew she made him suffer, but I thought he derived a certain amount of pleasure from her interest in him, from suffering for her.

And I would not let that continue.

I had four days until the dinner with the Duke and Duchess of Rells. Four days to get rid of Gwendolyn Marsh.

How to do it.

It wouldn't be enough to send her packing. She had her claws into Enoch, and he'd go back to her. I needed to sever her from him somehow.

She wouldn't respond to my showing her how wretched he was, because she already hated him, and she enjoyed punishing him. So, what did that leave? If I showed her that he was happy, would that anger her enough?

Possibly.

One thing that would probably get her out of the picture entirely would be if I broke my husband's curse.

Unfortunately, that would involve touching him again, and I was not doing that.

No, I didn't want him happy.

I wanted him to suffer.

Just… not for her.

Maybe she could be kidnapped. Put on a ship across the ocean. Sent far, far away so that we never saw her again. Would Mr. Higgins do it for me? He might. He hated her too, after all.

Of course, he might not, because it would likely anger Enoch, and Mr. Higgins didn't seem one to incur his master's wrath.

And anyway, she might find her way back. After all, she was reliant on Enoch to do whatever arcane magics he did that kept her from aging. She would likely have every inducement to get back across the ocean to him for that.

So, what did that leave, then?

Killing her?

Well, I couldn't kill her.

Not in cold blood.

One didn't do that.

Of course, she wasn't really supposed to be alive, was she? She would have been over a hundred years old. She'd lived past her normal life span, and she didn't have any right to continue on.

So, maybe killing her wasn't wrong.

THAT NIGHT, I went into a room in the upper part of the house, one near to my husband's bedchamber. There were a number of pistols in this room. Pretty things with polished wood or ivory handles. I selected one, and I went through drawers and looked on shelves and beneath various sundries until I found what I was looking for. A box of balls, another box of powder, some wadding, and a rod to jam it all into place.

Loading the revolver took time, but it was worth it to have six chambers ready to go.

Once I was ready, I went down the stairs, across the halls, and made my way towards Mrs. Marsh's part of the house.

At the door, I was arrested by a rather obvious problem.

What was I going to do after I killed her?

There would be a body. With a bullet in it. I would be holding a smoking pepperbox revolver. All the servants would know.

They would immediately run to the constabulary, who

would take me to prison, and then summarily hang me.

No matter that Gwendolyn Marsh was a crime against Nature itself, it wouldn't matter. I'd never convince the police I was simply righting a wrong done by arcane magics, would I?

I walked away from the door.

I paced a bit, trying to think of a solution.

Perhaps if I ran and then tucked the gun away, I could appear, pretending to have heard the shot, and act as though I knew nothing. Perhaps the servants might conclude that someone had broken into the house and killed Mrs. Marsh and then made a fast getaway.

Of course, I wasn't sure how quickly I could run. I wasn't sure I could get rid of the revolver. That all seemed to be leaving a lot to chance.

No, this was never going to work.

I went back and unloaded the gun, because I was afraid it might go off otherwise, and I was exhausted at that point.

I went to bed.

The next morning, there were three days to get rid of Gwendolyn Marsh.

Possibly, I could pay someone else to kill her. Possibly, I could go to the Collinses and say to them, "Look, I won't turn you in for killing my brother if you kill Gwendolyn Marsh for me."

Yes, because entering into an agreement with crime lords was an intelligent proposition.

I couldn't do that.

I turned it this way and that, and I eventually determined murder was not going to be the solution.

I turned instead to a solution I didn't really like, but one that I thought might be the best for everyone involved.

Mrs. Marsh had nothing and no one besides my husband.

Her hatred and twisted obsession with Enoch was all she lived for. She had never had anything else, since she had never been married, and she had never had children.

Well, what if I could change that?

The first thing I did was to write to the Duchess of Rells

and ask her if she would mind terribly if we had a few extra guests at dinner.

She said she was of the opinion that more voices meant more merriment, and I hoped this was true.

Then I sent invitations to two gentlemen.

One was the Baron of Truesdale, a man who had lost his wife to a fever the year before, leaving him with three children, aged twelve, nine, and four. He had been reportedly looking for a wife and having little success due to his strange requirement of not wishing to marry a young woman. Most men, no matter their age, no matter how many wives they'd already had, married women who were aged seventeen or twenty. Truesdale, however, insisted that he must find someone who was closer to his age. "I don't want some child raising my children," he was said to have railed.

The second was a knight by the name of Sir Matthew Peters. Sir Matthew had never been married and — indeed — seemed to have expressed no interest in doing so. However, he was always courting widows of the same age as Mrs. Marsh, and I thought perhaps, well, he might have a true affection for her.

I didn't know if either of them would like her, truth be told, but I told them that she was charming and just right for them, and that she expressed special curiosity about them both and that they must be careful for she would be snapped up by the other if they were not move quickly.

It was a bit of a hack job, truly.

I was not really skilled at matchmaking, having never really done it at all.

But both men responded in the affirmative that they would join the dinner party, even though it was sort of irregular what I'd done, inviting them myself. I was acquainted with them. It wasn't improper, I supposed, but issuing an invitation without my husband?

Oh, well.

It was over now. I couldn't undo it.

When I went to Mrs. Marsh's chambers, I brought a dressmaker with me.

"Do you like blue or lavender?" I greeted.

She was stunned to see me. "What are you about?"

"For your dress," I said. "For tomorrow evening. Miranda will have to work hard to get it done in time, but she is a wonder."

Mrs. Marsh gaped at me. "Dress?"

"Dinner," I said. "You'll be joining myself, my husband, the Duke and Duchess of Rells, and two gentlemen who have shown an interest in you, for dinner."

Mrs. Marsh's eyes widened. "An interest in me? For what?"

"Marriage, obviously, Mrs. Marsh," I said with a sigh.

Her lips parted. She couldn't speak. She simply stared at me.

"If you don't choose yourself, I shall say the lavender," I said. "A delicate color will suit you, I think. It'll bring out your eyes. You were once a striking woman, weren't you? We can make you so again, I think."

Mrs. Marsh sputtered, trying to find words.

"Well, if you've no objections, I say the lavender." I nodded to the dressmaker. "You may begin pinning." I settled myself down on a chaise.

Mrs. March found her voice. "You can't be serious about this. You think that if I am married, it will somehow get me out of Enoch's life?"

"Enoch is a very awful man," I said, blinking at her. "A very, very awful man who has wronged you over and over. Admittedly, you have been wretched in return, and you likely don't deserve any restitution. Even so, I am attempting to make it."

Mrs. Marsh pressed her lips together in a firm line.

The dressmaker began draping lavender fabric over Mrs. Marsh.

"Yes, it's quite a nice color," I said with a sigh.

"You still want him?" said Mrs. Marsh.

"Who? Enoch?" I shook my head. "I don't want anything to do with him."

"Then why—"

"He enjoys whatever it is you do to him," I said.
"No, he does not."
"Trust me, he does," I growled. "He still loves you."
"He absolutely doesn't."
"Separating you from him, your moving on from him, finding happiness without him? It will hurt him more than anything in the world," I said. I was just realizing this was likely true, which made my course of action rather a wondrous form of revenge after all. I smiled.

Mrs. Marsh considered this. She regarded me. "Well, what sort of men are coming?"

My smile widened. "If either of them accept you, Mrs. Marsh, hereafter, you will be addressed as 'my lady.'"

She let out a little laugh, looking down at the fabric. "It *is* a pretty color, isn't it?"

CHAPTER TWENTY

"WHY ARE THERE so many place settings?" came the low rumble of Enoch's voice.

I was surprised at how I responded to it, though I shouldn't have been. My entire body jumped, and I went taut all over. I wanted him. I wanted to be in his arms. I wanted his mouth, his hands, his...

Well, anyway.

I let out a shaking breath and smoothed at my hair. "I have decided to do away with Mrs. Gwendolyn Marsh, Mr. Granville."

He furrowed his brow.

"I am going to find her a husband," I said.

The furrow deepened. "She's too old for a husband."

"Well, she will need a husband of the right age, I suppose," I said with a shrug. "But if you think I'm going off and leaving you and her together? No. You don't get to have that, Enoch. I'm leaving you with *nothing*." I glared at him.

He flinched, looking away.

"You never thought of that, did you, while you were doing whatever it was you were doing for her? You never thought of trying to make amends. All you ever tried to do was suffer for her."

"No one is going to marry Gwendolyn," he muttered. "And I don't like your turning our dinner with the Rells into some matchmaking session."

"Well, the Duchess of Rells is delighted by it," I said. "She has already decided that if neither of the men tonight suit, she will put her mind to the task of setting Mrs. Marsh up with the right sort of man." Yes, even though Mrs. Marsh did not have the pedigree to be received into the uppercrust of society, the duchess had said this. When it was a woman trying to marry into it, it was all less threatening for whatever reason. "I assured Her Grace that Mrs. Marsh would have a respectable dowry."

"You mean, I'd provide that."

"Oh, you've been giving her money all this time, I didn't think you'd object now." I tilted my chin up.

He shook his head at me, his voice cold but wondering. "You're jealous of her."

"I am not," I said fiercely. "If I were jealous, it would mean I still wanted you, and I don't."

"You mean you don't *want* to want me."

"That is the same thing."

He laughed softly. "You know that I want *you*, of course."

"Yes, but you don't really. It's just some aspect of the curse that makes you want me. It's not truly you."

"Phoebe..." He sighed. "I told you, I have been near mounts before. I have rutted mounts before. When I tell you I want you the way I've never wanted anything in my entire life, believe it's true."

"Stop," I said. "That's not going to turn my head—"

"I want to find some way to fix this with us," he said. "I can't bear it, being parted from you. I need to find a way, to... what could I do in order to make you—?"

"*Stop.*"

He hung his head, letting out a noisy breath.

THE DINNER WAS a success, overall.

But it had little to do with either Enoch or myself, because neither of us did much during the dinner except concentrate very hard on not looking at each other.

I don't know if anyone else noticed that. No one said anything about it, but that wouldn't have been polite to have done so. So, the lack of commentary meant nothing.

The successful aspect was all down to the Duchess of Rells and Mrs. Marsh, who were in rare form, both of them, quite charming, making all sorts of witty comments, and keeping the conversation flowing. The two suitors both seemed taken with Mrs. Marsh, and I couldn't blame them, because she was altogether a different woman than I had hitherto seen.

I was gratified by the fact that Enoch didn't seem to notice.

He was only pointedly trying not to notice me.

Which...

Well, I didn't want to care about that. But I did care, I suppose. The way he'd said he wanted to fix things, it had stirred me. He didn't deserve that, however. He really didn't, and I couldn't simply forgive him.

The dinner seemed an anti-climax to me.

Here we had been, both of us, spending all this time building up to this dinner, the dinner that was supposed to change everything. It should have been the linchpin on which hinged our social climb, and yet here we were, neither of us able to even concentrate on it.

It spun past us both, a whirlwind, and when it was over, we were deposited back into our empty house, with Mrs. Marsh humming to herself and gazing out the window at the departing guests.

We were all in the massive foyer of the house, under that chandelier hung with real candles, each of us standing there in the brilliant whiteness of the room, ten feet of space between each of us.

Mrs. Marsh turned away from the window and surveyed Enoch. "I want you to rent me a house in town instead of that country house in Milluxe. I want you to secure me some dowry or income to keep me. We can negotiate the amount. And then I never want to see you again."

Enoch folded his arms over his chest. "Just like that?"

She laughed to herself. "Yes, yes, just like that. It's been nearly eighty years, Enoch. I think it's about time we were done with each other."

He rubbed a hand over his face. "All right. When do you want to negotiate?"

"Are you busy now?"

"So quickly." He blinked at her. "And if we do this, then... then the spells, the sacrifices, the blood—"

"No more of that," she whispered. "I've tasted enough of immortality, I think. It has fewer charms than one might think."

He bowed his head.

I surveyed them both.

"Your study?" said Mrs. Marsh.

"Certainly," he said, and they walked out of the foyer together.

I wished to be petulant and demand that I be allowed to witness the two of them negotiating, being alone together. What was more, I thought that if I did so, Enoch would allow it. But if I did, it would prove that I was jealous. And I didn't want to admit that. Not to him, but, even more, not to myself.

So, I retired to my room and had Janet undress me and set about packing to go to Enoch's country estate.

I could not believe it had been so easy to be rid of Gwendolyn Marsh, that all I had to do was to get her a nice dress and show her a lovely time with some gentlemen making eyes at her, and she would voluntarily walk out of Enoch's life.

On the other hand, why was I surprised?

What had it taken to get me to marry him in the first place? He'd paid me attention, complimented me, desired me, and then, well, there was that wedding dress.

Yes, it was easy to turn a woman's head, wasn't it, especially one who had been hurt and neglected over and over?

In the end, perhaps Mrs. Marsh and I weren't so different. Well.

I would never have cursed a man to become a centaur.

Then I wondered at myself. Perhaps I would have. Why had I stopped myself from murder, after all? Only because I was frightened I would get caught.

I went to bed.

I didn't sleep.

But when my husband came, much later, I pretended to be asleep.

He settled himself next to my bed, and ran his fingers through my hair. "I know you're awake."

I didn't say anything.

"She said she'd forgotten that life could be anything other than pain, do you believe that? She said that all she'd had for so long was suffering, and that she'd blamed me, but that she'd chosen it for herself. She said she couldn't believe that someone like you would have been so kind to her."

He'd come here to talk to me about *her?*

I stiffened.

"And I thought all she wanted was to live forever. I thought..." He swallowed. "The way she seemed to go after that. The things I went through to find a way to preserve her. The blood that I have spilled—both my own and the struggle with larger and larger animals. A bear once, actually." He let out a disbelieving laugh. "And you make her a dress, and she leaves me."

I rolled over and glared at him. "Are you hurt?"

"I knew you were awake."

I sat up in bed. "Are you devastated and destroyed by the loss of her?"

"I feel free for the first time in..." He shrugged. "I can't remember ever feeling like this." He smiled at me. "Thank you."

"*Thank* you?" I was appalled. He was supposed to be angry. This was supposed to be revenge.

"I don't think she forgives me, you know," he said. "She told me that I was a worthless piece of shite, in fact. But she said she wasn't going to waste any more time on me. That she realized she wanted something good for herself instead of pouring everything into hurting me. I wonder what it would feel like if I stopped trying to hurt myself."

"*I* want to hurt you," I said.

He laughed. "Oh." He reached out and touched my face. "Well, one mistress for another, then."

I knocked his hand away. "I'm not your mistress. I'm not your anything."

"You're my wife, Phoebe."

"Yes, but not in any way that matters."

"How do you want to hurt me?"

"Not in any way you'd like!"

He laughed. "You want to strike *me* with a riding crop?" He waggled his eyebrows. "There's one upstairs."

"We are not doing *anything* like that together."

He didn't say anything.

"I'm leaving you tomorrow," I said. "I'm going to your country estate, and we shall never touch, not ever again."

"All right," he said with a shrug. "So, are you sure you don't want to punish me before you leave? Just to see what it's like?"

"No."

"You'll be all alone in the country."

"Perhaps I'll take a lover," I said, jerking my chin up. "Perhaps I'll spread my legs for every single one of your footmen."

His jaw twitched. "You're trying to make me jealous. It's working."

I leaned forward. "I might like being with a man who I didn't need a wooden contraption to fuck, who I could kiss while his cock was inside me. I might like—"

"All right," he said, eyes flashing. "All right. You wanted to hurt me, you've done it."

Guilt washed through me.

"You could..." His voice was hoarse. "You could strike me and strike me. All over. You could force me to lick you between your thighs until you burst. You could refuse to give me relief. I'm hard now, you know, but you could torture me, make me harder, not give me a release. You could bridle *me*. You could—"

"This is what you want?"

"What do *you* want?"

"I want not to want you," I said.

He held my gaze for several moments. Then he got to his feet, and I was treated to the sight of his swollen prick, as hard as he claimed, between his hind legs. He gazed down at me from his full height. "I hope you're very happy with my footmen," he said dryly, and he left the room.

I went after him.

I KNOW.

RIDICULOUS thing to do.

I had won. I had crushed him. That last line of his to me, it was my triumph.

But he had an effect on me that was abominable, and all his talk of bridling him, and taking a riding crop to him, and seeing his huge, huge cock, it made my own body swell and ache.

I caught up to him in the hallway. I reached up my hands to him. "Put me on your back."

He looked down at me, his eyes dark. "What is this?"

"I don't know. Your punishment. Do as your mistress says."

His lips curved a little, a knowing gleam in his eyes. Then he reached down for me and lifted me, depositing me on his back.

I gripped him with my knees, his powerful body between my thighs. I pressed my breasts into his back and wrapped my arms around his waist. I leaned in, brushing my lips over his ear. "Upstairs."

He sighed, and he began to move.

We ascended the steps carefully. We entered his bedchamber and went through the other room, where the mount stood.

I climbed down from his back and gazed at it while he

pulled the chains to bring up the gas lamps.

"Well?" I said. "Where's the riding crop?"

He chuckled softly and retrieved it from the same set of drawers that contained the training cocks. He came to me and handed it over.

I ran my fingers over it, touching the small leather strap at the end, sliding my hand into the strap that would keep it from falling off my wrist. Then I slapped it into the palm of my other hand.

The sound was loud.

I liked it.

He sucked in a breath. "You look… it suits you."

"Hmm," I said. "Take everything off." I gestured to his clothing.

He immediately began to go to work on his buttons, gaze on me, expression hungry.

I set down the riding crop and yanked off my nightclothes so that I was naked.

Another noisy breath from him.

I picked up the riding crop and pointed at him. "You don't get to touch this."

"Of course not," he said. He shrugged out of his jacket. "Mistress." There was an insouciant lilt to his tone. It bespoke disobedience. Mischief. It made my body clench.

"Again."

"What?" He shrugged out of his waistcoat.

"Say it again," I said.

"I don't know what you're talking about." He grinned at me. "Maybe you'll have to jog my memory."

Oh. My body clenched again. I licked my lips and advanced on him. I didn't know where to strike him with this thing, but I thought perhaps against the upper swell of his hind leg's muscle? That might be where a rider would use it, I thought. I brought the riding crop down. It made that noise again.

He grunted.

"Well?" I whispered. "Say it."

"Mistress," he said in a voice like the deepest darkness of

a winter's night.

I shivered. I pressed into him, my bare breasts against his flank. I stroked his fur. I struck him with the riding crop again. And again.

He grunted each time, shedding his tie, unbuttoning his shirt.

"Your mistress is most displeased," I said.

"Apologies, mistress," he gasped. He took off his shirt. It fluttered to the floor.

"You're not really sorry, though," I said.

"Oh, believe me, mistress, I am," he said.

"I can make you sorrier," I said. I hit him on the other side, next to his tail.

His tail leaped and he grunted. "I'm sure you can."

"To the mount," I told him, bringing down the crop again and again.

He went.

I made him get up in it, securing his hooves, stretching himself out for me, presenting me with that very hard prick of his.

He gasped and grunted and rutted his hips at the air.

I smacked him near his tail. "None of that. Hold still."

He did.

I touched his cock with my hands and with the riding crop. I gathered up the heaviness of his bollocks and stroked them, and this made him wild. He moaned, his voice higher in pitch than I'd ever heard it.

So, of course, that's where I applied the riding crop.

He shrieked.

He didn't lose his erection, however.

I wormed my fingers between my legs and found my own clit. Oh, damnation, I was very, very wet, wasn't I? Well, I hadn't expected that, but I liked it. I liked the power, and I liked having him stretched out like this, at my mercy, so very vulnerable. More than anything, I liked having his cock to do what I wished with.

His thick, brown cock was incredibly arousing to me. I rubbed myself with one hand and used my other hand to toy with it. He leaked liquid and I smeared that into his dark, swollen head.

"Did you like it when I took the riding crop to your bollocks?"

"N-no," he gasped.

"Should I do it again?"

He grunted.

I took up the riding up and tickled his bollocks with the leather.

He sighed. "Please, yes, mistress, *yes.*"

So, I did. Maybe not as hard as last time. His cock jerked and I liked watching it. He made the most interesting of sounds.

My own fingers moved on my body, faster and faster. My pleasure was growing more and more intense.

"This prick of yours, husband," I said, tickling the underside of it. "It's gotten you in a lot of trouble, hasn't it?"

He moaned. "Fuck, Phoebe."

I smacked the shaft of him with the riding crop. "*What* do you call me?"

"Mistress, mistress," he groaned. "Apologies.

My pelvis was tight and twitching. My fingers nudged little warm-up trills of pleasure from me as I stroked myself.

"It's a very naughty prick, isn't it?"

"It is," he agreed. "Yes."

"Needs some correction, then?"

He was panting. "*Mistress.*"

"All over, I think," I said, and I delivered several smacks to the upper shaft of him. Then, using my hand, I gave him a few little soothing strokes, and his cock swelled and stiffened.

He didn't seem capable of words. He made a noise that sounded a bit like a whinny.

"And then here," I said, delivering a strike to the place where his cock met his bollocks.

He cried out.

"And here too," I said, landing blows on the sensitive underside of him.

"Mistress, please."

"Please what?" I realized that he had once given me a way to get him to stop if something became too much, by saying the word mercy, but he and I had not had that conversation before beginning this. Of course, this was... well, who was I fooling? This wasn't any real kind of punishment at all.

"Please..." He groaned. "Please again."

I smacked the head of him.

He shrieked.

I put my mouth on him.

He gasped. "Phoebe."

I sucked as much of him as I could into my mouth, soothing the sting of the riding crop with my mouth and tongue.

I pressed my fingers into my own clit, and I crested against him, and my own pleasure was like a stampede of centaurs, picking me up onto their backs and galloping over a cliff.

He spurted, and I swallowed every salty drop of him.

I kept his softening member in my mouth until he begged me piteously, telling me he was far too sensitive for any further stimulation.

Then, finally, I retreated.

I looked up at him. "Stay there in the mount until I'm gone, centaur."

"What about... shall I pleasure you?"

"I've taken care of myself," I told him, turning my back on him as I stalked across the room.

"Wait, Phoebe..."

"Goodbye, Enoch." I stopped to pick up my nightdress and then I left him behind without a backward look.

CHAPTER TWENTY-ONE

HE TRIED TO stop me the next morning.

He was actually pitiful, standing there as servants loaded up the carriage, his hair down, his expression twisted. "There's got to be something I can do," he said. "Tell me what it is."

"If I tell you, that defeats the entire purpose of your doing anything," I said.

"How does it do that?" he said.

"Well, by telling you, it means that you have proven yourself nothing more than particularly good at following orders."

"So, what? I'm supposed to guess?"

"No," I said. "You are supposed to know me well enough to know what I need."

"I don't," he said.

"Well, then," I said with a shrug.

"You're just toying with me, aren't you? There's nothing I could do to make it better."

"Likely not," I said breezily, folding my arms over my chest.

"What if I... bought you something?"

"No," I said.

"Something large. A house. An estate. A—"

"*No.*"

"What if it was something so expensive that I could

hardly afford it? What if I damaged my livelihood—"

"That's stupid," I said. "It's as if you've learned nothing from the decades with her, is it? I'm not her. I'm not gratified by your suffering."

He laughed harshly. "Oh, yes, last night, nothing about that was gratifying for you."

I looked up at him stonily. "Last night was a mistake."

He looked so hurt that I felt monstrous.

"Go away," I said. "I don't want to be near you right now."

His nostrils flared and he shifted on his hooves. For a moment, I thought he would leave, but he stood his ground. "All right, what if I threw a large party in your honor—"

"You're acting as if you can just do one thing and you can fix all this!"

"No," he said, then, with a sigh. "No, of course not. Not a grand gesture, of course. Time, then. A number of small things over time."

"No," I said, but my stupid voice broke. "No, because I shan't be anywhere near you ever again, Mr. Granville."

"I'll give you time away from me," he said. "But I shan't stay away from you forever. I can't do that, you see? I simply can't."

I snorted.

"Phoebe, I should have told you about her, but it's not... you act as though I was unfaithful to you with her or something, and—"

"You were unfaithful to *her* with *me*," I snapped. "You as good as married her all that time ago, and *I* was the other woman."

"No," he said. "No, no, it's not that way. No, you're my wife. My mount. My beautiful, eager—damnation, Phoebe, you're the most alluring woman to walk the face of the earth. Don't leave me."

I shook my head. "Stop that."

"I'm begging you. Please. Don't go. Stay, just stay, and let's try—"

"I can't be near you, or my presence will make you go

mad," I said. "If I'm close then, I'm compelled to..." I lowered my voice, even though we were out of earshot of the servants filling the carriage. "To come to your bed."

"It's not about that," he said.

I snorted.

"It's not *just* about that. Couldn't we... what you did last night? I won't touch you."

"Oh, is that enough?" I put my hands on my hips. "You went mad before, and wasn't that from not being inside me?"

"I don't *know* why that happened," he said. "Look, centaurs can go mad just from scenting a mount, you realize this? A centaur could be downwind from you and stampede a crowd. That didn't happen to me from you, though. And why it happened when it did? It's erratic and unpredictable. I can't tell you why."

"But if I'm close and we're not regularly fucking, then it's possible. And I don't want to fuck you." This was a lie. "I don't want to see you." This was true. How those two things could both be at the same time, I did not entirely understand, but there it was.

"Isn't there *any* way—"

"No," I said.

"I could keep you here by force."

"I know where you keep your pistols," I spat in his face.

He recoiled. "All right, fine. You're determined to go."

"I am," I said.

And I left.

On the carriage ride to the country house, I stared out the window at the scenery, and I couldn't help but think about what he'd said.

Wasn't there any way that I could be with him again?

Mrs. Marsh was gone. She had been the rift between us. Couldn't I find some way to forgive him?

It wasn't fair in some ways. He'd been in love with Mrs. Marsh for decades upon decades. How could I have expected him to have had no past?

But it wasn't that.

No, of course, before knowing me, his little perverse arrangement with that woman, it was nothing to me.

But after we married, after he began training me, after we began to connect...

He should have given her up.

He'd had both of us at the same time, that was the thing, and he hadn't even attempted to end things with her. In fact, he'd said things to me, about living forever, about not wanting to break his curse, those things. He'd wanted her, and he'd seen me as an inconvenience. A temptation he couldn't help but sample, even as he didn't want to give me his entire self.

Meanwhile, he'd been everything to me.

I'd tried not to let him be that, but he had been.

So...

Well, he needed to admit what he'd done wrong, for one thing. Admit it and apologize.

And then... then... well, I didn't know.

Something else besides that, though.

It was dark when we arrived at the country house, which was vast and old. Inside, it was just as horribly decorated as the town house, and I would have to do something about that. But for now, I sat down to dinner in the dining room and smiled wearily at the servants.

Afterwards, I fell into bed.

Now that I was away from Enoch, I could stop thinking about him.

I WOKE IN the morning, thinking of Enoch.

I wondered to myself, as Janet dressed me, why it was that I hadn't questioned my husband about my brother. I'd had every opportunity, and I hadn't even broached the subject. He'd spoken about wanting to make amends, and I remembered that he'd offered to kill my brother before.

But I hadn't asked.

Some part of me was afraid of the answer, I supposed.

I prodded at that thought for a bit.

Then I decided it was all best left alone, and I put it from my mind.

I spent the morning taking things off the walls. Well, not me personally. I instructed several of the servants. We went from room to room, and I tried to... to *reduce*. There was just so much. Enoch—ugh—he could not do simple. Everything was over-the-top, ostentatious, too much.

I ordered the removal of paintings, of draperies, of mounted deer heads and other such things.

By luncheon, we had barely gotten through half of the house, but I couldn't bear any more of it.

I decided to go on a walk on the grounds instead. I could have gone for a ride. There were horses in the stables. But I didn't like the idea of that, I found, so off I went.

I went on a path through the overgrown gardens. The path was overgrown as well, and I picked my way through it here and there. It wound close to the road at one point. There was a sturdy-looking fence, repaired here and there but as yet unpainted in the places where the new wood was.

I wandered off the path to look at the fence. It should be painted, but I should also commend whoever it was that was keeping it in good repair. Mmm. That was odd. The growth here, in this old part of the fence, it looked disturbed, as if someone had climbed it.

I supposed it wasn't exactly the sort of fence that would keep anyone determined out. It was more a symbol than anything. And it had probably been local children. There were nearby tenants, after all, on the grounds, and I certainly didn't begrudge some boys playing games.

Large boys, though, from the look of the disturbed undergrowth.

I kept walking. The path wound its way back toward the house.

When the figure appeared on the path, I was almost expecting it.

I wasn't, however, expecting it to be Laurence.

CHAPTER TWENTY-TWO

LAURENCE WAS WEARING the remnants of his suit—no jacket—and everything about him was dirty and shabby. His hair was greasy and practically standing up from his forehead. He had a wild look about him, as if he was ready to bolt or scream or fight.

He wasn't alone.

There were two other men with him, both dressed in tidy suits, as if they were well-to-do businessmen. There was something about the way they carried themselves, however, or perhaps the swell of their muscled arms beneath their clothes, or the deadliness of their expression, that gave them away.

They worked for one of the crime families.

Were they Collinses or Statteras? I couldn't quite say.

Laurence came for me. "Phoebe, it'll go easier for us both if you don't run."

So, I ran.

I turned, picked up my skirt, and ran.

I went back the way I'd come, which was toward the road, glad I was dressed for walking with boots and not the flimsy sorts of slippers I'd wear indoors. I rounded a bend and determined that when I made it to the road I'd go over the fence and try to flag down anyone driving through for help.

But when I looked over my shoulder, they were rounding

the bend and closing in on me.

I considered my options. The path went through overgrown gardens, and everything on either side was a tangle of vegetation. I could dart into there and they might not be able to see me, but if I moved at all, I'd make quite a bit of noise, and they'd hear me.

I picked up my feet and rounded another bend.

I slipped into the tangle of brush, hidden, and I went entirely still. I didn't even breathe.

They came into view, running.

They went straight past me.

I let out a breath.

Now what?

Should I wait? Would they come back if they saw I wasn't on the path? They must.

I needed to go.

I pushed out onto the road.

I took off running again.

A shout.

They had heard me!

I turned to see the men coming for me, Laurence bringing up the rear, looking exhausted.

I ran faster.

A painful stitch opened up in my side and my breath came in gasps.

I ignored it and pressed on.

I knew I couldn't hide again, and now I was running away from the road. I didn't know where this path led. I had never taken it before. I needed to get back to the *house*.

I glanced over my shoulder again.

They were closer.

I was panting. Sweat bloomed on my forehead, under my arms.

I glanced back again.

They were practically on top of me.

I skidded to a stop and looked around.

There.

A rock. I picked it up and brandished it, baring my teeth.

When the first of the men came for me, I brought it down hard on his skull.

He screamed and clutched his head and staggered away.

I turned for the other man.

Who grabbed my wrist and squeezed until I dropped the rock.

That man wrestled me to the ground and pinned my arms above my head, pressing me into the ground with his heavy girth. His breath smelled like onions, and he was sweaty.

I screamed. "Help me!" Why hadn't I yelled for help before? What an idiot I was! Perhaps, even now, servants from the house would have been here.

The man slapped his hand on my mouth.

I bit his fingers.

He punched me.

I had never been struck like that before. He hit me on the side of my face, and the pain radiated through my cheekbone and my jaw, and tears came to my eyes, and my head hurt, and I couldn't breathe.

"Shut up or I'll box your ears proper, missus," he sneered at me.

I quivered beneath him, so easily subdued. Tears flowed freely, but I didn't make a sound.

He wrenched me to my feet and tied me up, hands behind my back.

The other man, the one I'd hit, got up. He was bleeding from where the rock had hit his head. He swore at me. He ripped off a bit of his shirt and stuffed it into my mouth—a gag.

Laurence panted, hands on his knees. He looked up at me. "It would have been easier if you hadn't run, Phoebe."

I wished he was dead.

I wished my husband *had* killed him.

CHAPTER TWENTY-THREE

THEY FORCED ME to walk with them and they made me climb the fence. Then we walked along the road until a carriage came by and stopped for us.

I was loaded inside. Laurence sat next to me.

The other men sat on the other side.

The carriage took off. We weren't heading back to town, but in the opposite direction.

Laurence was talking to me. "You brought this on yourself, you know. I came to you and I asked you for your help and you set that wretched servant on me and treated me like trash. Your own flesh and blood? After everything I did for you? After all the years I fed and clothed you?"

I spit the gag out. "You worm. You squirming, ugly, disgusting worm."

Laurence pushed the gag back into my mouth. "Shut up."

One of the men, the one who'd punched me, laughed. "She's not wrong."

Laurence glowered at him. "Once your crime lord has his money and I have mine, we can go our separate ways and never see each other again."

"You *are* a worm, though," said the man. "Selling your own sister."

"Can't blame her for fighting, I guess," said the other man, clutching the place where I'd hit him. He glared at me. "But since she did, I can't say I'm going to feel bad about whatever happens to her."

Selling me?

Who would *buy* me?

Besides, slavery was illegal. Had been for decades now.

I didn't know what was going on, but I was very frightened.

I couldn't get out of the carriage at this point. Even if I could get a door open, throwing myself out at this speed would likely kill me. I'd simply have to bide my time and see what happened now.

I entertained a brief fantasy that perhaps Enoch would have come after me. He had tried to prevent me from leaving, after all, and if he arrived and discovered I had disappeared, he would...

Oh, it was hopeless.

First of all, he *wouldn't* come after me.

Second of all, he'd have no idea where to seek me.

I supposed that word would be sent to him when I didn't return home, but again, even if he went after me, he wouldn't find me.

Where were we *going*?

I glanced up at the sun, through the window. I put our direction as northwest.

The carriage sped off into the afternoon.

It went on into the night.

The men didn't stop to eat, even though Laurence complained peevishly of hunger. They only laughed at him, saying that he'd have to wait until he got his share of the money and then he could buy his own bread.

It was very dark, but the carriage rode on.

The men from the crime family slept in shifts, one awake and the other dozing. Laurence slept too.

I stayed awake for a long time, too anxious and frightened to relax. Then I determined that I might need my rest if I needed to attempt to fight or escape or anything that I might be able to do if the opportunity presented itself. So, I closed my eyes.

Still, I didn't think I was asleep at all.

Except when I opened my eyes, it was morning, and the carriage was stopped.

I had spit out the gag in my sleep, but I didn't say anything. Maybe if I was quiet, they'd leave my mouth empty. The gag had become disgusting, anyway, sodden with saliva, and it had been impossible to breathe through my mouth with that wad of wet fabric on my tongue.

The men were getting out of the carriage. Laurence did too.

They left me there.

I waited for a minute, and then I sat forward and looked out the window.

"Back!" cried one of the men. "You stay where you are, missus."

I ducked back, because I had not intended to be seen. So, all right, I couldn't see anything. I tried, instead, to listen.

I could hear their voices, but I couldn't make anything out.

Eventually, I slid over to the other side of the carriage and peered out that window.

I couldn't see anyone here. Just an expanse of grass and a wooded area, trees as far as the eye could see.

My hands were still tied behind my back, so getting the door open wasn't easy, but I managed it, turning around so that my back was to the door.

I eased it open and waited.

No one seemed to have heard anything.

I strained to see anything out of the other window, but all I could see that way was the sky from this angle.

Carefully, slowly, I climbed down out of the carriage. Feet on the ground, I rested against the side of it and gently, nearly silently, closed the door.

I could still hear the voices. I tried again to make out what they were saying. Too far away. Or maybe it was the sound of the wind in the trees. I looked up at the sky, and then back at the carriage.

The driver.

How had I forgotten about the carriage driver?

He was sitting atop the carriage, hand resting on a revolver at his waist, grinning at me as if I were the most amusing thing he'd ever seen.

My heart squeezed in defeat.

I didn't even know what I'd intended to do. I couldn't have thought I could run for the woods, could I? They'd have seen me.

My gaze locked onto the driver's.

His smile widened. Abruptly, he jumped down from his perch on the carriage. A long drop, truly, but he did it with ease, as if it was nothing, landing on his feet like a cat. Then he stalked over to me like one, still smiling, a beast of prey.

I was his victim and I backed away.

No.

Wait.

I turned, putting my face into the carriage. Then I waited, breathless, worried I'd miscalculated...

But no. He pressed into me from behind, one hand sliding over my hip, his nose going to my neck, nudging my earlobe. "What'll you do for me if I let you go, missus?" he breathed in my ear.

I scrabbled around with my hand at his waist.

He thought I was going for something else, and I felt him swell against my backside. But I pulled out the gun.

I pressed the barrel into his hardening member. "Untie me," I said hoarsely.

He jerked. "That's not loaded."

"Sure about that?" I said. "You sure every one of those chambers is clear of all powder and all debris? Sure it won't do any bit of damage to *this part* of your body?"

He swore softly. His fingers worked at the knots.

My hands were free, but I kept the gun on him. It was my leverage.

"There," he said. "Move off me, damn you."

But if I did, then what?

"Move off me, or I call for the others," he said in a harsh voice.

"Call for the others and I blow off your prick," I said,

turning, keeping the gun against him.

"I'm telling you, it's not loaded." Now, I could see his expression and he was still sizing me up in some awful way. Then again, his prick was still hard. Some part of him probably got a thrill out of this.

"You have balls and powder?" I said.

His face twitched.

"Give them to me," I said.

"All right," he said softly. "All right, it's loaded."

My eyes widened, and I lifted the thing and pointed it at his forehead.

He raised his hands, palms up. "Come on, then, think of how you'll sleep if you've murdered a man."

"How do *you* sleep?" I said, gritting my teeth.

"Why do you think I'm warning you off it?" He was fierce now.

I swallowed. "Well, let me go, then." I nodded for the trees. "Keep your damnable mouth shut while I—"

"They'll see you," he said.

He was right.

"Then I have to shoot you," I said.

But at that moment, I heard one of the men's voices. "What's going on over here?" He appeared around the side of the carriage.

I tucked the gun down the front of my bodice, between my breasts.

The driver's eyes widened. Then he looked me over with a different sort of look, appraising, approving, and heated. He was getting a charge out of this, to hell with him. "Nothing, I just thought the missus might want to stretch her legs," he said.

"You let her out?" said the other man. "You untied her?"

The driver shrugged.

The man looked me over and then snatched me by the arm and tugged me around the carriage. "Look, they'll be here at any moment, so I guess it doesn't matter."

"Who?" I said, gritting my teeth, as he dragged me along with him. "Who are you selling me to?"

"Why, centaurs, obviously," said the man. "There's a herd out here, and we've heard rumors of what they'll do for girls like you, girls that affect them in whatever way it is you affect centaurs."

I felt cold all over and I went entirely still.

The man tugged on me.

I didn't move.

A herd, like what Enoch had told me about. A herd, with pens and stalls and being strapped to a mount and taken by different centaurs, one after the other, being used...

It was sheer terror to me, not even remotely arousing, not the way it was when it was *him*, when it was *safe*.

Oh, hell and damnation, *when* had I started to think he was safe?

"Come on," snapped the man, yanking on me.

I pulled out the pistol and thumbed down the hammer. I shot him in the face.

He never knew what hit him.

The noise was loud, and he crumpled to the ground with a puzzled expression, as if he was confused as to this turn of events.

The other man and my brother both turned on me.

I shot the other man next. I hit him in the shoulder. He staggered, shrieked, came closer. I shot again. This time, the bullet went neatly into his skull, right between his eyebrows.

He fell too.

I turned the gun on my brother, my hands shaking.

Laurence threw up his hands. "What are you doing? Why must you ruin everything, Phoebe? You are a worthless, stupid, ugly—"

Bang.

I let out a mangled noise.

Oh, I'd just done that.

Behind me.

I whirled.

It was the driver, hands up. "Now, now, missus," he said in a very low voice. "Let's calm down."

"I'm not being sold to a herd of centaurs," I said.

"No, no, you are definitely not," he said. "I wouldn't dare. But, here's a question for you, missus. You ever drive a carriage?" He nodded at it. The horses were not calm. The gunshots had disturbed them and they were agitated, eyes wide, feet stamping.

"I can't trust you to drive me," I said.

"I'd sooner damage priceless art than hurt you. I swear it. Don't hurt *me*, please."

My hands were shaking. I regarded him for several minutes, lump rising in my throat, and then I lowered the pistol. How many shots left? Two? Three?

Two.

I turned back to the sight of my brother's lifeless body. I let out a sob. Oh, I'd *done* that.

Tears, unbidden, started streaming down my face.

"You didn't have a choice with that one," said the driver. He was right next to me now, his voice quiet. "He was going to deliver you over to be ravished by beasts. His own sister. That's not a man, you know. That's a worm. All that was good for him was to be crushed under your heel."

"I c-called him that," I gasped, wiping at one of my cheeks.

His hand closed over my hand, the one holding the gun.

I jerked back, bringing it up. "Stop that."

The driver backed away again, hands up. "Sorry, sorry. That was stupid of me. I'm not usually a stupid man, but I'm afraid you unnerve me quite a bit. I've never met a woman like you before."

"Oh, of course you haven't," I said, sarcastic. "Because that's the way to woo a woman, truly. Tell her she's not particularly feminine."

"I didn't mean it like that. It's actually, you with the gun like that, it's... it's perhaps the most erotic—"

"Shut. Up." I gestured with the gun.

"Very good, missus." He cleared his throat, looking at the ground.

I turned back to Laurence. I tried to remember anything, ever, good about Laurence, and I couldn't. I remembered him as a boy, teasing me, pulling my hair, telling me that he wished I'd been a boy so that he could have a brother instead of a stupid sister. I remembered him arguing with me over the expense of dressing me. I remembered, before I was ruined, being at a ball once, and he'd ridiculed me in front of everyone for being overly pleased at the taste of the punch served. *Anything excites my sister. She's rather simpleminded, I think.*

"Fuck you, Laurence," I whispered in a shaky voice.

He hadn't been all awful, it's true. I'd seen him show compassion and empathy—but only to other men of his class, truly. Never to me. Because I don't think he thought I was really a person. As a woman in his household, I think he thought of me as his property. Perhaps a bauble, a pretty accessory he could trade about for things he wanted. Or an annoyance when I didn't do as he wished.

I hated him.

I was not sorry he was dead.

I didn't know why I was crying.

I sniffed very hard and looked at the driver. "Well, where would you take me?" I didn't know what to do. I had just committed murder. Of course, I supposed it was all right. It was not only here in the country, but it was very far to the north, far, far from the reach of any constabularies, actually. So... well, I guessed disappearing and leaving the bodies was my best option.

I couldn't trust the driver, but perhaps I might have some power over him.

Then, the sound of approaching hoofbeats.

I turned back to see that a single centaur was riding out of the woods. He wasn't wearing a shirt, and he had long, long hair the color of sand and a long curling beard. I wondered why his beard curled and not his hair. There was hair on his chest. It also curled. A thatch of it appeared under his belly button before disappearing into his horse fur. Now that he was closer, I could see that it was peppered in silver.

I should have done something.

Lifted the gun, run, gotten in the carriage...

I don't know.

But I didn't. I stood there, staring at him, transfixed, and he came all the way up to me, maneuvering around the bodies, and looked down at me.

I stared up at him. He smelled good. It reminded me of Enoch's scent but different. Strangely, whereas Enoch had always frightened me in some exciting way, this centaur didn't scare me at all. I felt very, very calm.

He held out a hand. "Your hand, madam?" His voice was deep and rich and it reminded me of babbling brooks and dark hollows in the summer forest.

I put my hand in his.

He bent down and smelled me. He sniffed my knuckles, my palm. Then he let go of me. "Well. You're already mated. Curse-breaker, already bound. Odd how they didn't mention that." He glanced down at the bodies on the ground. "Of course, this... well, this isn't what I was expecting."

"What?" I said. "No, I am *not* mated."

"Is it Enoch Granville?" said the centaur. "Is that the scent on you?"

"*What?*" I said.

"My name is Nescuss," said the centaur.

"He talked about you," I said, furrowing my brow. "But he said that your curse was broken and that you changed things, and that centaurs didn't take women prisoner and—"

"All true," he said. "I've found, however, that when human men come to me with a woman that they're interested in 'selling,' that delivering that woman from those men is usually a favor to her. You seem to have things well in hand, however." He chuckled. He nudged the bodies of one of the men—not Laurence—with his hoof.

"Don't," I breathed. It was disrespectful. I bit down on my lip. "I should bury them."

"Oh, that's what you'd wish?" said Nescuss.

I looked at the driver, who was staring slack-jawed at the centaur. He shrugged at me. "I heard, but I didn't... I must not have thought it was real. Really like a horse. It's..." He swallowed. "I don't understand, actually. What could you even *do* with a human woman? How would that even *work?*"

"Do you want me to leave you with this man?" said Nescuss. "Or would you like to come back to the herd's village with me? You might like to meet my wife, Maribelle. There are other women in the herd, as well. Some wives, a few mounts, those that prefer it that way. You'd be safe there. And we can send word to Enoch to come for you."

I trusted him.

It was ridiculous, but I felt it in me somewhere, a strange tranquility that promised that he wouldn't harm me.

To be truthful, I did not think I would be as safe with the driver.

So, I agreed, and Nescuss swung me up onto his back, and the driver called after me, "Couldn't I see you again somehow?"

I just laughed.

Nescuss called back that it wasn't wise to tangle with a centaur over his bonded mate.

And then we ducked into the trees and left him behind.

I was still clutching the pistol.

CHAPTER TWENTY-FOUR

AS WE RODE, I thought about what Nescuss had said. I couldn't believe it.

"You can scent that I'm bonded?"

"I can," said Nescuss. "A funny thing, however, because I could not scent it when my own wife and I formed the bond. I didn't know until she was with child, truly, though when I think back, I seem to remember the day that it happened. I know when things changed between us."

I considered. "Changed from... she was your captive at some point? You used her, hurt her? And she fell in love with you anyway?"

"I don't understand that myself," said Nescuss. "I don't deserve her, of course. But centaurs, as a rule, are not particularly good men. We wouldn't have been cursed otherwise."

I supposed there was some truth to that.

"At any rate," said Nescuss, "you oughtn't think that it's odd that you were unaware of your bond, that is all."

"Well, I don't think I do have a bond," I said. "I think you must be mistaken. Couldn't you just somehow smell him on me because of... of my having touched him?"

"No, it's a distinctive scent, I assure you."

"It's only that I don't love him," I said. "I hate him, in fact. He's a horrible, horrible man and I never want to see him again."

Nescuss turned to me, looking over his shoulder. "Ah, yes. Well, I never liked him either."

I let out a laugh.

He turned back to the forest ahead, laughing as well. "When he came to the herd, he caused all sorts of trouble. He insisted we were doing violence to the women, and he let go all of the mounts and said we should all be executed for our crimes against the women in the camp. Perhaps he wasn't wrong, though I couldn't see it at the time. There's also the fact that he mounted exactly one woman there."

I stiffened. "Your mate."

"Yes," he said, and he wasn't happy about it.

"And *that's* who you're taking me to meet. Hell and damnation, if I have to meet any other of his women—"

"You're jealous, then," said Nescuss.

"I just hate him," I said. "I mean nothing to him. There are so many other women, and—"

"I am jealous, too," muttered Nescuss. "He let her go free. He rescued her. It should have been me to do that. I should have noticed. But I didn't until he made me see her. I suppose maybe I owe him the introduction, but I hate it."

I let out a long, slow breath. So, I was going to be taken to the woman who my husband had raped, and was there a way out of this now?

"And he told you about her," said Nescuss. "Which means... it's significant. I keep trying to tell myself it's not significant and then..." His voice had grown scoured and sulky.

"Let me down," I said, trying to scramble off his back.

"Don't be ridiculous," he said. "There's nowhere to go."

"I don't want to be taken to see your wife!" I said.

"Well, good, because I need to have a talk with her alone anyway," he said sharply.

"Why, what did *she* do?" I demanded. I'd just been thinking about my brother treating me like property, but this was all the same damnable thing. I managed to slide down off of Nescuss's back, landing awkwardly.

He let out a whinny of frustration.

But it hardly mattered, because we were practically there. I could see the centaur village through the trees, the mounts rising amongst the leaves, the cottages lining a makeshift street. More than that, I could see groups of small, human children running through the paths, screaming with laughter.

Nescuss groaned. "Nothing. She did nothing."

I looked up at him.

He sighed. "It's not *her* fault. It's Enoch's."

"You're right, it is."

"Fuck Enoch Granville," muttered Nescuss.

"Fuck him," I agreed stoutly.

MARIBELLE WAS BEAUTIFUL. Even though her hair was threaded with strands of silver and her face was lined, she seemed to have this inner glow of youth and energy. She held me at arms' length, beaming.

"Oh, really? She's Enoch's?" She smiled up at her husband.

"Don't be like that," muttered Nescuss.

Maribelle snorted. "Don't be like *that*."

Nescuss grunted. "I'm going to send some centaurs after him, tell him to come and collect her."

"Oh," I said. "You are?"

"You don't wish him to come?" said Nescuss.

"Of course she does," said Maribelle.

At the same time, I said, "No."

Nescuss's eyebrows shot up.

Maribelle shoved him. "Send for him."

Nescuss huffed, eyeing her darkly.

She lifted her chin imperiously.

He left the cottage.

The cottage was bigger than one might imagine a typical cottage to be, but it would have to be if it would house a centaur, of course. It had high ceilings. There were furs and tapestries hanging to divide sleeping areas from a sitting room and a kitchen area. The kitchen had wooden countertops surrounding a hearth. Something was bubbling over the fire there. It smelled delicious. It was warm and light and cozy here.

Maribelle squeezed my hands. "How is Enoch? It's been quite some time."

Yes, indeed, he said he hadn't been with a woman in nearly fifty years and how old *was* she? She could be in her seventies, I supposed, but she didn't look that old to me. I didn't know if I could ask her age, however. It seemed frightfully rude.

"Oh, he's fine," I said. "He's perfect. He doesn't care about anything or anyone except himself."

Maribelle laughed. "Truly? I don't think he was ever that way." She considered. "Well, perhaps he was overly concerned with punishing himself. Perhaps in that way, I might agree with you."

I looked around the kitchen. There was a large clay pot on the hearth, bubbling away. I hoped she wasn't going to expect me to help her with the dinner. I didn't know anything about cooking. I was far too highborn for such a thing.

"He told you about me," said Maribelle. "You don't like me."

I looked down at my shoes, ashamed of myself. "That's not fair. He told me he… that it was against your will."

"They were all brutal back then," she said in a low voice. "It's true."

I looked up at her. "I'm sorry."

"It was a long time ago."

"Yes, how long?" Then I shook my head and looked away again. "Oh, pardon me. My apologies for asking."

"Centaur mates do seem to age a bit differently, it's true," she said with a laugh. "I am seventy-seven years old."

Did that mean he was telling the truth? I tried to puzzle it out.

However, she was talking again. "Enoch helped us, you know, when he freed the women."

"But you didn't leave," I said.

She shrugged. "I didn't have anywhere to go. When Nescuss tried to bring me back, though, I negotiated. That was when things started to change between us. And the centaurs as well. There was a spirited debate amongst the herd. Many of the centaurs had felt the treatment of the women was wrong but been afraid to go against the dictates of the herd, you see. Many more didn't wish to share mounts, wanted a woman of their very own. They didn't even know the curse could be broken back then. None of them in the herd had ever fallen in love. They couldn't, not with the way they treated the women."

"Well, I'm so very happy that you and Enoch have such a deep and abiding bond," I said, nostrils flaring.

"Oh, it's not like that," she said with a laugh. "You and Nescuss, truly." She rolled her eyes. "That man. The *things* he did before he met me, and he still gets so very pained about *my* past."

"Yes," I said. "What sort of things? How could you forgive him?"

She let out a surprised laugh. "Straight to it, then? You do cut right to the quick, don't you?"

I grimaced. "Apologies," I said again.

She gestured to the table in the kitchen. It was very high, high enough for a centaur to eat at it standing, and it had tall stools. We climbed up to perch on the stools, her and I, facing each other.

"Well, I can't say I have a good reason," she said. "I suppose I didn't want to go back to where I had come from, that is true. I had fled a bad man, a man who had married me and got a child on me, and then beat it out of me. I knew if I went back, he would claim me as his again. Perhaps I thought there couldn't *be* anything different. Perhaps I thought that at least with the centaurs, the, er, the sex was good." She ducked down her head, her cheeks reddening as she laughed.

I found myself blushing too.

"He was horrid at the beginning," Maribelle said.

"Enoch?"

"Nescuss," she said, laughing, throwing back her head. "My, you have a one-track mind." She winked at me.

I blushed deeper, embarrassed.

"When I was first brought to the herd, I'd run from my husband, who I had been frightened was going to beat me to death. I had gone to my father about it, and he'd given my husband a long, stern talking to, which had resulted in no change other than that my husband was now threatening to kill me if I told anyone about it. One night, I got away from him and ran off into the forest. I ran and ran until a centaur scented me. He was mad with it, chased me literally up a tree and mounted me. It was... it should have been awful. It *was* awful. But something about it..." She looked at me. "I'd never been wanted like that before. Do you have any notion what I mean?"

I lifted my gaze to hers, and I nodded, slowly, my stomach turning over.

"Well, there was a novelty to it," she said. "A power, even. It came with all these... unpleasant consequences, of course. Being trapped. Being, well, owned. Being kept and treated... And they were brutal, as I said. All of them. So, there was pain. They were not gentle with me, or with the other women. They kept us like animals. They had—have— a sort of sexual interest in horse accoutrements?"

I was certain my entire face was a deep scarlet. "No, I'm aware."

She let out a knowing laugh. "Of course. They liked to call us fillies. They liked to call it breaking, training, riding... well, anyway, it should have been awful, but it wasn't always. There was a pleasure involved as well. I had never had that sort of pleasure with a man. I don't know if it's some sort of fate, as if I was always meant for a centaur? Or if somehow, being brutalized as I was before, it made it easier to accept such things? I don't *know* why, you see. I can't say I'm proud of my decisions. And I can't even say that after Nescuss's curse was broken that he changed enough, at least not right away. Of course, he wasn't interested in sharing me, that was true enough. And, of course, it hurt him if I was at all uncomfortable, so he wouldn't hear of me being penned up or treated badly. And of course I had influence over him so I could convince him to make sure the other women were treated better. But... was he the most giving and considerate of mates? Was he a good man? *Is* he a good man?" She shrugged, eyeing me.

I furrowed my brow, unsure of how to respond.

"Look," she said, "when he is awful, I fight back. He likes that. I can't say for sure he's a good man, but I know this. The human man I was with before, he wanted to beat everything out of me. He wanted to make me into some vessel for him to use. He didn't want me to be a person. And Nescuss... what he likes best about me are the parts of me that are, well, me. He loves *me*." She touched her chest. "He loves the parts of me that make him angry just as much as the other parts of me, and I love him that way too. So, I guess I don't care, in the end, how it all started, whether or not he deserves it."

I regarded her, thinking about my brother, thinking about my earlier musings, that my brother had not seen me as a person. If I was really bonded to Enoch, if I'd broken his curse, that meant Enoch loved me.

But...

Well, if he loved me, why hadn't he given up Mrs. Marsh? Why had I had to *take her* from him?

I swallowed. "It's not like that with Enoch. He doesn't love me at all. I think there's some mistake. His curse isn't broken."

"Do you wish to talk about Enoch?"

"No," I said.

"All right, then," she said.

I opened my mouth and words started spilling out anyway. I told her everything. I told her about Mrs. Marsh and how she hadn't aged, how he'd been doing sacrifices and giving her centaur blood.

"Hmm," she said. "I wonder if centaur bodily fluids ease aging. Maybe I and the other women have aged gently because of all the centaur seed."

I did not think this was the salient point. I kept going, telling her about how I'd gotten Mrs. Marsh to leave him, how I'd meant it as revenge, and how he'd barely seemed bothered.

"Because it's already you, of course," said Maribelle.

"Then why didn't he give her up?" I said.

"Because he felt responsible for her. He seems to feel responsibility very deeply, if I remember correctly."

"But what about me?" I said.

"Well, with you it's entirely different," she said.

I snorted. "I don't forgive him," I said. "You might forgive your centaur for keeping you in a pen and letting other men rape you constantly and now you two are all thick as thieves, but I can't do such a thing. Anyway, Nescuss is still jealous of Enoch, so he cares about you. Enoch, on the other hand, only cares about Enoch."

Maribelle opened her mouth to speak.

But the door opened and two children peered in, both girls. One was smaller than the other. They both had curly sandy-colored hair. "Grandma, do you want to see how well we can cartwheel?"

Maribelle smiled at them both. "No cartwheels in the house, girls."

"Well, come out and look," said one of them.

"Please?" said the other.

Maribelle shrugged at me, and we climbed off the stools and went outside to watch the girls do wobbly cartwheels until they both became giggling masses of tangled curls and limbs who hurled themselves into their grandmother's arms.

Maribelle kissed them on their foreheads until another centaur came by and the girls cried "Daddy, Daddy!" and he tossed them both onto his back and saluted Maribelle, calling out he needed to get home to her daughter in time for dinner or there would be hell to pay.

Maribelle smiled after them. "One of our daughters mated a centaur, which Nescuss wasn't the least bit pleased about, believe me. But it's been nice having them close. Our other children left eventually for the human towns and cities. We don't see them or our other grandchildren as often." She turned to me. "Enoch is right, perhaps, to settle you amongst the humans."

"How many children did you have with him?" I said in a small voice.

"Four," she said. "All entirely human, of course, though I sometimes wonder what a small centaur would have been like. It's funny how love makes you wish for odd things." She sighed.

"You think I should forgive Enoch," I said.

She shrugged. "I think he apologized, didn't he? You said he begged for you to tell him some way to make amends. I think he would have done anything you told him. He said he would have ruined himself financially for you. Does that not sound like he cares about you?"

"But he betrayed me," I said. "All along, it was *her*."

"You can't get past that?"

"Should I?" I was angry. "Who would get past that?"

"I don't know," said Maribelle. "Perhaps no one." She was quiet. "But it occurs to me that what you said about Gwendolyn Marsh, realizing she had marinated in hate and anger for all those years, and then deciding to let it all go and seek happiness—"

"But I can't reward him," I said.

"You must make him suffer?"

I sighed. "No, he'd like suffering too much."

She laughed. "Perhaps you're right. Oh, look, here comes Nescuss."

"I can't trust him ever again," I said softly. "I'd be stupid to give him my heart now."

"Ah, true," she said. "Love makes us fools. Did I not just get done telling you how foolish I was to be with this one?" She raised her voice. "You'd best get back here and check on your stew, husband!"

"You haven't touched it, have you?" said Nescuss, breaking into a trot.

"No, no," said Maribelle, shaking her head. She chuckled

to me. "I can't boil water, you know. I'm wretched in the kitchen."

"He cooks?" I said, eyeing Nescuss.

"He does," she said. "I hunt from his back with a bow and arrows. He's stewing up the last rabbit I shot, you see. So, we have the labor divided well, between us." She was grinning up at her husband as he approached.

"If you've done a *thing* to that stew," said Nescuss, ducking past us into the cottage.

"You'll what?" she said.

"I'll take a riding crop to your arse," said Nescuss from within, gruff.

Maribelle only giggled. "Oh, not that, husband," she called. She turned to me. "Once, I tried to salt it, and the whole cap came off the salt. It was very salty and quite inedible. I ate it anyway, just to spite him." She laughed again.

The stew was delicious, actually, the meat tender. It was flavored with onions and it had chunks of carrots and potatoes. It was perfectly seasoned.

I didn't inquire about Enoch, and Nescuss didn't bring him up either.

Instead, the two spent the evening pleasantly ribbing the other, teasing and laughing as they ate, and there was such ease between them, such love, it made me feel… well, I liked it, but it sort of terrified me. The thought of accepting such a thing…

If I had this with Enoch, I might grow to need it. And then, when I lost it, I would be inconsolable. I couldn't take the risk.

He wouldn't come for me, anyway.

I was given a place to sleep in one of the little partitioned-off alcoves of the cottage, and I settled under blankets and slipped easily to sleep, wondering about Nescuss and Maribelle, who obviously couldn't be intimate in that bed.

The mounts in the village, they were all so… public. Was that…? How did that work?

I went to sleep thinking about being mounted by Enoch in

front of a whole village of centaurs, of him praising me, telling the others to look how pretty I was, to observe how well I took his cock.

I dreamed tight and shivery dreams.

And I woke to Enoch's voice.

CHAPTER TWENTY-FIVE

HE LOOKED SO out of place in his suit and tie here, where all the centaurs were bare-chested and bearded and wild. He stood outside Nescuss's cottage and beckoned for me, all the while glaring at Nescuss.

"What is she doing here with you?" Enoch said.

"I don't know how it was you lost track of your own mate," said Nescuss. "I certainly don't lose track of mine."

"Mate?" said Enoch, turning to look at me.

"I scent it," said Nescuss.

Enoch's face gentled. "Phoebe?"

I looked away.

"Come to me," he murmured.

I stayed where I was.

"She was with four men, three of them dead. She was holding a pistol. There were rope marks on her wrists," said Nescuss. "So, you were protecting her so very, *very* well."

"What happened?" said Enoch to me.

I lifted my chin. "Laurence."

"Your brother?"

"He wanted to sell me to a centaur herd to make enough money to settle his debts."

"Oh, yes, he came to me to ask for money," said Enoch. "He called you such names I nearly killed him. But I knew you didn't wish me to."

My chest tightened. My jaw jerked. My eyes stung.

"One of the dead men was your brother?" said Nescuss quietly. "You didn't tell me that."

"You shot him?" said Enoch.

I was going to start sobbing.

"Phoebe, what happened?" Enoch closed the distance between us.

I glanced up at his agonized expression.

"I should have been there," he said. "I know you didn't want me there, but I should have—"

"Why did you come?" I said. "Nothing's changed. I don't want to be near you."

Enoch flinched as if I'd slapped him.

It was quiet.

Nescuss cleared his throat.

Enoch turned on him. "You said you could scent—"

"I'm afraid having a broken curse doesn't mean the fillies don't still get angry with you," said Nescuss. "They get angrier, I think, actually. And, of course, you care that they're angry."

"Nescuss," said Maribelle, clearly appalled.

"See?" said Nescuss, sighing.

"If you call me a filly again—"

"What? You're an old, gray mare?" said Nescuss.

"You're the one who's going to have a riding crop taken to your arse," she said, eyes flashing.

Nescuss winced.

"And you'll be sleeping outside," she said.

"Oh, Maribelle," he said. "Come, now, I don't think I said anything that bad."

Maribelle disappeared into the cottage.

Nescuss went after her, calling her name plaintively.

Enoch and I were left alone.

He reached down and touched my face in that way of his. He gazed at me with a wondering look on his face. "I think it must have been when you let me have you to ease my madness. What a sacrifice. When I came back to myself, when I saw I'd hurt you, I never felt such—I think the curse broke then."

"Such what?" I said. "Guilt?"

"Well, yes, but also grateful. No one... people don't do things like that for me, Phoebe. Women definitely don't..." He shrugged. "I wish there was some way I could do something of the same magnitude for you."

I ducked out of his touch. He always said things like that, and I used to let them turn my head, but I couldn't now. I had to protect myself.

It was quiet.

"I'll take you back to the country estate, then," he said. "I'll make sure that you're better protected this time before I leave you alone."

"How will you take me back?" I said. "How did you get here?"

"I galloped through the night, of course. The other centaurs who had come to give me the news were tired, so I went on ahead." He sighed. "You don't wish to ride me. You don't want to be close to me at all."

I twisted my fingers together. That wasn't true, exactly. I did wish to ride on his back. I wished to be close to him. I wished it all to be exactly as it had been before, when I didn't know what his secrets were. I wished I could pretend that he hadn't betrayed me and that he was my dark, handsome rescuer. But that was all impossible now, and riding on his back would only confuse me.

"I'll get you a horse, how about that?" he said. "I'll send someone to a nearby village for one. I'll give him coin."

"Fine," I said.

"Fine," he said, defeated.

It was quiet again.

I stepped out of the shadow of the cottage and spied one of those mounts rising up between the trees. I eyed it. "So, it's all out in the open here?"

Enoch turned to look where I was looking. "Ah, yes, the herd is very voyeuristic."

I looked up at him. "Everyone?"

He shrugged. "There are other mounts, ones you can't see, off in the woods." He gestured with one hand. "So, no, not everyone, not anymore. But when I first arrived here, it was common enough for everyone to watch, yes. If they didn't have women, they'd watch each other masturbate." His lip curled.

I laughed. "I see what you think of that."

"Would you wish to be publicly mounted?"

"No," I said, very quickly, because I wouldn't, shivery dreams notwithstanding.

He laughed again, softly, leaning down. "Is that a no that is quite similar to the way you don't wish to be penned, or the way you don't wish to be bridled?"

I glared at him. "Stop it."

"I don't know why I ask, anyway," he said. "I don't like being watched. It's difficult for me to, er, perform. I find it abominable, not the least bit arousing. And as for even teasing you with it when we are together, you have made it clear we're never going to be together, haven't you?"

"I have," I said.

"I'll see to the horse," he said, turning away from me.

I leaned into the door of the cottage, where I heard the high-pitched sound of Maribelle still railing at Nescuss. I jerked back. "Wait," I said. "I'll come with you."

He gave me a long look. "Suit yourself."

Halfway across the village, I decided I was being ridiculous, but I didn't say anything.

No, I waited until he was talking to a young human man, obviously a child of one of the centaurs and the women here, asking him if he minded going to procure a horse.

Then I spoke up. "It's really fine. I can ride on your back."

Enoch glanced down at me, eyebrows raised. "No, you didn't wish to—"

"It will be fine," I said firmly.

Enoch regarded me for several long moments and then turned back to the young man. "Well, never mind, then, I suppose. Sorry to have troubled you."

Then there was no reason to wait at all, but I said I wished to say goodbye to Maribelle.

We went back to the cottage, and I interrupted their

argument to tell them that I'd be going.

Maribelle came out and embraced me. I waited for her to give me some parting words of wisdom, but all she said was, "I wish you all the best."

Nescuss shook hands with Enoch and said he hoped he had a good journey. He said it had been very nice to meet me and wished me well also.

Then Enoch picked me up and deposited me on his back, and we left.

We rode in silence and I tried to hold on mostly with my knees rather than touch his torso. After about an hour of this, I realized that this was not going to be the most comfortable of ways to travel.

A saddle might make it easier, but that thought took on a decidedly sexual tinge, and I did not voice it.

Instead, we rode on through the day, and I had to put my arms around his torso, and if I began to feel chafed or uncomfortable, I didn't say anything about that either.

We stopped for food. Enoch was ravenous, and his eyes were drooping. If he hadn't been so hungry, I thought he might have fallen asleep at the tavern where we'd stopped. We hadn't been able to eat inside either, because the place wasn't big enough to accommodate centaurs, so they'd put up a makeshift table for us outdoors, and we ate there.

"You can't go on," I said to him.

"Absolutely, I can," he said.

"You've been riding all night and all day," I said. "Now, with me on your back, you've got to be sore and very tired."

"I'd rather get back to our country estate," he said. "There's nowhere comfortable for me to rest on the road."

I supposed this was true. I offered to walk for a bit.

He said this would only slow us down.

But the rest of the journey back, which took us until after darkness had settled, I felt awful for him. I didn't know why I cared. I was not supposed to be cultivating any feelings for him at all.

We finally made it back, however, and he practically collapsed at the threshold. With help, he was able to make it to his bedchamber. It was on the first floor in this house, because the steps had not been made to his specifications and it was very difficult for his hooves to navigate their narrow steepness.

The servants were all in a tizzy.

Apparently, when I disappeared, they'd sent word to Enoch, who'd come to the estate. This was where the centaurs had found him and given him the news of me. The servants had all been frightened that I'd been killed or worse and they fussed over me and asked me a thousand questions.

Most of them had not realized that there were a great many other centaurs besides their master. They wanted to know all about the herd and whether or not there were female centaurs and that sort of thing.

I answered questions until Janet rescued me, saying that I seemed tired and she took me up to my own bedchamber and shooed everyone away.

Then it was only Janet and me, and we were alone.

I flung myself down on my bed, lay on my back, and patted the space next to me.

Janet laughed a little and lay down too.

"Thank you for that," I told her. "A little peace and quiet is what I need."

"Are you all right?" she said. "You really weren't hurt?"

"It was Laurence, Janet," I said. "He did it. He was going to sell me for money to pay his debts."

Janet turned on her side, propping her head up on an elbow, her eyes very wide. "You can't be serious."

"I wish I was lying," I said. "I wish my brother had been utterly different than he was."

"Was?"

I blew out another breath. I loved Janet. In some ways, I was closer to her than anyone. But she was a servant, and I was not an idiot. I couldn't tell her what I'd done. "He's dead, yes," I said.

"Did your husband do it?" said Janet.

I shook my head. "No, it was just an accident. A freak

thing with the carriage. I got away afterwards, and then I happened upon the centaurs who helped me and sent for Mr. Granville."

"Well, if your husband had rescued you, perhaps that would mean you'd forgive him," said Janet.

"No," I said.

"So, you haven't forgiven him?" said Janet.

"Of course not," I said.

"Of course not," she repeated.

I looked up at her, propped up next to me in the bed. "You think I should. Everyone thinks I should."

"I don't know," she said with a shrug. "I'm not sure what we're doing out here in the country, however. This isn't what you want, and I know it. You want dinners with dukes and duchesses. You want balls and teas and people who'd been awful to you eating their words. You're not going to get it out here. Forgive him or don't, but it seems a waste to be parted from him."

How could I explain to her that being near him meant I needed to have sex with him?

Oh, dear.

I'd ridden all the way back here on his back. Would that have driven him close to madness?

"Look, Janet, do you remember when... when Mr. Granville was tied and chained and brought through the house by Mr. Higgins?"

She sat up slowly, looking down on me. "Everyone remembers that."

"Well, it's my fault that happened," I said. "When he's near me, his desire for me drives him out of his head. And I have to give in to the desire or else that will happen again. So, he and I need to be apart."

"Oh," she said, sighing. "Seems a pity, though."

"Just get me ready for bed," I moaned. "I don't think I've ever been so tired or sore in my life. Never ride bare back, Janet. I don't recommend it."

CHAPTER TWENTY-SIX

I WISHED FOR the shivery dreams of the night before, shameful as they may have been. Instead, I had a dream about Laurence. He was dead, shot in the head, rotting, but up and moving, his skin gray. He was with Oscar, also shot, and they were laughing together, playing whist and drinking port.

"After Mr. Higgins is called in to shoot poor Mr. Granville, it'll be a threesome of men you've murdered," said Laurence to me, smiling. His teeth were stained red.

When I woke up, I hurriedly pulled on a wrapper over my nightdress and rushed through the house to Enoch's bedchamber.

He was asleep, torso propped up on a mass of pillows against the headboard of his bed—well, it was not a raised bed, but cushions on the floor, as in his town house. If I'd been there, he would have been pillowed on my breasts, of course, and that made my body twist, especially considering why I was there.

I nudged him between his bare shoulder blades until he woke up.

He blinked at me, bleary-eyed. "Phoebe."

"Good," I said. "You haven't gone mad."

"What?" he said. "If you've broken my curse, that won't happen anymore."

I stepped back from him. "You could have told me that."

"I feel certain I did?"

"No, you did not," I said, folding my arms over my chest.

"Well, now you know." He yawned, stretching, and then flopped back into his pile of pillows and looked at me through slitted eyes. "I love the way you look after you've been asleep, with your hair in disarray and the hints of your body without any structured undergarments. You're beautiful."

"Stop saying things like that to me."

He yawned again. "You were coming to fuck me, weren't you? To make sure that I didn't go mad?"

"Well, I don't need to force myself now," I said. "Besides, I wasn't even sure. Is there a mount here?"

"Obviously." He yawned again. "Through that door over there. It was a sitting room at one point, but I had it converted. There's a big window. We could pull the curtains wide if it'll give you a charge. Maybe we'll get an audience."

"You... how dare you?" I kicked him—not hard, on his horse body which was under the covers.

"Ouch," he said mildly.

"Obviously there's a mount?" I was going across the room.

"I told you we use them to pleasure ourselves," he said.

"Yes, but I don't see how."

"Don't you? The platform can be used as something to rut into, of course. Or one can get quite creative and mount all sorts of greased pockets. I've never gotten into that myself."

"Well, I suppose you'll have to now." I threw open the door to look at the mount, which was mostly like the one in town, only not nearly as new looking.

"Because you're never going to touch me again?"

"No," I said.

"Well, then," he said. "I'll break my fast here and then head back to town. I'm sending Mr. Higgins here to guard you for the time being, and—"

"Actually," I called, stepping into the room and approaching the mount, "it seems to me if there's no danger of proximity between us, then there's no reason for us to be separated. You still want to rise in society, I suppose?"

"Well, now that I'm limited to the span of one human lifetime, the pressure is considerable," he called back. "So, yes, I suppose I haven't a moment to lose. You want to help?"

"I want to rise as well," I said. "You know this." I ran my fingers over the straps on the mount. "You know I wouldn't have married you otherwise."

"Is that why you married me?" He chuckled.

"Well, not entirely," I said with a little sigh. "I suppose I was stupid and naive. I suppose I believed you could care about me, even though no one ever has."

There was no response to this, but I heard rustling from the other room and then the sound of hooves on the wooden floor.

I moved out to lean against the side of the mount.

He appeared in the doorway. "I do care about you, Phoebe."

"Well," I said, "perhaps. In whatever way is alloted to me, I suppose."

"What's that supposed to mean?" he said.

"Nothing," I said. "Being accepted back into society will be enough. It'll have to be."

"Is this about your brother? About the way he treated you?"

"No," I said.

"About shooting him?" Enoch stepped closer to me. "If you wish to speak to someone about—"

"I wish to pretend that never happened, actually," I said breezily.

"I know I hurt you," he said. "I only... Gwendolyn—if I hadn't been connected to her, I would never have become a centaur, and I would have been dead by now, and you and I never would have met, let alone fallen in love—"

"This is love, is it?"

"I suppose so," he said. "I admit it feels... well, wretched. It's odd, because I've spent what feels like my whole life in pain, and I didn't think it could be worse, but you... hurting you…" He hung his head.

"I'm not hurt," I said. "I'm entirely beyond it now. I'm fine."

"Now, that's a lie," he said. "Because all I want to do is stop your hurt. I feel your hurt like—that's why it's worse. Before, I was only able to feel my own pain, and now *your* pain hurts me."

"I'm not *in* pain," I said. "Maybe I was, but I've gotten past it, and I won't let myself feel that way anymore. I'm not going to be stupid anymore. Let's not speak of this again either. Let's simply pretend it's always been thus between us. A marriage of convenience."

"That's not—"

"Actually, we don't even need to pretend. It always has been."

"Nothing about being married to you has been convenient," he growled.

I snorted. "Well, not for me either, I suppose." I tilted my head. "But I can help you achieve your greatest desire, the only thing you've ever really wanted for yourself. I can help you rise."

He swallowed. His voice came out raw. "You've told me again and again that was impossible."

"It is," I said. "They'll never truly respect us, of course. We'll always be an oddity to them, and they'll always talk about us when we aren't around, and most of it won't be complimentary. But we can make them accept us into their balls and their dining rooms. And we can make them wish for *our* favor. It'll be enough. It has to be." It was all I had left, all I could dare to let myself wish for anymore.

He drew in a breath, held it for a time, and then finally let it out. "What if I said I didn't care about all that anymore?"

"I'd call you a liar."

"What if I said I wanted only to pave the way for our children not to be ridiculed, but that otherwise, I thought the whole of the gentry could go straight to hell?"

"We're not going to have any children."

"What if I said what I really wanted was you? That since I

saw you, I knew you were all I wanted, but I was afraid to admit it to myself, because every time I've ever felt anything for a woman, it's gone badly? What if I said you terrify me, but that I want to walk right into my fear and hold your hand, and that I think together we could face anything at all?"

"I would say that you're good at pretty speeches and at making me think you care about me. But that no one cares about me. That whatever it is that some women have that makes men devoted to them, I don't have. And I don't need pretense anymore, Enoch. I'll be satisfied with what I can have that is real, even if it's very little."

CHAPTER TWENTY-SEVEN

WE TOOK A carriage back to town. I had never traveled with Enoch in one of his larger carriages, but he had it designed so that he and another person could fit inside it handily.

He wanted to talk on the way back, but I didn't let him.

He kept trying to say things to me. "You said something like that before. That the only way you knew things were real is if they were bad in some way. You said you couldn't trust it when things were too good. I remember that."

I ignored him.

"Phoebe, what I feel for you isn't pretense. Love *can* be real."

I stared out the window.

"And there's nothing wrong with *you*," he said to me. "It's not as if you're not lovable."

I only breathed.

I supposed I didn't engage him because I knew I wasn't making sense.

Well...

If I looked at it from a certain perspective, anyway, it *did* make sense. I had never really been able to count on people for my entire life. Perhaps my parents to some degree, but they'd *died*. My brother, Oscar Smithy, the people of society I'd been acquainted with, Enoch... eventually, people simply let me down. It was what they did.

Now, I knew that people didn't always let people down, of course, so, one way to make it make sense was to assume that it was *me*. There must be something about me that was making this happen again and again.

I had known it was foolish to give any of my trust to Enoch Granville. I had tried, even, not to do so. I had cautioned myself, and then... it had happened anyway. And once I trusted him?

Betrayal.

It was simply what happened to me.

Maybe I should have realized this earlier in my life. Maybe if I had, I wouldn't have been so stupidly hopeful about him. No matter how hard I tried to guard my heart, I hadn't been able to. However, with this knowledge—the knowledge that I was simply flawed, that other people could be happy but I could not—that made it easier to shut everything down.

I needed to shut everything down.

I needed to protect myself.

I'd spent all this time hoping someone else would protect me. Hoping for my brother to care about me. Hoping for Enoch Granville to put me first. Hoping...

No more of that.

I didn't care if it didn't make sense if it was held up to scrutiny. I needed it. I needed it because I couldn't bear disappointment again. I couldn't bear *pain*.

So.

I would no longer expect anything else. As long as I was steeled for it, I'd be safe. Nothing could hurt me ever again. No more pain.

Eventually, Enoch stopped talking and fell silent.

Eventually, there was nothing except the scenery out the window and the sound of the wheels on the road.

Eventually, I was left to shore up the walls of myself, to lock myself away inside my new fortress, to make my defenses impenetrable.

We all arrived back in town, and I set about planning how Enoch and I would take the gentry, how we would get ourselves into an unenviable place within society. The first step was to accept that we would never be respectable, I thought. We could not be revered, but we could be formidable. If we embraced the idea that we were a carnival attraction and played that role, that would mean that we gave the upper echelon pleasure. We would charm them by entertaining them and by never asking to be anything other than beneath them.

Then, we would use the secrets he had amassed through underhanded means—paying coin to strumpets like Arabella and getting Mr. Higgins to strongarm them from others—to incite fear when necessary.

We would appear to be harmless and silly. Until we were lethal.

I thought it would work. No, I *knew* it would.

It was all I wanted to talk to him about.

At first, we would meet in one of the vast, ostentatious sitting rooms in our house, and he kept trying to speak to me about our relationship. He made soulful and stirring declarations of love.

I ignored all of that, and eventually, he stopped.

Within several weeks, he knew that all we would speak about would be our plans for rising within society and that I was serious when I said I was never going to touch him again.

And within a month, my plans began to take root.

At first, I missed him.

I missed touching him, kissing him, and I missed, well, the sheer maddening sensuality of everything about him. I missed his urgent, dark voice, his eager tongue, his massive cock, even the straps of the mount on my ankles and the jeweled bridle on my face.

But then, we were invited to the home of the Duke and Duchess of Rells, and we were both brilliant, if I do say so myself. We came home with the promise of three other invitations, all of which were issued formally within two days.

I was so pleased by this that I was able to stop thinking

about whatever I'd left behind with Enoch.

It hadn't been real, that was the thing.

I knew the curse was broken — well, I had Nescuss's word for it, anyway, but I didn't see any true signs of it. It wasn't as if a month was long enough for Enoch to begin aging — and that should indicate true feelings.

But I thought that whatever it was to truly be in love with me must be different than what it was to be in love with someone else. Because I was, of course, flawed in that way where people couldn't help but betray me. So, it was as much love as I could get, because of my flaw.

But it wasn't real love. Not like what other people got. And so, I had no use for it.

I didn't mind getting less as long as what I had was real. What we had, climbing society, it was less, but it was real, and I was in control of it. I had no illusions that people really liked me or that I could trust any of them. No people were trustworthy, at least not when it came to me. I knew how it was, and I didn't mind.

It was enough.

Enoch was gratified by our rise, too.

When we schemed together, he would smile at me and say that I was brilliant and that there was no way that this would be possible without me.

It wasn't quick, and it wasn't even steady.

I waited six months — six months of invitations, six months of making impressions, of being seen with all the right people — before we hosted another ball. Enoch kept saying we should do it earlier, but I said we must wait.

Even so, the ball was more sparsely attended than I would have liked, and I didn't throw another one for eight more months while we slowly amassed the right sort of people.

Enoch's secrets — the ones he was getting from Arabella — proved useful on occasion, when necessary. Sometimes, we could not charm our way and so we knocked the door down.

Within two years, however, there was not a household in

town who would deny us entry, and I daresay any event that was worth having included us. I had no illusions that we were not—in some ways—a spectacle, a sort of circus act that the upper classes enjoyed parading around for their guests, but it didn't matter.

We had power and influence and it was all we'd wanted.

Mr. Higgins had retired from our service about seven months after the curse broke. He felt the decline of his aging rather quickly, I think. He had given years and years of his life to Enoch, and now he wanted what was left of it for himself.

Enoch gave him a fine severance, a great deal of coin, and let him go.

I missed him.

We had become friends in our way. But, as I've noted, one cannot really be friends with someone whose salary one pays. And anyway, the fortress I'd built within myself—the one that kept Enoch out and kept all the pain out? It seemed to close me off from, well, everyone.

I think Mr. Higgins noticed.

When he left, he held my hand for too long, gazing into my eyes, shaking his head. "I thought you might change him, Mrs. Granville," he said. "I should have realized he'd change you."

But what did Mr. Higgins know?

I had changed myself.

At any rate, he sent letters. He bought himself a little plot of land to work, and he settled in a small cottage. He went into the tavern in town each day, he said, and he was teaching himself to play the piano-forte there. When he managed it, he would play long ballads for the gathered townspeople, singing as well. He said they'd crowd about and clap for him, begging to hear more.

It is enough, he wrote. *I am content.*

Funny that he chose that turn of phrase, I sometimes thought.

I tried to tell myself that I was also content.

But somehow, the word turned sideways, brushing at my

insides with sharp, shard-like edges.

What had become of my brother's inheritance? Well, a cousin of ours was the new Earl of Crisbane. He was not nearly as bad with money as my brother had been. My brother had been declared dead after a year of no one being able to find him. I had spoken to the constabularies on many occasions, but they had never made any arrests. No one hanged for that crime.

I was not close with what remained of my family, who were slightly embarrassed that I was married to a centaur, I think. Before that, they had cut me because I was ruined.

So, I could not bring myself to care much about them.

Indeed, I had not needed them to get where we were. It was my triumph, and I gloried in it.

It was enough.

But it wasn't enough for Enoch. Oddly, even though this had been *his* dream, he seemed restless. I caught him looking at himself in the mirror, examining his face, looking for lines that hadn't been there, searching for gray hair, making comments about whether he had new aches and pains.

He started drinking.

I had never seen him drink alcohol, and I soon realized why. Centaurs did not do well with it. Sometimes, he was all right, but sometimes, one glass of wine would send him into a rage. He'd knock over furniture and scream about being trapped and dead and dying.

He'd beg me to release him. He'd say, "Why must you bury it all? You can't feel the wounds, Phoebe, but I still feel them. I feel them all. I want us *healed*."

One of these nights, I told him he should simply start paying whores. "I don't want to see them, if you don't mind. Bring them up the servants' stairs when you put them on your mount."

He was in the middle of one of the sitting rooms, standing over a splintered couch that he'd trampled. He threw back his head and laughed, a hollow echoing sound. "Yes, that's what it's about. It's about quim." He laughed and laughed and laughed.

"It's all I won't give you," I said. "I think, otherwise, I'm everything a wife should be. Everything you ever wanted from a wife, more than you thought you could possibly have."

"I didn't want a wife," he said to me. "I saw you, though, and I lost all control of myself."

"Well, sincere apologies," I said. "I don't know what you want me to do about that."

"Get on the mount for me," he said. "What if I say I want that from you?"

"I just told you to hire a whore," I said.

"I don't want a whore," he said, mouth twisting. "You broke my curse. You're *all* I want."

"You were quite happy not fucking Gwendolyn," I said.

"Yes, well, that was different," he said. "She took pleasure in denying me, in hurting me. You won't let me touch you because you're afraid of feeling anything."

"That is not why," I said, glowering at him. "You're too drunk, anyway. I doubt you could stay stiff."

"That a challenge, wife?" He stalked over to me.

"No," I said.

"Mine is," he said. "I dare you to let me touch you. I dare you to let me make you feel something."

"I am not afraid of you," I said, my voice rising, my hands clenched in fists.

"It can be all filth, if you want." His voice broke. "No affection, nothing like that."

"There it is," I said. "You wish to hurt me. You're angry. You want revenge."

"Afraid of that?"

"Fuck you!" I snapped.

He swallowed. "How would it arouse you to be hurt? With the riding crop you used on me all that time ago? Or just with my hands?"

"I haven't been penetrated in so long that if you took me now, I'd need trained again."

"Afraid of that, then? Afraid of my cock?"

"Never," I said, glaring at him. "Nothing about you

frightens me."

"Yes, because nothing frightens you at all. You are cold, through and through, Phoebe. You're all hard ambition and nothing else."

"I tire of this conversation. You're drunk."

"I know what it's like, being cold like that," he said. "It's how I was before you warmed me up. But why did you do that if you were just going to freeze me out in the cold again?"

"I didn't do anything to you! I tried as hard as I could to keep you out, not to let you in, and you got in anyway, and then—" I suddenly felt dangerously close to tears.

That terrified me, so I turned on my heel and stalked out of the room.

He came after me. "Don't you walk away from me. Don't you shut me out."

I did walk away, but for some reason, my steps took me all the way up to his room, to the mount.

When he realized where we were going, he got different. His breath started coming in harsh gasps, and he tried to whisper things to me, and I turned on him and put my finger in his face and said, "Just filth, you said."

"All right," he said.

We stared at the mount, together.

"What's your pleasure, then?" he said softly. "Are you my wild filly? Am I breaking you? Do you wish to punish me?"

"I want you to pretend people are watching us," I said.

He laughed, and there was true humor in it. "I knew you wanted it."

I didn't have it in me to be angry.

"Who's watching us, Phoebe?" His mouth was kissing the top of my head, his voice going scoured around the edges. "Is it a herd of centaurs, or is it the humans at a ball?"

I shut my eyes, sagging into him. "We're already their entertainment."

"Oh, yes," he said. "Think how many would come to watch me mount you."

I swallowed, my body feeling loose and eager. "They'd crowd around the mount and gaze up at us."

"You'd preen and show them your breasts, wouldn't you?" he said. "You'd like to face outward so that they could see your body."

My body clenched. "Yes," I admitted. "I want you to bridle me again, Enoch. Did you ever get reins?"

He groaned, hands roaming over my body. "Wait here, Phoebe." He kissed my temple and then took off to go through his drawers.

I started trying to work on the buttons of my dress.

He came back with glittering, jeweled, slender leather straps all balled up in his hands. He turned me, and he unbuttoned my dress and unlaced my corset, and I felt the bridle's straps brushing against me as he did so.

"Think," he said, as he helped me out of my clothing. "Think of them all gathered around as I divested you of your clothes. Think of them commenting to each other, the men's gazes appraising, the women jealous of your perfect curves."

I gasped, and I didn't even argue or say that I wasn't perfect, that my body wouldn't make women jealous. In that moment, I felt as though maybe it would. I wanted to at least pretend it would. I wanted that, just for *this*.

He reached down to cup one of my breasts. He curved his palm under the underside, as if he was offering it to someone else. "What would I say to them about you? What would you want?"

I looked up at him. "Would you be jealous of them looking at me?"

"Would that arouse you?" he whispered. "If I wanted to shield you from their view, if I said that you were for my eyes only?"

My body clenched again, and I felt heavy between my thighs. It had been two years since I'd been with Enoch, so I'd pleasured myself now and again, but this kind of arousal, well, I hadn't managed anything like this. It was heady and sweet and good.

"Or," he said in a velvet voice, "would you like me to be secure in my claim of my pretty mount and proud to show you off? Would you like me to call out to men in their ties and tails, ask them if they did not wish they could be fondling a pair of lovely teats like yours?"

I groaned, bending my head back. "Kiss me."

He did, upside down, bending at the waist to lower himself enough to get his mouth on mine. His upper lip against my lower one, our tongues rough side against rough side.

As he kissed me his other hand found my other breast. I had forgotten the feeling of the pads of his thumbs on my nipples, the way he stroked and tickled and teased. I moaned into our kiss, my nipples standing at attention for him.

He broke the kiss. "So? The second one?" He continued to toy with my nipples. "Then, after that, I'd have you turn around and bend over for them. I'd tell you to show off your pretty wet slit. I'd tell you to reach back and part your folds for the audience."

I groaned, a shudder going through me.

"And, as the men pressed forward, their wives shocked and angry that they were so eager for you, I'd tell them that you were like slipping into the warmest, tightest slick glove, that fucking you was a perfect, slippery ride to sheer bliss." He pinched both of my nipples at once.

I cried out.

"Then," he murmured, his voice going even lower, "I'd tell you to straighten up for your bridle."

Oh, where was the bridle? He wasn't holding it anymore, because he had his hands full of my breasts. He let go of me and produced it from one of his pockets. He was still dressed, after all. I was the naked one.

"You haven't undressed," I said.

"I don't think I shall," he said. "Wouldn't you like that? Me dressed, you bare. Me, the gentleman monster, tidy from the waist up, with my beastlike hard cock sticking out for the women gathered round to ogle. Would you like them seeing it? Would you like them wondering if they could take it all, if they could manage to get crammed full of me like you do?"

Another shudder went through me.

He began to put the bridle on me. "Would you like the bit in your mouth, Phoebe?"

I convulsed.

"*Yes*," he hissed, gentling it into my mouth, tucking my tongue down under its cold metal. He hummed. "You look very pretty with the bridle on, and all the people watching would think so too." He did have reins. He hooked them into the little metal rings on the bridle and draped them down, making me put my arms through them. They lay between my breasts, at my sides, and he gathered them up at my back and pulled them taut.

They cut under my breasts, making them stand out, lewd and bulging.

"I'd show you off like that, Phoebe," he said. "And everyone would see how my cock was pulsing because of how hard I was."

I mewled. I wanted to touch his cock, I realized. It had been too long since I had. But when I tried to move, he caught me by my reins, and I couldn't go anywhere. My pelvis twitched. I was very, very aroused.

He loosened the reins, gave them a little thwack. "To the mount, then, Phoebe. Let's go."

I walked, and he came with me.

I climbed into the mount, and he strapped in my ankles and removed the reins from under my arms, letting them dangle in front of me, before he strapped in my wrists. He lifted me and spread my legs and put his hands between my legs to fondle my quim. He rubbed me there.

"My, my, you're very wet, aren't you?" he breathed.

I gasped.

His finger circled my clit, slow, nearly torturous. "You're soaking wet, Phoebe. Tell me, did you miss my fingers on you here?"

I cried out. He very well knew that I couldn't talk with

the bit in my mouth.

"Come for me if you missed it, wife," he said, his voice low and grating. "Crest on my fingers, give me all your pleasure, fall apart against me. Show me how much you wished for this over these years of separation."

I tried to move my pelvis away from his hand, but the mount held me in place, and my body betrayed me anyway, my eager quim seeking his finger, seeking the pleasure he gave me.

The climax he took from me came like a lightning strike, no warning, just blinding bright pleasure that splintered through my body, making me go rigid and then exploding in thunderous quakes through my pelvis and thighs.

He pressed his fingers into my clit, letting me twitch out the aftershocks against him and he kissed my jaw, whispering in my ear. "I wanted you, Phoebe. I wanted to make you come. I missed the smell of you, the feel of you, the noises you make."

Stop. But all I could do was let out an agonized noise.

He kissed my mouth.

I couldn't move my tongue with the bit in there.

He massaged my trapped tongue with his, and then he took the bit away. He kissed me hard, and I kissed back.

Then he was gone, rearranging me on the mount.

I remembered what he'd said. "I thought I was going to face out?" I said. "Show off my breasts for the gathered audience."

He chuckled, gathering up my reins. "I'm going to burst, Phoebe." He put his hooves into the grooves, stretching himself out in front of me, presenting me with his cock. He tugged on my reins.

His thick hardness was level with my face, and it was as big and swollen as it had ever been. The dark head of it was glistening with his own arousal, weeping out of him.

I licked him, the flat of my tongue going over the sensitive underside of him and all the way over his slit and to the top of his head.

He shuddered, letting out a groan.

I had missed his prick. I wished my hands were free. I wished I could run my hands over the silkiness of his skin, feel him pulse and jerk when I squeezed him. But I was secure, so I had to use my mouth.

Still, I waited, and he gave a tug on the reins, pulling my face forward. "Suck me, wife," he ordered in a gravelly voice.

That made my body clench. I sucked him into my mouth, stretching my lips, taking as much of him as I can. I massaged him with my tongue.

He grunted and convulsed, emptying himself into my mouth that quickly.

I swallowed, practically choking on it. It was *a lot*.

"Sorry," he muttered from above me. "It's... been a while."

Certainly, he'd been pleasuring himself in the interim, hadn't he?

I swallowed him down. I kept him in my mouth, suckling him gently, liking the way he felt there. I supposed I liked having him in my body, actually. I liked him joined to me.

But he slid his cock free. I noted that it was still rock hard, as if his orgasm had done nothing to abate his arousal.

He took his hooves down and then we were kissing. He caressed my face, thoroughly claiming my mouth.

Then, panting, he rested his forehead against mine, his eyes closed.

I kept mine open. I was breathing too hard too. "I-if you're not going to take me from behind, I want you to take off your clothes." My voice was small.

He pulled away to look into my eyes. "All right." He began to peel off his jacket. He tossed that off, and I watched it land next to the mount.

"You've..." I chewed on my bottom lip. "You've pleasured yourself with this since we were together on it, haven't you?"

"No," he said.

"But—"

"A normal human man," said Enoch, undoing his tie, "if

he doesn't empty his bollocks, will have emissions—it'll come out when he's sleeping. A nonmagical body would work that way. But a centaur... we're cursed not to have sex. So, no, I don't have to do it. No reason, not even maintenance. And this mount makes me think of you. And when I think of you, it's pain."

For no reason I could fathom, tears sprang to my eyes. It was stupid. What did I care if he didn't pleasure himself? And why did he always say that he could feel my pain? I had worked hard to ensure I wouldn't *be* in pain. I had protected myself entirely.

Enoch shed his tie. He started to unbutton his waistcoat. "I want to make you come again before I try to put my cock inside you. I think maybe try to stretch you a bit with my fingers also. I don't actually want to hurt you, so if it's too much, you'll tell me."

"No training cock?" I said.

"I only want me in you," he said. "My skin, my fingers, my prick. The devil only knows when you'll let me back inside you again after this."

"I'm not cold," I said.

He took off his waistcoat. He fiddled with the top button of his shirt. His shirt was tailored differently than a normal man's might be. He didn't have any trousers for it to be tucked into, so it was hemmed short and fitted to his torso.

I gazed at the V-shape of his beautiful chest, thinking about how handsome he was, how greedy I was for a look at his body bared. I wished again that my hands weren't bound. I wanted to touch him.

"You *are* cold," he said. "You want to talk about this now?"

"No, I don't want to talk at all," I said. "Stop stalling and take everything off, Enoch. Show me your stomach. Show me your chest. Show me your *arms*."

A smile quirked his lips. "You like my arms?"

"When you were with the centaur herd, did you have a beard?"

His smile widened. "You like beards?"

"It's just a question. Trying to imagine you all wild and unkempt, I suppose."

"What if we were performing for a crowd now?"

I licked my lips. "Are we back to that?" I didn't mind, I supposed. It quickened something inside me.

He was unbuttoning his shirt. "What do you suppose they'd have made of you swallowing down my seed?" He raised an eyebrow. "How many of the wives in proper society do that for their husbands?"

Well, I supposed I had no notion about that. I hadn't thought it through. But it didn't seem to be very useful in terms of making children, I supposed, and perhaps it wasn't entirely cleanly. I thought of the tidy countesses in their gloves and coiffed hairstyles. "Probably none of them," I breathed.

He reached out and rubbed a thumb over my lower lip. "What would all the gathered men make of you, then?"

My body tightened.

"You'd never, never let them see you like that." His voice was gentle as he slowly peeled his shirt away, baring the swells of his muscular stomach to me.

"Well, no," I said. "Not truly. You're the one who told me these things were pretend. You said being vulnerable makes us aroused."

He pulled his shirt further off, showing me his broad, strong shoulders. "You're never vulnerable in front of them, not truly. So pretending to be vulnerable for a crowd, for *that* crowd, it makes you very wet."

Now, I felt uncomfortable for some reason. "I'm always vulnerable. You know this. We had to work hard to get them to accept us, and they could have crushed us at any second—"

"You're never vulnerable for anyone anymore, though, Phoebe," he interrupted, his voice a little dull. "Definitely not for me. Even this..." He shrugged out of his shirt and reached out to caress my face. "All filth, you said."

"*You* said that," I protested. My eyes stung again.

He rubbed his thumb over my lower lip again. "My

pretty filly in her bridle and reins. I can take her now, but she won't ever really let me back in."

"No," I gasped. "I won't. I can't."

"You could," he said.

"I would be stupid to do that," I said.

He drew back as if I'd struck him, hurt all over his face. "Stupid?"

"I can't trust you, Enoch!"

"Yes, you can. I haven't touched another woman—not even before you, I hadn't. I told you that you were the first in fifty years—"

"But that wasn't true, because Gwendolyn—"

"But that... that's not fair, Phoebe. And what do I need to do to prove to you that I'm yours? How can I show you—"

"Nothing, there's nothing you could ever do!" My voice rising in pitch. "It's not you, anyway. It's something flawed within *me*. People just hurt me for whatever reason and no one is good to me and so I shan't let *anyone* else *ever* get close enough to do that again."

He stepped back from me, shifting on his hooves, blinking, gaping at me.

I was shaking. I tried to rip my hands free from the straps that bound me to the mount.

"Oh," he said. "Oh, of course. I'm so sorry. Oh, for fuck's sake, Phoebe." Now he was kissing me.

There were tears in my eyes, and they were going to spill out, and I was confused. I jerked my hands at the straps.

His hands came up, never breaking our kiss, and undid the straps.

Now, my hands free, I thought I might push him away or possibly hit him or dig my fingernails into his skin or—

I sank my hands into his mane and pulled him closer. The tears slipped out and I kissed him and he put his hands on my skin.

He stroked my breasts, gentle. His fingers grazed my nipples until they were stiff again.

I gasped into his mouth.

"It really was me, Phoebe," he whispered. "It wasn't you.

There's nothing wrong with you."

"Stop that," I said, my voice cracking. "Don't *do* that."

"It was me, and it was that horrid brother of yours, and that wretched Oscar Smithy, and it was the entire society, all of whom turned their backs on you after violence was done to you, and it was *them*."

"No, that doesn't make sense," I said. "I'm the one common thing between them all, so it must be me."

"Everyone is hurt by other people, Phoebe," he said. "Everyone." He was still toying with my breasts, and I wanted him to stop so that I could think better, so that I could argue with him, but I didn't tell him to stop. I just let his fingers run softly over my hard nipples and I let the tears fall down my cheeks like little rivers, and I shook my head as hard as I could. "People aren't all bad, of course, but they do have a capacity to hurt others. They have as deep a capacity to care for others, I think, but there's that darkness, too. You... you can't really stop that from happening, I'm afraid. It's the price we pay for trust."

"Too high a price," I gasped out.

"All right," he breathed. "Keep me out forever, then. Then you'll never have to worry that I'll hurt you, it's true."

"I won't," I said. "Because I don't trust you, and I never will."

"All right," he said, and one of his hands went lower on my body, between my legs. I was still ridiculously wet, and his fingers slipped between the lips of me. His thumb found my clit and his forefinger plunged inside me.

I cried out at the intrusion, at the way his thumb brushed up and down on my clitoris, which jerked—already sensitive from the last orgasm he'd given me.

"But you'll never have anything else with me, then," he said. "It'll never be like the time we made love, when I felt like I got lost inside you, like I gave you pieces of myself to keep safe and you accepted them."

"You felt like that?" I whispered.

"And we'll never have those nights in each other's arms, holding each other, and we'll never have the feeling that we could have—the feeling that we can protect each other from the rest of the world, that even when everyone else is horrible to us, we have one another. We'll never have that." He slipped another finger inside me. "But it's quite worth it, I'm sure, all so that you never feel any pain. Yes, it's a good trade. No pain, but no pleasure either. Nothing but cold."

I bit down hard on my lower lip. "Just fuck me now," I ground out.

"No, you're not ready," he said.

"I don't care if I'm ready. Just fuck me and do it hard. Hurt me now. I want it to hurt."

"No," he said, shaking his head, his thumb working my clit, his other hand rubbing my hard nipple.

"You said it would just be filth."

"I don't deserve anything else, I know," he said. "I know I did this to you. I don't have any right to demand anything else from you. I know that."

"You don't," I said.

"Because it is my fault, isn't it?" His eyes flashed. "Is it you who is to blame for the rift between us, or is it me?"

"Oh, does it matter, just fuck me!"

"It does matter, because you can't forgive me if you don't blame me, Phoebe."

"I'll never forgive you." My voice was rough.

"But it was my fault, wasn't it?" He eased another finger into me—three fingers now, stretching me, a *good* stretch, his thumb doing unimaginable things to my clit. "Wasn't it, Phoebe?"

I gritted my teeth.

"Do you blame me?"

"Yes," I said finally. "Yes, yes, I do. It was you. You hurt me."

"You trusted me, and I betrayed you. And you didn't do anything to deserve that."

I was going to sob. I wanted to sob. But his fingers—the way he was touching me—it was confusing. My body crested instead. I cried out.

The pleasure was hot. It was white. It was everything.

"You didn't do anything wrong, Phoebe, and you didn't deserve it," he whispered in my ear. "It was me. It was them."

I came, a white roaring rush of heat and release. I clung to his shoulders, gasping, and the sobs came now.

I was kissing him for some reason. Him, even though he was right, of course, that he was to blame. Even though he didn't deserve anything from me.

He groaned into my mouth, holding onto me, his fingers—all three of them—jammed tightly as far as they could get inside me.

I ripped my lips away. "I won't forgive you."

"All right," he said. "You don't have to." He touched the bridle. "I want this off."

"No," I said. "Fuck me with it on, Enoch."

"You want me to fuck you now? After that?"

"Break me like a filly," I said. "Treat me like nothing. It's what you did, after all."

His gaze searched mine, his fingers sliding out of me. "You're not nothing to me."

My nostrils flared.

"You're everything," he whispered, voice strained. "And I'm sorry I was afraid of it. I tried to hold you at arms' length at first, but the pull of you was too strong. You're right, I treated you badly. You're right. I'm sorry. I'm more sorry than you could—"

"Stop," I said. "Just fuck me." I yanked on his mane, pulling his head back.

He sucked in a harsh breath. "Yes, mistress," he said darkly.

But when he was inside me, I felt invaded. Even though he was above me, even though I had to look up to find his gaze, even though I could have closed my eyes or gazed at his belly, or done anything like that, I didn't.

I looked up at him, looked into his dark eyes, and looked at whatever expression that was on his face. I didn't want to think it was adoration, but some part of me knew it was.

And his cock was so very fucking big, and it did that

thing to me again, where it hit me in too many places—stretching my clit, rubbing against the sensitive ring around my opening, and then hitting that spot inside me, and all at *once*.

Being fucked by him was being possessed by him. It demanded surrender, and I tried to fight, but I couldn't. I gave in to him, and I climaxed again, a ring of burning intense fire that sizzled me.

And when it was over, when he pulled me into his arms and pillowed his head on my breast, I knew I should put a stop to it.

But it felt so good and so familiar and so safe here against him, our skin pressed close, the feel of his warm and strength wrapped around me, that... I didn't want to be away from him, so I clung to him for dear life.

CHAPTER TWENTY-EIGHT

THE FOLLOWING MORNING was stormy, and rain lashed the windows of his bedchamber. It was gray and threatening, and I didn't want to get out of bed, so I lay half-dreaming in his arms for longer than I should have. He was awake too. We were both awake, but we chose not to acknowledge that the other was.

His valet came in and left immediately, clearly cheered at the sight of us in bed together. "Oh!" he said brightly. "I see. Quite good, sir. I'll be going then. Ignore me." He practically sang the words as he scurried right back out again.

And neither of us acknowledged that or spoke to each other.

We simply held on to the other.

I think we knew if we talked, it would get more difficult, and we wanted the ease of each other's touch for now. Perhaps that was only how I felt. I could have asked him, but I didn't wish to.

Eventually, the need to find a chamberpot became too pressing to ignore, and I had to slip out from beneath him and go off behind the screen in the other room.

When I got back, he was still lying in bed, chest bare, head pillowed on his beautifully muscled arms. He watched me coming back through the room, totally nude. He was smiling at me.

I felt embarrassed and exposed. I wanted to climb back

into the bed with him. I wanted…

It had happened again, hadn't it?

I had started to trust him, just like that. I wanted him for comfort, for protection. I even expected him to give it to me, if I asked for it. I supposed, in some way, some part of me had always known he'd be willing if I gave him the chance to do so.

I stopped, bowing my head, twisting my hands together in front of my naked body.

"Phoebe." His voice was gravelly.

"Scoot over, you big lug," I said. I lifted my face to look at him, giving him a small smile.

He scooted, lifting the blanket for me.

I slipped back in and wrapped my legs around his horse body from the side. He twisted his torso to face mine.

I shut my eyes.

He touched my cheek in that way of his. "I drank far too much last night. I have a hellish headache."

I laughed, not opening my eyes. "It can't be this easy."

"No," he said. "I'm sure it can't."

And then he kissed me.

IT SORT OF was, though.

Easy, I mean.

Trusting him was easy. I'd had to work not to, actually. I wanted to trust him. I had wanted it all along, and he'd wanted it too. We'd both put up all these barriers, and then… when we were both ready, it was just a matter of relaxing into what seemed natural.

But then I was with child within three months, which shouldn't have been a surprise. We both knew it would likely happen, and we even talked about it, and we both vocally expressed that we wanted it to happen.

Some part of me was shocked, though, because I had somehow decided a long time ago that such things weren't for me. Happiness, love, motherhood…

Suddenly, I had them all, and it was so good that I didn't know how to experience it. I wasn't equipped for good things. I had spent too long preparing for ill, protecting myself from ill.

Happiness felt odd.

But, well, I got used to it.

I managed it just fine.

Enoch seemed similarly shocked at the notion of it all. I think he'd felt the same way. I think, all those years ago, when that Deborah woman had thrown herself to her death and taken the child he'd put in her along with her, he'd shut a door in his head on the idea of being a father.

It took him a while to adjust, too.

But once that was accomplished, we were both breathless with gratitude for it all. We wanted to savor every minute of it, even the unpleasant parts. When I was exhausted because of the pregnancy, he wanted to be there, so we both went to bed early. When I was ill and sure I was going to vomit, he was there, holding back my hair while I gagged. (I never did vomit, though. It felt as though I would, numerous times. Sometimes I wished I would just for the relief I thought it would bring. But I didn't. And that stage passed more quickly than I had anticipated.)

Indeed, that was what I learned was the truest bit of parenthood. Its speed. Just when I thought an aspect of it was too difficult to bear, it would flit off, bringing a new challenge, and I'd find myself strangely wistful for it now that it was gone.

Our first child was a little boy. He looked enough like Enoch that it seemed as if my husband had been duplicated perfectly and smaller (and with human legs, of course) but when his hair grew in, it was like mine. He was a bright and happy child. Well, he cried as much as babies are wont to do, I supposed, but I remembered the bright times better. Maybe that was that wistfulness within me.

Maybe that was why he was barely a year and a half old before I was gone with child again.

Maybe that was why I had four little boys by the time that

our firstborn was seven years old. They grew so quickly, you see. It was difficult not to crave another, not to crave the tininess of fingers and toes and noses, the small wondrous bundle of a sweet newborn in my arms. And I couldn't say that Enoch wasn't just as enamored with his children, so he didn't much attempt to deter me, that was the truth.

When we got our little girl a year later, I finally decided that it was time to purchase a charm against conception. Five was enough.

Well.

That charm was entirely reversible, of course.

Made in United States
Troutdale, OR
10/12/2023